LOVE YOU LATTE, SOPHIE

Love You Latte, Sophie

JULIE STÉVIGNY

First printing, 2023

ISBN - Paperback: 9789464776669
ISBN – E-book: 9789464776676

*"Be fearless in the pursuit
of what sets your soul on fire."*
- Jennifer Lee

Julie started this story in 2010 while battling depression and burnout. Writing was a way to escape her frantic mind. Having risen from her own ashes, she dedicates this book to all women who struggle to bring out their true selves, to those who are afraid to follow their dreams or trust their own voices. She found the courage within to pursue one of her dreams and so can you.

CONTENTS

NEW YORK, MY KINDA CUPPA

"Ladies and gentlemen, as we start our descent, please make sure your seat backs and tray tables are in their full upright position. Make sure your seat belt is securely fastened and all carry-on luggage is stowed underneath the seat in front of you or in the overhead bins. Thank you."

I was only half listening to the captain's message. I was too damn impatient to get off the plane.

A few months ago, I'd gotten the biggest news ever: The advocacy firm I worked for in Paris had offered me a transfer to the States. I wouldn't be stationed in one of their offices in some cheesy little town. I'd be in New York, at their headquarters. I was thrilled. Well, no, that's an understatement. I was ecstatic. New York was "the" place I wanted to work and live. It had been on my bucket list since, I don't know...forever. After all the marvelous stories I'd heard about the city that never sleeps, I was excited to see what it had in store for me. What had I been missing? Would I find myself? Reconnect with Carol? I couldn't wait to find out. And here I was — well, almost. The plane had to land, of course.

I took a glimpse around and saw everyone had taken their seats. I could see the impatient faces of the children sitting two rows behind me. *Probably their first trip overseas*, I thought. An elderly couple — I guessed mid-seventies — sat in front of them. The worried look on the lady's face said it all. She was afraid of flying. I suppose the landing is the worst part of the whole trip. She was gripping her husband's hand firmly and resting her head against her seat, eyes closed, while the plane dove through the clouds. I turned my attention back outside and saw New York's famous skyline looming. *A few more minutes, Sophie, a few more...*

Years had passed since my last visit to the States. I had turned my back on America for years. At first, I was hesitant about the transfer. I'd lost sleep over it for a few weeks. Would this be a good idea? Would this be my step up the ladder? Would New York City be *my* city? Would I finally be less restless?

Paris had grown on me over the years. It was nothing compared to New York. And New York was nothing compared to Paris. But I was born and raised in the States, so I couldn't escape it forever. In the end, I would have to face it.

Seeing those little girls — one even had a Care Bear on her lap, the pink one with a rainbow on its belly — made me think about my parents and growing up. Carol had a pink one, I had a yellow Care Bear. Just the thought made my eyes teary.

To be honest, since both of my parents had died in a horrible car accident eight years ago, leaving my sister Carol and me behind, I was a barrel of emotions, and the slightest thing could bring me to tears.

So the loss of our parents was something that hit very deep inside. I couldn't hide it. I cried for months in the beginning. This was something I handled differently now. I no longer had the time to sit with my emotions. My work controlled my entire life, 24/7. If I wasn't traveling to see clients, I was in a court-room defending a case or behind my laptop drawing up some legal paperwork. So, nope, far too busy with other things to look at my emotions or even feel them deeply.

Carol, on the other hand, she hid her emotions like a pro. She never told me or anyone else how she was feeling. In the begin-ning, she locked herself in her room, safe in the comfort of our family home, safe from the town rumors and the endless pitying glances. That was the hardest part, people who stared at you when you walked by or when you went to the bank, even when you ventured into the local market. Vultures. Drama seekers. That's what I called them. I heard them talking behind my back. There was nothing to do in our little town, so they devoured every new sad story, filling in the silent gab of boredom. I hated them. I hated that town.

Of course, a few people wanted to help out. They brought dozens of lasagnas and pies, but no one offered to clean the house, help us pay our bills, or any of the other stuff a household needs. They were only helping so they could soothe their conscience, find peace with themselves. Even back then I knew who was in it for the long run, who would help us through rough patches, whatever the outcome was. But I could count them on one hand. It toughens you up and changes your vision about friendship, loyalty, support. It was an extra life lesson I never wanted to learn. But now I knew. If I wanted something to happen, I had to take matters into my own hands. I was done believing in utopian ideas.

After a few months I noticed changes in Carol's behavior. She went out every night, came home early in the morning, didn't mention where she'd been, and, of course, dated the strangest and scrappiest guys in town. She confided in a new group of friends, people I didn't trust for a second. They were a terrible influence. They drank excessively. Some of them even used drugs. Why couldn't she handle it differently? I wanted her to find an outlet so she could deal with it, to process the loss, just like I was trying to do. But she never found a way. I know she was too young. No one taught us how to deal with that grief. So Carol stayed in our hometown and coped in her own way. That's when I lost all connection with her. Carol locked me out of the emotional world she'd created for herself. She put up a wall, driving us apart as sisters.

It's strange because, growing up, we were inseparable. We did almost everything together and were a united front against our parents. Like most siblings, I guess. But after the accident, it felt like she was miles away. I needed her so badly. It wasn't easy for me either. I just couldn't bear it.

It was the year of my eighteenth birthday when they passed away. I was an adult now and had to take care of my sister. Since we needed the money, I looked for a job after school. My first job was waitressing in a bistro downtown. I worked every weekend and after school. Soon enough I found a job as an apprentice in a law firm called Johnson & Carter. I helped with the filing, I checked the office mail, I forwarded requests to the right lawyer, I did some other administrative work. Easy tasks in the beginning. Eventually, they taught me how to build up a case, where to look for information. It was there that I got a taste of the legal system and grew interested in becoming a lawyer. My senior year, I applied for scholarships at different schools, in the States and abroad, but I kept getting rejection letters. I desperately wanted to leave town, leave our house. It was smothering me.

And then, one day, out of the blue, I finally received the letter I had been dreaming of for so long. I had been accepted at the Sorbonne in Paris. They had even granted me a scholarship. Johnson & Carter had written a recommendation letter telling the Sorbonne they'd been thrilled with my work and it would be foolish of them not to accept me. And it helped, I guess. Finally, I could leave town. I could complete my education. I left Carol, our house, my grieving and moved to France. I know, it sounds selfish. But it was the only way to stop me from falling apart.

I graduated a few years later with a law degree and an expertise in environmental law. Like most of the graduates, I stayed in the city where I studied. I found a job at Leaf, a law firm in Paris's business district. Well, to be more specific, in la Défense. La Défense is "the" center of Paris when it comes to business. I couldn't dream of a better start.

The Paris office was a small division; the headquarters were in New York. Traveling had never been an issue for me. During my stay in Paris, I went along to support some of the lawyers on environmental law cases. Sometimes I stayed a few weeks to support a case; sometimes I stayed abroad for months. The complexity of the case defined my stay and made me live out of my suitcase. I didn't need to settle in one place, and seeing more of the world — when I could leave the conference room, of course — was a big bonus.

With climate change, a lot of focus was on the environment. So my knowledge in environmental law, especially water quality law, was handy. It's one of the reasons they offered me the job in New York. They didn't have any lawyers specializing in that area. After debating every pro and con of my move to New York, I persuaded myself I was ready to go back to the States. I couldn't let my past stop me from doing what I loved. So I signed my new contract, sold my apartment in Paris, handed over my active cases — and it brought me to this point, here, on a plane from France.

The plane landed smoothly on the tarmac at JFK and was taxiing toward the terminal. A happy sigh escaped my lips. I was back on American soil. I waited for the unlock seatbelt sign to switch off and glanced quickly at my watch. 10:25. Right on time. The minute I heard the beep, I hauled myself out of my seat. I grabbed my purse from the overhead compartment and followed the other passengers off the plane. Luckily, my seat was in the first row, so I didn't have to wait too long.

I hadn't planned anything for the next two days. Unpacking, settling down, exploring the city a bit. That was it. On Monday, I would start my new job, in a new office, in a new city, with new colleagues. I smiled broadly at the thought of this new, exciting chapter in my life and walked slowly toward the luggage area. Most of my belongings had already been shipped to my new apartment, so I only had one suitcase to pick up. For once, I wasn't rushing. It felt fabulous.

The minute I stepped out of the airport to hail a cab, the heat and humidity wrapped itself firmly around me. "Humph, hot." This was definitely something I needed to adapt to. I took off my navy-blue trench and my blue-and-gold-thread woven scarf, draped them carefully over my arm, and waited for the next cab.

As my cab crossed the Brooklyn Bridge, I soaked in the fantastic view of the city... I loved the mix of ancient buildings with the colossal, sturdy, and some elegant skyscrapers and the buzz of the city oozing out of it. Fifty minutes later, I arrived at my new home on Duane Street. I didn't know how long I'd stay because, with my job, it could change quickly. But I hoped it would be for a considerably longer period than I was used to. I had been dreaming of living here for a long time, and it gave me time to properly reconnect with Carol, so I didn't want it to be fleeting either. Time to settle in and explore this amazing city. That would do it.

Stepping out of the cab, I looked up at the prewar building from 1920 and had to catch my breath. *Wow, this building is even more spectacular than I'd imagined,* I thought. I felt an immense sensation of happiness washing over me. Being an expat was superb, especially in my situation. I was single and a hardworking woman with no family. My employer could send me anywhere in the world. No one was waiting for me at night, so mostly I worked in the evenings and on the weekends. Free time? A personal life? Haven't got any of that. Strangely, I was fine with that because I don't know where I would find the time to maintain a relationship or manage a family.

Leaf had invested in me over the years, and I'd delivered. They had arranged everything, from the search of the apartment to the interior decoration and the move. Nothing left for me to do.

They had found a superb loft apartment, with sixteen hundred square feet on the fifth floor. There were only two units on the floor. It was gorgeous. The entire space was bathed in light; it filtered through the skylit and oversized windows at the front of the apartment. It had been newly renovated with handsome exposed brick walls, soaring ceilings, new maple floors, and four slender cast-iron columns. There was a partially open kitchen with beautiful high-end stainless-steel appliances, stone countertops, and custom-made cabinets.

That open kitchen reminded me of home. Being quite close, the kitchen was where the four of us had gathered the most. It was the very center of our family history. Most things we did, we did in the kitchen. Reading, studying, discussing our next holiday or what to do during the upcoming weekend. My mother always had something baking in the oven. Cookies, a cake for teatime, a marvelous roasted chicken for supper, or one of her signature quiche dishes. In our family house, the house that Carol had kept as a holiday home, every room reminded me of them. Even the smallest things threw me back into memories. The vanilla-scented hand soap while washing my hands, the distinctive crackling sound of the front door opening. All of it was too confronting for me, and I hated every bit. I wanted to explore the world, I wanted to see new places beyond American borders. I needed to get out of that small town thinking pattern, out of that house, and expand my horizons. I needed to go further with my life and stop grieving once and for all — it's what my parents would have wanted. I needed to do something with my life before it was too late. And that was my motivation to move abroad.

From the kitchen, I continued to explore the rest of the apartment and peeked into every room. The primary bedroom had a walk-in closet, and there were double sinks, a claw-foot tub, and a shower in the bathroom, ideal for my nightly destressing bath. There was even a small laundry room with a utility sink, a pantry, and some generously sized closets. The apartment was only a few steps away from Tribeca and a few blocks from the financial district where I worked. What more could I ask for. Others could only dream of such a prime location in New York, while I'd had it thrown in my lap. Okay, I worked really hard for it. I spent all of my time at work or on work — and they even had me on call for interventions. This was the least they could do, right?! I was starting to love New York already. It's a city where anything is possible. I had already discovered this, the moment I'd entered the loft.

THANKS A LATTE

Since I still had a few days left before I started work on Monday, I asked Carol to have breakfast with me on Friday morning. In all those years abroad, I'd tried to keep in touch with her. Not weekly. I didn't have time for that. But I tried to call her once a month. Time passed, though, and over the years we had grown further and further apart, calling each other less. She'd never visited me. Not in Paris. Not in any other country. And I had never gone back to America to visit her. It had been a while since we'd seen each other in the flesh.

My plan revolved around taking some time for coffee and breakfast, catching up with her, and hopefully building a better relationship than the one we'd had for the past several years.

We'd agreed to meet at the Starbucks on 38 Park Row. I'm a Starbucks addict and I hadn't found a good one in Paris. I'd missed it. A good American latte could make my day.

It was a lovely day. The sun had already cleared the morning chill, so I decided to walk the short distance from my apartment to the coffee shop. It was an ideal way to get to know my way around. I walked onto Broadway, left city hall on my right, and entered City Hall Park. While looking at the map on my cell, I crossed the park toward the coffee shop. A small breeze ruffled the leaves gently and made them dance to the rhythm of the wind. My mind wandered off. How much would Carol have changed? Occasionally, she sent me some pictures, and from time to time we Skyped. In most pictures she was partying, being a goofball. She lived mostly out of her comfort zone and changed jobs constantly, just for the thrill of it. This was how I knew her. Carol is the youngest; we're two years apart. She is playful, sociable, not the brightest sometimes, but I love her just the way she is. Like all sisters, we had our quarrels as kids. We probably drove our parents nuts. But it always ended in a good way: making up and laughing about how stupid our fight was. On the other hand, I was the serious one, sticking to my secure plan in life. It was me, myself, and I. Maybe I had changed in her eyes?

I was too busy working. Or maybe I'd suppressed the thought of what we had as a family. Something to examine with a shrink, if I had one. But now that I'd set foot on my homeland, I had to see her. It had been six years since I'd seen her in person, since we'd been in the same city, in the same room. Maybe pick up where we'd left off so long ago.

But this would take some getting used to.

Since the age of six, I'd been looking forward to traveling the world. It was only through my work at Johnson & Carter — and my parents' passing — that the idea of finishing my education in Europe took hold. My dad and I had made a chart of all the places we wanted to see. We never had the money to travel but dreaming felt just as good. He was the one who kept believing in me, who told me it would be possible to travel around the world one day. I'd even put money from birthdays, Christmases, and chores aside to save up. But everything changed after their sudden passing. At the age of eighteen, I became a parent to a girl in search of herself, a girl who got lost in her grief. I didn't know how to help her because I needed help as well.

Europe stayed on hold. It stayed a dream for me, like I always thought it would.

The inheritance from our parents' death only covered the funeral costs and other household expenses. Carol couldn't cope with life without our parents, especially without our mother. They had a good relationship, and our mother wasn't there for her anymore. Carol was constantly getting in trouble. I struggled to manage everything. Working, studying, paying the mortgage, cooking, and cleaning — and keeping an eye on Carol. I had no authority over her. She didn't listen. She wandered in and out like she lived in a hotel. I was a graduate, wanted to travel the world, study abroad, but I couldn't anymore. I hated the position I was in. *Why now? Why me?* I could have been anywhere but here. But I couldn't leave Carol; she was still my sister. I wanted to leave, but who else would take care of her? Where would the money come from to support her?

A few months after the funeral, our aunt Lynn — my mother's eldest sister, who was divorced and had no children of her own — moved into our house in Tillamook. She had seen me struggling with Carol and thankfully came at the right time to my, well, our aid. She was the one who gave me the push I needed to go to Europe. Lynn decided she would keep an eye on Carol while I was studying in France. I escaped our little town and studied real hard. I wanted to show Aunt Lynn I was worthy. I only had one shot, and this had to be the one. Dating and going out? Not part of my itinerary. I would be the ace of my class. And I must say I did a fantastic job.

Carol was already waiting for me in front of Starbucks when I crossed the street. She wore dark-blue ripped jeans, a white halter top, and a yellow jersey. Yellow All-stars matched her outfit. Her dark brown hair was cut into a messy pixie. She looked very thin — or was it just the jeans? When she saw me, she ran toward me and hugged me firmly.

"Oh my god, you're here! Finally. I missed you, Soph, I did."

"Me too, Carol, me too," I said and hugged her back tightly. It felt so comfortable and familiar.

Carol was the only immediate family I had left, except our aunt Lynn of course. Even if we hadn't seen each other in years, it seemed like she'd missed me as well. When we called or texted, we'd shared our loves and heartaches, the good and the unpleasant moments in our life. I didn't have much to share because my personal life was non-existent, so Carol knew all about my work and the cases I'd been working on. I was literally glued to my job. Work, work, work. And maybe because of that, I missed out on a lot of things. I was still single. I met a lot of men, but none deserving of the "boyfriend" label. I had a few good friends, scattered all over the world, and that was it. So my sister meant a lot to me. I hated myself for not being there for her when she was sixteen. Or even in these last six years. I had made a promise to myself: From now on I would be there for her, no matter what. I hoped we could spend more time together. Just like before the accident, as sisters, one front. She looked up at me and held me at arm's length.

"So, let me take a good look at you. Gosh, you changed, Sophie. Your hair — it's shorter, but the color is fantastic. It's brown but with a golden blonde touch in it. And are these curls? Damn, who's your hairdresser?"

"Thanks," I said. "It's a permanent on top of a double coloring. I had a great hairdresser back in Paris, so I'll have to look for another one over here."

"Pity he's in France, but I love the cut. It suits you. Come on, I'm dying to hear all about your new apartment and your new job, and it goes so much better with a good cup of coffee and some muffins." She beamed at me brightly. After what we'd been through, she could have made it difficult for me from the beginning. To my astonishment, I could sense she was upbeat. Her mention of muffins made me relax because I knew how she'd struggled with her diet. I could still see her sitting there, at the kitchen table, tearing little pieces from her lunch, eating agonizingly slow, only to suddenly say she'd had enough and leave an almost full plate on the table.

We stood in line chatting casually, waiting for our turn to order. Suddenly, Carol grabbed my elbow and pulled me close.

"Soph, I have to go. I can't stay." She looked around in panic. I watched as she turned pale.

I looked at her in disbelief. What happened to her happy mood from moments ago? "But, Carol, we just got here. What's wrong? If you don't like Starbucks, we can go to another coffee shop, you know."

She pointed toward the outside terrace and nodded at a man with curly blonde hair wearing an expensive-looking grey-striped suit. He was in his mid-twenties, maybe even a bit older. Why was she making all this fuss over a guy?

"Carol, what's wrong? I don't understand. What does this guy have to do with it?"

"Sophie, I can't stay," she said. "I can't stand to be in his neighborhood. I'm sorry, I'll make it up to you."

"Carol, wait. Stay, please..." I pleaded.

Giving me no choice to stop her, she ran out of the coffee shop. It wouldn't make any difference if I ran after her. I knew her. She needed space for whatever had just happened. And so I waited alone in line. I'd been looking forward to this moment. Sipping our lattes together, reliving memories from our childhood... And all of the sudden, she's out the door. For what? A guy?

I glanced back in the direction Carol had looked and felt a tingle of recognition. The guy still sat at the same spot, totally at ease, sipping his coffee and reading the *New York Post*.

I know that guy! But what was his name again? I kept staring, but it didn't come to me right away. And then it hit me. Yes, of course, it's Patrick Downey, the quarterback from our high school in Tillamook. If I recall, his mother was from England, but he grew up in the States. So he was the guy every girl wanted to date. Not me. I wasn't busy with guys back then. I was kind of a late bloomer. But it was definitely him, a few years older and somewhat more mature. And he looked trim in his fancy suit.

Carol was a few years younger than him. If I remember correctly, they even dated, nothing serious. Right, she told me the story once in an e-mail when I was in my first year at the Sorbonne. Their relationship, or whatever you called it at that age, was before the crash. She had never trusted me enough to share the story until I was gone. But when I was abroad, she wrote about him, their dates, how gentle he had been with her. One day she found him in the locker room, making out with another girl. She was heartbroken. The toughest thing for her was knowing the girl he cheated on her with was a cheerleader. She blamed herself. According to Carol, Patrick's misstep was all her fault. She assumed it was because she was fatter than that cheerleader. She'd always been chubby as a kid, but I never thought of her as fat at all. But at her age girls were quickly influenced and she started to doubt herself. If you saw her now, you'd be afraid to hold her. She is so thin and looks super fragile. I remember a phone call with my aunt Lynn when I was already in Paris. She told me Carol was acting strange. She had lost a lot of weight and had become more and more introverted. Her grades stayed the same, so she didn't look into it. She chalked it up to puberty, in combination with the loss of our parents. But it got worse. Carol became anorexic. Didn't she see it coming? Didn't I see it coming? I can't recall. I was too busy with school in Paris. I had other priorities back then. And my aunt did the best she could. But she had no grip on Carol or control over her either. Carol always reminded Aunt Lynn that she wasn't our real mother, which was never easy for her to hear.

Carol eventually got hospitalized. We stayed in contact by mail but not as frequently as I wanted. I never went back to see her, not even when she was hospitalized. So I was a bit shocked when I saw her tiny figure just now. She had color in her face, her hair was beautifully cut, but when I held her, I felt her bony structure through her clothes.

Clearly, Carol didn't want to be in Patrick's presence. I decided to call her in the afternoon. Why did we have to run into this dreadful guy? He ruined our reunion. It made me more furious as minutes went by.

"Miss, miss!" The waiter shouted and waved at me. I looked up and found myself at the front of the line. It was my turn to order, and I had kept people waiting. *Way to go, Soph.*

"I'm sorry, sir. Uh, a grand latte with caramel. Extra foam please."

"To go or for here?" He sneered at me, clearly irritated.

"Uh, to go."

"Name?"

"Sophie."

I paid for my latte and waited at the pickup counter. Latte in hand, I headed toward the outside terrace. I'd decided to go back to my place and unpack some boxes. But then, I saw Patrick Downey still sitting outside. Still livid about the brusque end to my meetup with Carol, I decided right then and there to do something about it. Avenging Carol was the best thing I could do. We'd probably laugh about it later, and she would feel a lot better. Perhaps we could order pizza and make some margaritas. That would be nice.

Walking outside, I undid the lid of my coffee cup. I was feeling extremely confident, and it felt right in that moment. I wouldn't harm him — I wasn't that vile — but it was payback time.

As I walked by, I pretended to trip right in front of him and threw my entire coffee all over him. He was soaked. *What a shame to spill a good coffee,* I thought. I regretted it instantly. I stood up and clasped a hand over my mouth. I quickly glanced at him and saw the splashes of brown and golden caramel dripping off his white shirt and grey suit jacket. *What did I do? Sophie, you're way out of line. You're a grown up. Get a grip, girl.*

With a shaky inhalation, I apologized. "Oh, sir, I'm so sorry. But I tripped right there, and... Are you hurt?" Stumbling over my words, I looked at him, getting redder by the minute. I couldn't stop babbling.

"The lid must not have been placed on the cup correctly. I'm so sorry..."

Sophie, you threw a cup of hot coffee on the guy and you're lying? I had to save myself. These days they could sue you for almost anything. I should know. I'm a lawyer. Okay, not a personal injury lawyer, didn't like that part in law school. I wanted something with more impact. Environmental law let me advise large organizations and businesses on their risks, responsibilities, regulatory concerns, and damage limitation and defend them if litigation ensued. So my knowledge wouldn't be helpful if this turned into a case.

A few people sitting on the terrace looked at the odd scene, but nobody helped Patrick out. Typical. Patrick swung between anger and bewilderment as he held his coffee-smeared shirt off his chest. His gaze darkened and his voice trembled with fury as he looked up at me and then back down at his smeared shirt.

"My suit, you ruined my suit! Do you know how much a tailor-made suit costs?" He scowled.

I noticed he was wearing a vintage Patek Philippe around his wrist, which was obviously an heirloom. They don't make that model anymore, so I should have known it was an expensive suit. My mind spun frantically. How could I save myself from this awkward situation? Save myself from a lawsuit? Because he certainly had the money to drag my ass to court.

"Sir, I only live a few blocks from here. I can bring your suit to the dry cleaners, and in the meantime, you could clean yourself up. I'll pay for the damage, the dry cleaning, everything."

I was perplexed by my answer. Why the hell did I propose that? I wanted revenge. Not him at my place. But I couldn't really leave him standing there with his shirt and suit all filthy. *Aaargh.* I had to leave before this got even more out of hand. I revealed my loveliest smile and hoped he would accept my offer so we could leave the premises.

He took another long look at his suit then back at me, pausing and rethinking what I'd proposed. Leaving his gaze on me a little too long. He calmed down, thank god, and said rudely, "It's the least you can do." He wiped the last bit of dripping coffee from his suit, dried his hands on a napkin, and grabbed his brown leather briefcase from under the table. I followed him through the tables and out onto the sidewalk.

"Okay, off we go," I said, trying to sound upbeat as I hailed a cab. I didn't want him walking around looking like a giant latte, even if it was just a few blocks. Luckily, we had a cab within a minute.

Patrick got into the cab first. He didn't hold the door for me or let me get in first. *Asshole. Can't he be a gentleman?*

While the cab drove toward Duane Street, I gazed outside and wondered how on earth I got into this messy situation. This was my first real day in New York; how would the rest turn out?

Oh yeah, before I forget, mental note to myself, I thought. *Make sure no one recognizes me if I ever go back to that Starbucks.* I knew Carol would get a kick out of this. I planned to call her once Patrick left my place, so we could have a good laugh about it. But for the moment I didn't find it funny.

The cab parked in front of the building on Duane Street and Sammy was standing outside. Sammy was the building's doorman. I call it an in-house manager, but what's in a name, right? He was approximately six feet tall and had brown-cropped hair and hazelnut eyes. At first glance, he looks scary with his bodybuilder's torso, but once you talk to him, you see he's helpful and a good listener. When I arrived yesterday, he kindly showed me around the block. He gave me a map of the area, indicated the best places to eat, and crossed out the ones I'd better forget about. Plus, he showed me every Starbucks on the map. A man after my heart. Sammy didn't just open the door or handle security for the building; he also arranged other stuff, like housekeeping and dry cleaning. And he could always hail a cab in advance. The building was five floors, and most of the apartments were occupied by expats. I'd already discovered there was one student living there. Don't ask me how he could afford an apartment like that. He was probably from a wealthy family. This morning, I'd met a shy elderly woman named Laura when I took the elevator down. She worked at the local newspaper and wrote the obituaries. I would get acquainted with the other residents as well, but come on, it was my first day. I'd have plenty of time for that later on.

I paid the cab driver and stepped out of the car. Patrick was already waiting on the curb, cleaning his expensive watch. Sammy greeted me and the guy soaked in coffee and held the door open. Patrick hadn't introduced himself, let alone spoken more than five words, and I wasn't holding my breath. Stubborn asshole.

"Hi, Sammy," I said, stepping into the lobby.

"Hi, Sophie. You had a good time with your sister?" he asked politely, ignoring the strange situation. Like he hadn't noticed Patrick's stained suit. Or maybe he had noticed it but was being polite.

"Oh, it didn't go so well. I'll tell you the details later on," I said. "Hey, could you come up in about ten minutes? I've got some urgent dry cleaning to do. Would it be possible within the hour?"

Sammy looked at the guy standing next to me and nodded. He understood instantly. "Sure, no problem," he said and closed the door behind us.

As soon as the elevator doors closed, Patrick suddenly found his voice. "Wow, he's curious. My doorman only knows my name and that's about it."

I looked at him, puzzled. What did he want me to say? Sammy shouldn't ask any questions simply because he's a doorman? *My god, what a weirdo.*

His eyes softened a bit when he saw my reaction, and he recovered quickly. "Oh no, don't take it the wrong way. It's cool he's so accessible. In my building, I'm always "sir." I've known my doorman for years and still it's "good morning, sir," "good night, sir." Nothing more." He sighed and leaned against the chrome bar behind him.

I snapped my mouth shut before I could say something atrocious and stared straight ahead, hoping this whole thing would be over real soon.

Silently, Patrick followed me out of the elevator, and I unlocked my door.

I'd already grown fond of this apartment. It was spacious for a New York apartment, and there was plenty of light coming in through the huge skylit window spanning half of my apartment. I didn't have a special view, but most apartments in New York don't. Only if you live in a penthouse in Central Park, I presume. The whole place had been neatly arranged already. The items I brought from home — books and pictures, mostly — were stacked on the shelves against the kitchen wall. The two large framed posters I bought in Paris, by the famous French photographer Robert Doisneau, hung in the living area. I liked things to be abstract, neat, and clean so my mind stayed clear. I was kind of a perfectionist, and the apartment's generous storage made it so much easier for me. I still had a few boxes to unpack, but everything would find its place in time.

"Come on in," I said, waving Patrick into the entryway. "So, this way to the bathroom." I led him to the bathroom, which was at the rear of the apartment, next to my bedroom. It was weird having a guy around. I wasn't used to it, so I was a bit nervous as I showed him everything he needed for a shower. I took some towels out of the cabinet underneath the sink and folded them neatly over the space heater that hung against the wall so they'd be warm.

"If you need anything else, give a scream. I'll be in the kitchen," I said.

He laughed at the word "scream."

"Oh, can I have your clothes so I can take them to the dry cleaner?"

Both of his brows shot up, stunned by my directness. Understandable, because I was still standing in the bathroom and he needed some privacy to get undressed. He cleared his throat, my cue to leave, and I immediately understood my inappropriate request. I blushed and looked away. "Sorry, sir, I... I'll wait outside," I said hurriedly and took a step toward the door.

He shrugged out of his jacket and stumbled a bit, feeling embarrassed. "No, no it's fine. It's... Well, I... I'm Patrick, by the way, Patrick Downey," he said, holding his hand out to shake mine. Something shifted in the air, changing the atmosphere in an instant.

"Sophie," I said. I shook his warm, soft, and a bit sticky from the coffee I'd spilled hand, sending goosebumps dancing across my skin. Was he feeling it too? Because he held my hand a bit longer than necessary.

"I hate to be called sir. This makes it easier." His lips curled into a slow, heart-stopping smile, lighting up his entire face, highlighting some wrinkles around his mouth and eyes.

"Indeed, it does make things easier." I left the bathroom, giving him some space to undress in private.

He cracked the door open slightly and handed me his suit and smeared shirt. After Sammy gathered the dry cleaning and promised to have them cleaned as soon as possible, I made some fresh coffee while Patrick showered. In case he wanted a cup. You never know.

I listened to the water running while I read an article about interior design in a magazine I'd bought in the airport in Paris.

Nothing interesting, but I was just passing time. The coffee was dripping silently into the pot and filling the kitchen with a divine burned smell. It's a smell you only get from using fresh coffee beans. I propped my chin in my palm, scanned the pictures, browsed the articles, but they couldn't keep my attention. What was I going to do for the rest of the day? Except unpacking those last boxes, I had nothing on my schedule. In fact, my get-together with Carol had been the only item on my agenda. Maybe I could order in some food? I wasn't in the mood for going out alone, so couch potato-ing was a good alternative. The sound of the shower shutting off sent an instant charge of awareness through me. I sat up, checked my hair in the oven's reflection, and passed my tongue over my teeth. *Why the hell did I do that?*

Patrick came out of the bathroom wearing only my fluffy cream towel around his athletic waist, showing off his marvelous curves. His curly blonde hair, still wet from the shower, was now combed back. The shower did him good because he looked self-assured and at ease. I, on the other hand, was hyperaware of him standing half-naked in my living room. I had to admit, he was cute. Correction, the guy was steaming hot. That body of his, gosh. A six-pack, strong arms, a light tan, mmm, mmmmm. Easy on the eyes, that's for sure. Shivers went up my spine. Was it noticeable that I'd been out of the game for a while?

"Sophie, do you maybe have a bathrobe or a huge t-shirt? It's a bit chilly out here," he said.

"Yeah, robe. Got it." I quickly closed my mouth before I started to drool and jumped off the kitchen chair. What would he think of me? *Shame on you, Sophie.*

I hurried past him, and I could smell a hint of musk combined with soap, my soap. He smelled divine. I got so distracted I almost tripped over my own feet.

You know those thick cotton bathrobes you get in a spa or in a superbly posh hotel? The kind you can stay in for hours? Well,

I owned one. And it was crisp white. I handed him the robe, hoping he would remove the towel in front of me, but he was decent enough not to and stepped back into the bathroom.

The dry cleaning of his suit would surely take an hour, so we had some time to kill. We sat down at the kitchen counter, Patrick on a high wooden chair wearing my thick, white, and lush cotton bathrobe. The sleeves only covered his upper arms, and he could just close the rope around his torso, but it fit. Sort of. I had bought it as a memento several years ago after my first hotel stay while working for Leaf. I had been in the UK for a few months, working long hours on a contaminated waste land case and practically living out of my hotel room when I wasn't in a meeting with my clients or in court. That robe had made my stay so much cozier.

I sat at the other end of the counter, facing him, two coffee mugs and a freshly made pot of steaming-hot Arabic standing between us.

"Would you like a cup?" I asked, pointing at the coffeepot. "It's freshly made."

"Sure, if you don't spill it all over me again." He emphasized the "again" and showed off a crooked smile.

"I'm so sorry. I never did anything like that before." I peered at him through my eyelashes, feeling remorseful.

"What? The coffee throwing or having strange men at your place?" he teased.

He had me there. I was locked in the grip of his eyes, his gaze searingly intense. I started to blush but couldn't stop staring into his beautiful blue eyes. Shivers crossed my back — the good ones, of course. My breathing quickened. I didn't reply. Well, I couldn't squeak out a word. My mouth felt dry and my head was spinning, overwhelmed by his presence.

"So, Sophie, what do you do for a living?" He said it so casually.

I swallowed. "I'm a lawyer."

His brows shot up and he cocked his head to the side. "Tell me," he said, gazing back into my eyes, "can I sue you for this?"

I don't know how he did it, but I transformed into a shy eighteen-year-old girl on a whim. My heart started to beat harder and my mouth became even dryer. He surely knew what his presence was doing to me and which strings to pull.

With my chin propped on one hand, I bit my nail and exhaled loudly. "Would you?" I asked sheepishly, lowering my eyes out of embarrassment. I had to undo myself from his grip, something I didn't want to do, but something I needed to do so I could keep my head clear.

"I thought about it but no, I wouldn't. Not after you've been so accommodating." He leaned back and smiled. I swallowed hard and sat up straight as I poured some coffee into a white porcelain coffee mug that read "life begins with coffee." These mugs meant a lot to me, even if they were just white with some funny lines on them. They were from my dad. He'd collected them over the years. He was, just like me, a real coffee lover. Everywhere I'd moved, I'd brought them with me. So I had some familiar stuff with me.

My heartbeat started to settle down and I breathed out slowly. *I can manage this,* I thought. *He's a man, an ordinary man I just met. I'm a grownup, dammit.*

We drank our coffee, talked a little bit more.

And then, once again, I saw that quizzical look on Patrick's face. The same one he'd had after I proposed him cleaning up at my place.

"Sorry to ask, but you look familiar to me. Sure we haven't met here in New York?"

Oh fuck, he knows. Quick, Sophie, divert the conversation.

I shook my head. "Nope. Just moved to New York so can't be that."

"Oh, okay." He still wasn't convinced but a quick knock on the front door cut his thoughts off. It was Sammy with the dry cleaning.

I got up to open the door and saw an hour had passed. Patrick was easy to talk to. That must be why time passed so quickly. I paid Sammy to cover the expenses, gave him a large tip, and thanked him for his quick assistance.

Patrick finished his coffee in a gulp, certainly scorching his throat, took his clothes, and got dressed. I had hoped we could talk a little longer, but he had to get to work. Of course, not everyone had a day off like me.

He glanced at his Patek Philippe, and when he looked up, that beautiful smile was gone, his face all businesslike.

"Sophie, thanks for the hospitality, but I have a business meeting to attend." He shook my hand firmly.

I must say, I was hoping for a kiss on the cheek. But what more could I expect? I threw coffee all over him. I was just a random girl offering him a ride and a chance to clean himself up. Normal, so I thought. No matter how many silly romantic novels I had read — and loved — I knew he wouldn't come flying into my arms and kiss me. *Dream on, Soph, dream on.*

"You're more than welcome," I said. The earlier tension between us was now gone.

Once Patrick left, I took my cell out of my purse and dialed Carol's number. I wanted to tell her the whole story, from the moment I threw coffee on Patrick as an act of revenge to him being at my place and our conversation...

The phone rang once, but hearing it ring made me rethink things, and I quickly ended the call, placing my phone back on the table. *Come on, Soph, Carol doesn't need to know about this. It would only hurt her more,* I told myself. Clearly, she'd been smitten with Patrick in high school and was still recovering. *Keep your mouth shut, nothing happened.* Besides, what were the odds of seeing him again?

FIRST COFFEE

I went to the Starbucks on 38 Park Row every morning. Not for a particular reason. Of course not. It was the Starbucks on the way to the office, so I had to pass by there anyway. And I'm one of those people who needs a coffee to kickstart the day. My day can't get started without a good hot caramel latte with extra foam. I even convinced myself this morning ritual would make my day. So I stuck with it. Plus, it would be offensive not to stop there after what happened on my first day in New York. I owed it to the place.

Okay, okay, I admit it. It could also have been because I met Patrick there for the first time. "Met" is in fact a euphemism for me spilling coffee all over him and entertaining him briefly in my apartment, almost naked, but still. I was hoping I would run into him again. I wanted it desperately. But it had been a month since the Latte Incident, and I hadn't seen him.

But I had — surprisingly — made some friends over the last month. Alex was one of them. Well, it's actually Alexander, but his friends call him Alex. He was the type a guy you'd love to date. Cute, kind, a good listener, knows a lot about fashion, and, boy, can he gossip about anything. With his spiky black hair, blue eyes, and pronounced jawline, he could make any head turn. But sadly, he's for the other version of me. He's gay. I don't mind. It's amazing to have a male friend who doesn't want to sleep with you because he'd like to test your friendship.

Alex was the manager of the Starbucks on 38 Park Row. And every morning at 7:45, he waited at the counter with my latte.

He knew my coffee preferences, and I never had to get in line to order. And my coffee was accompanied by a side of morning gossip because Alex had a lot of stories to tell. All in all, my days started utterly relaxed.

Alex and I met a few days after the Latte Incident. I was waiting for my coffee at the pickup counter when he addressed me by name. He'd recognized me from that infamous day, so we started to chat. I confided in him that it wasn't an accident but a setup and told him the reason I did it. That was enough to make him a huge fan. In the beginning, we exchanged hellos when we crossed paths, but we became fast friends after a few weeks.

Alex saw me entering the shop and urgently waved me to the counter.

"Hi, Alex."

"Hi, gorgeous." He gave me three kisses on the cheek, European style. I quickly sat on the chair he placed at the counter for me so I could drink my coffee at ease in the morning before heading to the office.

"So, are you in for drinks this evening? You know, that new hot place called Vitello in SoHo?" he asked.

"Yeah, it got great reviews, and everyone is dying to get in," I said, sipping my latte. "Rumor has it the waiters are models, and they're extremely hot."

"Well, guess what? We can get in without any trouble." He smiled naughtily.

"Noooooooooooooooo. Really?" Alex had a huge network and could get us into the newest and hottest places in town. Even better, we never had to think about where to go on Friday nights.

"Yep, I made a new friend when I went to Santorini last week. You know, that new club in SoHo I told you about? Well, he's a waiter at Vitello. We kind of hooked up after his shift. I must've made a good impression because he put our names on the list. So, sweetheart, this evening, you, me, and our dearest friend

Jane are going out." He was practically shouting. Some people in line shot strange looks at him, but they quickly returned their gaze forward, waiting for their turn to order.

"Wow, Alex, you amaze me every time," I said.

"I know," he replied with a smirk. "Oh god, heavenly creature! Don't look, Soph, but there's a cute guy — he's for sure straight — and he's been watching you since the minute you walked in."

"Wait, where?" I wanted to look behind me, but Alex clasped my hand to stop me.

"Don't turn around, dear. He's coming toward us," he whispered.

"What?" I stood up and turned halfway, bumping into the guy behind me.

When I looked up, I recognized him right away, his stature, his curly hair, his crooked smile. It was Patrick. My heart started racing and an electric kinda chill crossed my entire body.

"Hi, Sophie," he said, his voice like velvet. "It's been a while. Got coffee on anyone else lately?" He chuckled quietly.

"H-hi," I stuttered and started to blush. I couldn't tear my eyes off him, and again I didn't know what to say.

"Would you like another coffee?" He pointed at my empty mug.

"Oh, no thanks. I was just heading out. I... I have to go to work." I placed the mug back on the counter, grabbed my vintage tote bag from Whipping Post from under my chair, waved goodbye to Alex, made a sign I would call him later, looked at Patrick one last time, and exited the coffee shop as quickly as I could before he could say another word. Or before I could reply with something stupid.

The instant I stepped outside, it dawned on me. *What did I do? Patrick asked me for coffee, and I ran away from him! Oh my god, why did I do that?*

I barely grasped what had just happened. I turned down coffee from the guy I'd waited what felt like an eternity to see. I hurried toward the office, hoping for a busy day so I could forget about my latest faux pas. But on the other hand, I was hoping the day would end soon so I could talk it through with Alex and Jane over a good glass of wine or a cocktail. *I have to work on my social skills with men,* I thought. *I'm so not good at it.*

Alex, Jane, and I ordered some drinks and were making dinner plans when Alex blurted out the question I didn't want to answer.

"Soph, I have to ask. What happened this morning? I called you on your cell, but you didn't call me back. Who was that gorgeous guy at my counter this morning?" Alex looked at me, his gaze intense.

I looked away, feeling uncomfortable reliving the moment. "Hum, that's Patrick," I whispered. I started to blush as I spoke his name.

"Oh dear, the coffee guy? The guy you spilled your coffee on and got almost naked at your place?" Jane screamed. "No! You're kidding? But you hadn't seen him in weeks."

"One month and two days to be exact," I muttered.

"You're still keeping track? Come on, Sophie, you're better than this," Jane retorted.

I met Jane through Alex. If you met her for the first time, you'd think she was a cocky and patronizing New York bitch. But it's a false first impression. Once you get to know her better, you see how wise and sweet she is. But you have to dig through her tough exterior. She is so in tune with herself. She chooses her own friends and doesn't let anyone dictate her life. Her quirky attitude is a way to keep people at a distance.

She and Alex grew up together and moved to the city when they were twenty, looking for success as actors. They shared an apartment those first years, but when Jane met her husband

Gerald — now a renowned banker — she moved out. But they kept in touch and saw each other on a regular basis.

One night, Alex and I bumped into Jane and Gerald. We'd shared some drinks, and because Alex approved of me, she'd accepted me too. It clicked. Since then, we'd been out a few times together.

Jane and Alex knew the whole story and with a lot of detail. I couldn't stop talking about Patrick. I couldn't stop thinking about him. He took over every conversation, every thought. They were trying to set me up with some guys they knew to help me get Patrick out of my head. I couldn't blame them. I was talking nonstop about him. Must have been terribly annoying.

Alex took my hands in his and looked me straight in the eyes "But, dear, it won't help if you're running away from him."

"You did what?" Jane asked in disbelief.

I sighed and cast my eyes down. I had no choice but to tell her what had happened. My version. I knew she'd drag it out of me eventually.

"Patrick was at the coffee shop this morning. Alex and I were drinking our coffee, like every morning. He came over and asked if I wanted to have another coffee. But with him. I kind of stood him up and ran out before he could say anything else." I paused for a moment, sinking into my embarrassment. "Look, I didn't know what to say to him, okay?" Tears filled my eyes. "This was my chance, and I blew it." I dropped my head between my hands. "I'm a hopeless case when it comes to men!" I sniffled loudly.

"Not entirely, dear," Alex said calmly.

My eyes shot up in surprise, and I wiped away a few tears with the back of my hand. I noted Jane's surprised reaction. Neither one of us knew what Alex was talking about.

"When you bolted, he asked if I knew you."

"What?" I couldn't believe it. "So, what did you say?"

"Well, I told him I knew you. That we're close friends." He hesitated. "And that that wasn't normal behavior."

"Alexxxxx, no you didn't," I moaned. "He'll think I'm totally deranged!"

"What did he say?" Jane asked.

I was on the edge of my chair. Literally. I couldn't keep myself calm. I wanted to know what he'd told Patrick — and what Patrick had said.

"He wanted to know if there was any possibility you'd go out with him." Alex smiled brightly.

"He wants to go out with me? How is this even possible? And what did you say?" I lost it. I was impatient, rattling off question after question.

"I told him he had to do his best."

I blinked. "You what?"

People around us turned our direction. My response was apparently a bit too loud.

"Soph, calm down," Alex said. "He's worth a shot if you ask me. Play hard to get. It'll pay off. You'll see."

"Hard to get? But how?" I cried. "I threw coffee all over him, I stood him up, and he still wants to go out with me? I don't get it."

"Me neither," Jane said.

"Ladies, you have to make them work. This way, it's a lot more fun and a guaranteed success." Alex declared it with such ease, like it was something he announced every day. I had a fleeting image of him as a dating counselor.

He leaned forward. "Okay, this is what you do. If by any chance you see him again — and I'm sure you will — ignore him. Don't immediately say yes if he asks you out. Leave him hanging. Because if he thinks he can't get you, he'll try harder to win you over." Alex was practically singing, as if this were the most brilliant idea he'd ever presented in his entire life. Sometimes he had the strangest theories about dating, but what the hell? If it could help change my status from single to dating, why not? I wasn't an expert, so what harm could it do? Besides, it sounded like good advice.

"Okay, I'll try." I nodded, determined. I didn't know how I'd do this, but I was sure Alex would help me get through it.

On Monday morning, I went straight to the counter where Alex was directing one of his staff members. He ended the conversation as soon as he saw me. I was terribly nervous, had barely slept last night. What if Patrick wasn't there? And if he was, what would I do? What would I even say? My mind kept buzzing with questions and different scenarios.

Alex beamed at me. He was in a good mood, certainly better than mine. "He's already here."

My nerves were kicking in, and my hands started to shake as I sat down. "Alex, what do I do?" I felt a bit desperate. If Patrick asked me out, I'd say yes. In a heartbeat.

"Get your coffee to go. When you pass him, just say hi. Try not to accept any of his invitations. Say you have a presentation, a client visit, or whatever. But no matter what," Alex warned, "DO NOT ACCEPT. You'll see. It'll work."

"Okay." I nodded in understanding. I mustered up all the courage I had, grabbed my coffee to go, and walked toward the coffee shop's exit. And there he sat, in the corner of the coffee shop, reading the morning paper with his coffee. I must have passed him when I entered, but I only noticed him now. He looked up at me. Clearly, he'd seen me come in.

"Uh, hi." I was so surprised I could barely utter a word.

"Good morning. You have time for coffee?" He held up his mug.

"Uh, not really. I have a meeting in ten minutes and I'm already running late. Sorry," I added.

The sorry convinced him. He nodded understandably but tried again. "Perhaps another time this week?"

"Yeah, maybe. Bye." I walked out as fast as possible. I did it! I did what Alex had told me. So now what?

This game between me and Patrick went on for a few weeks. Patrick persevered. Every morning he sat in the same spot, reading his paper and drinking a cup of coffee, simply waiting for me, hoping I would stay and drink a cup with him. I, on the other hand, always had an excuse at the ready: too busy, a client visit, already had a coffee, had a presentation to give. Patrick was a patient man and was presumably waiting for the day I'd finally accept his offer. I started to like our little game. It made my day, seeing him waiting for me every morning. Okay, fine, his divine smile made me walk on air, even when I refused his offers.

One morning, Alex greeted me with a heartwarming smile. Right away I thought, *What is he keeping from me?* I had to know. Patrick wasn't sitting in his usual spot, so maybe he was late or sick or maybe he'd gotten tired of waiting for me. Alex was still looking at me, that bizarre smile on his face. I couldn't figure out what he was hiding.

"What? Why are you looking at me like this?"

"Soph, I have to tell you something. Can you go to the back, where we usually sit after hours? I'll bring the coffee."

I looked at him, puzzled. We only sat in the back when there was something seriously wrong or when he wanted to tell me something his staff couldn't hear. My gut told me it wasn't the second option.

"You okay?" I asked. Now I was a bit worried.

"Yeah, go," he said. "I'll be there in a minute."

Why is he acting so strange? Okay. In a few minutes, you'll know more, so just go to the back, Sophie, and stop your frantic reasoning.

Alex had made a relaxing corner in the back of the coffee shop with a grey three-seater sofa with nailhead trim in the center. An elongated industrial coffee table, which perfectly matched the sofa, sat on a white and grey patchwork rug. The room also featured small cozy corners with comfortable vintage armchairs. Every seat was packed with matching pillows. There was a bookshelf with magazines and books you could borrow against the back wall. The huge brick fireplace made it even cozier, especially when it was cold outside. It was my favorite spot on Sundays. I could sit there reading a good book and sipping a hot chocolate for hours. It was like a cozy little living room.

The moment I turned the corner, I knew it was Patrick, even from the back. He was staring into the fireplace, two mugs of steaming hot coffee on the low table in front of him. I came to a stop, not expecting him there at all. He must have heard me stepping into the room because he looked up in my direction. "You want to join me?" he asked, again in that deep velvety voice. He patted the sofa invitingly.

I turned around to make sure he was actually talking to me, that I wasn't daydreaming. When I didn't see anyone else, that it was only us in the room, I responded eagerly. "Sure." I walked slowly toward him and took a seat knowing it was okay to accept. Alex had obviously tricked me into this. Patrick and I sat next to each other, quiet for a few minutes.

"I already ordered you a coffee. Caramel latte with extra foam, right?" Patrick asked.

"Mmmhmmm, thanks. Alex gave it away, did he?" I smiled softly, avoiding his bold look. I didn't want to gaze directly into his eyes. If I did, I knew I'd lose myself in them all over again.

"Yeah, he did," Patrick admitted. "I had to find a way. You're hard to get for some coffee, you know."

"Who? Me?" I couldn't help myself. I looked dreamily into his eyes.

"Well, to be frank, you're easy to talk to, and I enjoyed the other day at your place. And yes, Alex helped me a bit as well," he added.

Did he admit he liked being in my company? "Yeah, it was lovely," I replied, not finding other words. *What else can we talk about?*

"So, since you have such a busy life, we'd better set a date. When are you free this week? I want to take you to dinner. If it suits you, of course?"

Wow, he got right to the point there. A guy on a mission.

"Well, you're catching me at the wrong time, Patrick. I... I'm leaving in a few days," I said.

"You're leaving New York? For good?" he asked.

"Oh no! Not for good! Heavens no. I've got a case in India, but I'll be back in two, three weeks max." I could barely contain my scream. Would he wait for me? Was he thinking I was standing him up again? Or that this was one of my umpteenth excuses?

"Oh, I see." He was perplexed. I could tell he was trying hard to be upbeat. But something had shifted in his mood. "India, wow. That's great! Never been there."

"It's New Delhi, to be exact. But maybe we can meet when I'm back?" I bit my lip. I wanted to tell him I'd prefer a date with him more than going to India. But something stopped me, and we sat wrapped in complete silence.

In one gulp, he emptied his coffee mug, just like he'd done at my place, and stood up quickly. "So I guess... I'll see you around? Have a wonderful time in India. Goodbye, Sophie."

I nodded. He lifted his hand in a gesture of goodbye, didn't kiss me on the cheek, and left the room in a few strides. Tears welled up in my eyes the instant he was gone. How could this moment change so quickly into something so odd? I wanted to go out with him. I really did. But my job didn't allow it. Not right now.

Oh, he probably thinks I'm a player and this is his way of showing me he's had enough? I had to accept the first time he asked. Gosh, why did I even listen to Alex? Why can't I make up my own mind about him? Why do I even need someone else's opinion or approval for my next action? I sighed loudly in frustration.

Alex was by my side a few seconds later. He had seen Patrick briskly leaving the coffee shop and immediately sensed something was off.

"Soph, what happened?" He looked at me with concern.

"Why do they have to send me to India? Why the hell now!" I shrieked loudly.

Alex took me in his arms and held me tight, soothing me with a few tender words. "It'll work itself out. You'll see."

I didn't want anyone to witness my gloomy mood or see my red and puffy eyes, so I called the office to tell them I was making the last preparations for India and wouldn't come in today. Working from home was the only solution. Besides, being productive would already be a huge task. Tomorrow was my last day of work before flying to India Friday morning. Maybe a change of scenery would get my mind off Patrick.

Alex and I left the coffee shop together. He offered to help me pack my suitcases. But to be honest, I knew he came along because he was feeling remorseful. He'd put me in that situation. He felt responsible and wanted to be there for me. He said he blamed himself the morning went wrong. He had pushed a little too hard and too much and didn't leave me any room to find out things for myself. We spent the rest of the afternoon packing and drinking wine. I accepted refills gratefully.

I thought I had opened up a bit at my apartment that first time we saw each other, giving the guy a chance to get to know me, to woo me like Alex had told me.

Okay, I *thought* I had opened up a bit, but maybe in my head it was better than in reality. Since I'm a real workaholic and hadn't dated in years, opening up wasn't the easiest thing for me. This is a point of attention for me, something to work on. Otherwise, I'm convinced I'm destined to be alone.

Jane showed up later that evening with pizza and a few extra bottles of wine. I was lucky to have such good friends. Some people could discuss things like this with their family. Maybe a brother or a sister. Someone very close to them. I only had Carol, but I couldn't talk about it with her. After our failed meetup, we talked a few times over the phone, we went to see a movie, we grabbed a quick burger. I didn't mention a thing about Patrick, not then, maybe not ever. She wouldn't understand. Well, I just didn't want her to feel hurt again if I talked about him. She was really upset when she saw him at the coffee shop. I hated seeing people upset and certainly my sister. We'd had our share already. So I just put my focus on her and her life; when she asked about my dating life, I turned the subject quickly back to work.

Alex, Jane, and I got hugely drunk. We downed three bottles of wine and two bottles of tequila. And then we passed out on the couch. Thankfully, Alex's loud snoring woke me up the next morning. I'd forgotten to set the alarm on my phone. When I peered at the kitchen clock, I saw it was a few minutes before eight. *Dammit, I'm running late.* Stumbling across my living room, I frantically searched for clean clothes, a cup of coffee, and some painkillers. My head was throbbing heavily — courtesy of lack of sleep, the accumulation of emotions, and an overdose of alcohol.

I left a short note for Alex and Jane. Lucky for them, they didn't have to go to work. Alex could take a day off since he was his own boss and Jane never worked on Thursday. I hurried to the office, accompanied by a huge hangover. I didn't bother stopping for my usual morning coffee, scared I would run into Patrick. The day literally crawled by. My hangover didn't help. I couldn't concentrate at all. I hoped this wouldn't affect my trip to India. I had to make sure all the paperwork for the settlement with Ultra Cement Limited, the largest cement producer in India, was finished and ready to sign. The contracts were already drafted. But the settlement needed some adjustments, just a few, so it was perfect. This was the biggest client I'd had to deal with since my arrival in New York, and if I threw myself into this case, if I did a good job, I could land the whole account. It had been my goal since the beginning: to execute my job to perfection, so people were proud of me. I had to work hard so I could make something out of my career, get a promotion, support myself on my own, like I had always done. So I had to concentrate on this trip. Nothing else. What was I even thinking? I didn't have time for a relationship! And why would a guy like Patrick even be interested in me? He could get any girl he wanted. *Get a grip on your life, Soph. You were on the right track. Okay, it's been a bit emotional but leave it behind and look ahead.*

When I got home later that evening, Sammy was waiting at the elevator.

"Hi, Sammy," I said.

"Good evening, Sophie. How was your day?" he asked.

"Horrible!" I confessed. "I had a lot of work to do before leaving for India. And it wasn't easy with a hangover." I touched my throbbing head and smiled self-consciously. Sammy nodded empathetically.

I was exhausted and another huge headache was setting in. All I wanted to do was lie down, as soon as possible. While I waited for the elevator, I remembered I needed a cab in the morning. "Oh, Sammy, before I forget, I have to leave for the airport at eight o'clock tomorrow morning. Could you hail me a cab a few minutes before eight please?"

"Sure, will do. Have a good evening, Sophie," he said.

"Thank you, Sammy. And a good evening to you too," I said as I stepped onto the elevator and the doors closed.

Everything was set for my trip. I didn't need much since it was a business trip and I always packed lightly: some casual and professional dresses, three pairs of shoes that matched all my outfits, the necessary lingerie, and of course my swimsuit. After a long day of work, I always enjoyed a good swim. It was my ideal way to relax. Irene knew me extremely well and always booked me a hotel with a pool. When I arrived in New York, Irene was the one who'd welcomed me with open arms and managed all my trips. She's my boss Kate's secretary, so any time Kate puts me on a case abroad, Irene arranges every part of my trip. Plane tickets, hotel bookings, restaurant reservations with my clients... She has it covered. Irene's a petite blonde with a love for France and an organizational talent Marie Kondo would be jealous of, so I wasn't surprised we clicked.

My head was still throbbing after I finished packing the last items. After a long hot shower and putting on some freshly washed pajamas, I settled myself on the couch with a fleece blanket and started watching *Gone with the Wind.* It was the only movie I had on DVD, *old school,* and I'd already watched it a hundred times. A real classic and one of my favorites. It has a quote I love tremendously. Nowadays, you'd never catch a man saying it to a woman. Rhett Butler says to Scarlett O'Hara, *"No, I don't think I'll kiss you, although you need kissing badly. That's what's wrong with you. You should be kissed and often, and by someone who knows how."* If a guy said this to you, you'd be swept right off your feet, right? *Ah, Soph, you're a romantic fool.* As I watched the movie, my headache slowly ebbed. I'd needed this moment for myself badly.

The intercom woke me. I must have fallen asleep on the couch. Warily, rousing myself from sleep, I dragged myself off the couch and pressed the button.

"Hello?"

"Sophie, it's Sammy. I have a visitor for you."

"Oh okay," I said. "You can send them up." I forgot to ask who it was. But Sammy only let someone up if I knew them. It was probably Alex or Jane. I switched off the TV and DVD player and headed for the door, hoping they wouldn't mind my PJs — and that they wouldn't stay long. I was looking forward to going to bed and enjoying a deep comatose kind of sleep. I needed to recover from our booze-filled night. A quick look in the mirror hanging next to the front door showed my sleepy state and unflattering hair. As the doorbell rang, I quickly rearranged my hair in a high bun. A few pinches to my cheeks gave me a healthier look. A bit better.

Opening the door, I was shocked to find Patrick in the hallway, holding a brown paper bag. He was dressed casually in washed blue jeans and a dark blue woolen cardigan. He was the last person I'd expected tonight.

"Hi." I faltered, half asleep, half guarded.

"Hi. I woke you, didn't I?" Patrick looked embarrassed when he saw my white-and-red cherry-dot pajamas. I could see him questioning if he should stay or go.

"No, it's fine," I insisted. "I fell asleep on the sofa watching a movie." *Why on earth was he here? What about yesterday when I told him I had to leave for India?*

Patrick was still standing in the hallway, one hand in his pocket, looking at his toes nervously.

"Well, I was in the neighborhood, and I wanted to see you before you left. I brought some dinner. Hungry?" He held up the bag.

He brought dinner. Oh my god, how thoughtful of him. Still, Soph, it doesn't explain his presence. You have to find out.

"Thanks. That's so nice of you. I... C-come on in." I opened the door widely. This was awkward. It was the second time he had visited my apartment. The first time we had a nice chat. But what could I expect now? Tomorrow I was leaving for India, and he was here, at my place, bringing dinner. Weeks, days, hours had passed. I'd been thinking about him, hoping something would finally happen between us. But then, yesterday, he left the coffee shop with barely a goodbye.

I could sense his nervousness, but it wasn't noticeable. He looked impeccable standing in my kitchen. But there was something about him. I didn't know what exactly. I couldn't explain it. A *je ne sais quoi*, as the French say. It made him extremely attractive, and I felt myself falling for him, real hard. I was taking a dangerous road and I was quite aware of it. I was opening up to him, letting my guard down when he was around — and that's always dangerous. Because I could get hurt again. Well, I already felt hurt after yesterday. My confidence took a hit. I thought it was the end of something that hadn't even started.

It made me think back on my time studying at the Sorbonne. My friends had taken me out to a Lambda fraternity party. They knew I'd set my eyes on a certain guy, so they thought going to that party would stack the odds in my favor. Nothing happened that night, we didn't even talk. A few days later, I started getting some texts from him, out of the blue, and I fell in love with a guy I'd never even kissed or spoken to. Weeks went by and we just texted. A lot. Eventually, I gathered my confidence and asked him to meet me for a proper date. He suggested we meet at a party first and grab some dinner afterward. I just went along with his proposition, didn't question any of it.

When I approached him that night, he said he didn't know me. That it wasn't his number. I'd fallen into a trap. A terrible joke by my so-called friends. The boy I'd developed feelings for, the person I thought had been sending me sweet messages for the last few weeks, had no idea who I was. I was devastated. I felt naïve. I'd let my guard down, so now trusting people wasn't my forte.

I looked at Patrick. *How do I react to his presence? He brought Chinese takeout, out of the blue? I like his thoughtfulness, but it won't change a thing about yesterday and how I'm feeling right now,* I thought.

We stood quietly in the room, a tangible tension hanging between us. Patrick put the takeout bag on the counter. Since I had skipped breakfast and dinner and was recovering from my hangover, I was famished. The smell of Chinese delicacies filled the kitchen and my stomach rumbled. We started unwrapping the boxes, both of us happy to have some distraction. I put two plates and wine glasses on the counter. Patrick, still standing on the other side of the kitchen counter, watched my every move from the corner of his eye. He'd also brought a bottle of red wine and started to uncork it.

It's strange, I thought. *We aren't accustomed to each other, aren't familiar with each other's habits, but miraculously he found his way around.*

The bottle of wine opened with a loud popping sound and startled me. I looked up and a warm, heart-melting smile spread across his lips. I had to ask him. He had to give me some explanation for his presence. This wasn't just an evening between friends or a casual dinner for two. There was more to this, and I needed to get to the bottom of it. But did I really want to dig? Maybe I wouldn't be happy with his answer. Maybe he pitied me. Maybe this was a pity dinner. Was this heading somewhere or was I imagining things?

Patrick was facing me, his beautiful curls wrapping around his face, showing off his fierce blue eyes. I popped the question I had wanted to ask the moment I'd found him outside my apartment.

"Why did you leave the coffee shop so suddenly yesterday?" There it was, in the open. No turning back now.

He hesitated, clearly startled by my bluntness. "I don't know, Sophie… It just happened."

"Everything happens for a reason." I pushed through, letting him feel embarrassed.

He looked down at his shoes and twisted the cork between his fingers. "Okay."

I could almost hear him thinking. He was looking for the right words.

"I hate the fact that you're leaving for India. I understand it's for work, but still I don't like it," he said.

"Why? It's my job. You have no say in the matter," I said.

"Why not? Come on, Sophie, don't tell me you're blind." He ran both hands through his hair in frustration.

I wasn't stopping at that answer. I'm a lawyer after all. I wanted all the information. "Why, Patrick? Really why? You left me at the coffee shop without saying a word, without an explanation."

Taking a deep breath, he looked away from me. Suddenly, his posture changed, his back straightened. He swallowed hard and strode toward me until he stood right in front of me. His nervousness had changed into something raw, primal. It alerted all my senses, making me much more aware of him. He was standing at arm's length. If I reached out, I could easily touch him. I could pull him closer. But I didn't. Inhaling deeply, I tried to compose myself. But it was hard. My heart picked up, making my mouth feel dry. I wet my lips.

"Don't do that," he said.

"What?"

"That thing with your lips. It's distracting me."

He was aware of what I was doing, I had an effect on him? I could challenge him. Slowly, I passed my tongue around the edge of my bottom lip, wetting it again. I held eye contact carefully, gazing at him from underneath my lashes. I saw him swallow hard again.

"You still didn't answer my question, Patrick. Why did you leave? Why did you come here this evening?" I asked.

"I'm here because of you. Because I can't stay away from you. Because I like being in your presence. Is this what you want to hear?"

"Mmm." Was that a rhetorical question? I stared into his deep blue eyes, drowning in them. He gazed back at me. Neither of us moved or looked away for a few minutes. The tension built up even more. My body responded to his gaze without hesitation. My cheeks turned red, my pupils became more dilated, and my breathing grew more irregular.

Patrick's breath quickened, he inhaled deeply, and with a short "what the hell," he pulled me against him, kissing me fiercely on the lips. Looking for some stability, I cupped his face with both hands, responding eagerly to his kiss. The stubble on his chin tickled my hands and chin, lightly scraping my lips. His hands felt warm but strong as he held me by the waist, keeping me close. He deepened the kiss by opening my mouth gently. I didn't react fast enough, and our teeth collided with a loud thump. In reaction, I threw my head back a little bit. But it didn't stop him, and he kissed me again but much slower this time. He waited for me to deepen the kiss. So when I opened my mouth, I let him explore mine with his tongue, caressing it carefully. Following his rhythm, we lost ourselves in the kiss. My stomach growled loudly, and I took a few steps back. I looked at Patrick in embarrassment. What would he say?

He took me in, a bit startled, but then started to giggle. "Someone is feeling hungry," he teased.

I wrapped my arms around my stomach, smiling.

"Come on, let's eat," he said and slid the chair back for me before opening the rest of the boxes.

"Good idea," I said, grabbing a plate and a glass and placing them in front of him.

"I didn't know what you'd like, so I ordered a bunch of dishes," he said.

"I'm not difficult but thank you."

He opened a few drawers. "Sophie, where can I find a fork and a knife?"

"Over there, in the top drawer on your left. Why do you need cutlery?" I asked. "You brought chop sticks." I split mine in two.

"Well, I admit, I love Chinese, but chop sticks aren't my thing. I assure you it'll be a mess if I use them, and I don't want you to clean up after me."

"I'm willing to take that chance," I replied, grinning widely. "Come on, I'll teach you." I took another pair of chop sticks out of the paper bag, broke them in half, and handed them to him.

Patrick accepted them hesitantly, watching my every move.

"Well, aren't you skilled." He laughed while I showed him how to use the sticks. I couldn't contain myself and laughed along with him.

"Never thought I'd teach someone how to eat with chop sticks," I said as I caught my breath.

We ate chicken dumplings, Chinese greens in oyster sauce, sesame lotus balls, and stir-fried noodles with scallions, onions, bean sprouts, and soy sauce. All accompanied by a glass of pinot noir. It couldn't be more perfect.

I was stunned to see how easy our conversation was, how much we laughed. What a kiss could do to break the tension.

After dinner we tidied up the kitchen. Well, you don't have to be a rocket scientist. It's easy with Chinese. You throw everything in the garbage bin: boxes, sticks, and done.

I was drying off my hands when Patrick came up behind me, startling me. He took my hand, turning me toward him and caressing it softly with his thumb. An electric jolt shot through my body, his gaze searingly intense.

"Look, I want to try something, if you'll let me." His chest expanded on a deep breath. I couldn't stop staring at him, couldn't move. Wouldn't move. I was mesmerized by him, by his presence, by what he was doing to me. And he was only caressing my hand. My heart started to rattle again. Seeing that I wasn't objecting to his touch, he kept going. His other hand softly stroked my face, sweeping a few strands of hair that had loosened from my knot behind my ear. I closed my eyes and enjoyed the tingling underneath my skin, sensing the path he was tracing with his fingers. He caressed my lips gently with his thumb, nudging them apart. My heart skipped a beat and my breath caught for a moment but quickly adopted a more violent and heavy rhythm, keeping every word locked away. Still no protest from my side, he closed the gap between us, our faces only a few inches apart. His lips slowly curved into a heart-stopping smile. I tilted my head back a little bit so I could get a better look at him. But he cupped the back of my head with his left hand and pulled me closer. I could feel his warm breath on my face and closed my eyes, enjoying being this close to him. He started to trace a path with his nose from my ear down to my neck. I surrendered myself completely to his touch, hoping my knees wouldn't buckle beneath me. In the hollow of my neck, he left a soft kiss. My whole body was on high alert, and he knew it. He moved further up and kissed my left cheek, my temples, my forehead, linking every kiss gently with the top of his nose. I didn't move, didn't want him to stop, my body scintillating with every well-placed kiss. He kissed my left eyelid and headed down again, finally kissing the spot next to my lips. He smiled contentedly, provoking me with just the twirl in his lips. I turned my face toward him and responded to his touch with a tender kiss. I couldn't wait any longer.

Sealing his mouth over mine, he took control of my lips, parting them slowly while deepening the kiss. This time I didn't bungle it. I put my arms around his neck, and he grabbed me by the waist and pulled me against his upper body. I could feel his heart racing through his chest, a low rumble vibrating intensely. For several minutes, there was nothing else but us, kissing, grabbing, being all over each other. We were still stand-ing next to the kitchen counter when we broke apart and took a breath.

"Wow." He exhaled excitedly.

"I agree." Half-drunk by that intense kiss, I smiled back at him. I couldn't stop smiling. I had never been kissed like that before. It reminded me of what Rhett had implied to Scarlett. This was a guy who knew how to kiss. *Would he know the movie?*

I needed a few minutes to pull myself together, so I tidied up the rest of the kitchen while Patrick took our glasses and the bottle of wine to the living room. He took a seat in the corner of my soft grey linen couch, one leg tucked beneath him. He watched me in the kitchen, his arm loosely draped over the back of the couch. I was hyperaware of him watching me but also of having him around. He was such a self-assured, graceful, and handsome man. I, on the other hand, with my self-esteem and trust issues, hadn't the slightest idea why he wanted to be with me. I hadn't had good experiences in my relationships. Why would men even be interested in me? I was naïve, a perfection-ist, and a workaholic. I didn't see myself as attractive. I couldn't believe he was there. Okay, he made it a bit clearer when he kissed me in the kitchen. But what if he changed his mind? What if this was all a game to him? A plan to get me back for throwing coffee at him?

I didn't want to take a chance, or let my thoughts take over too much, so I joined him. A sweet yearning filled me the minute I sat down. It was such a rush being near him. *I could trust my body, right?* A simple look from him drew me into his arms, and we started kissing again. My mouth had only touched his for an instant, but the jolt raced through my system again. He must have felt it too because he pulled me onto his lap, wrapping my legs around his torso. His hands traveled down my spine and cupped my ass firmly, making my skin burn through my paja-mas. His hands moved up and down, and he skillfully slid them under my pajama top, caressing the sides of my breasts. It was so excruciatingly good. It was like I hadn't been touched or kissed by a guy in ages. Okay, it's true. It had been a while. My whole body was aching for him. I wanted to lose myself completely in the moment, in him, in his eyes, but I couldn't go through with it. My rational mind took over completely. We had only met a few weeks ago.

I took his hands from under my top and held them in between mine, pushing him back against the couch. Leaning forward, I kissed him gently on the lips and slid slowly from his lap. I had a hard time restraining myself, but I didn't want it to be a one-night stand. Strangely, he didn't argue. Maybe he didn't want me to do anything uncomfortable. I could see he had a hard time as well. But he showed a tremendous amount of willpower and didn't throw himself at me. He wrapped his arm around me, pulling me closer, and I laid my head on his chest. After a few minutes of enjoying the silence and each other's presence, we talked till early in the morning until I finally fell asleep on his shoulder around one o'clock.

SLOW LATTE

When my alarm went off the next morning, I was alone on the couch, covered by my grey fleece blanket, still wearing my cherry-dotted pajamas. I glanced at the clock on the kitchen wall. Seven thirty, damn. I hurried into the kitchen where my phone's wakeup alarm was blaring. My cab would arrive in less than half an hour, and I had to shower. *But where did Patrick go? Did he leave in the middle of the night? Did I ask him to leave?* I couldn't remember. I was so fucking tired. The alcohol from two nights ago and the lack of sleep were taking their toll. I had no time to think everything over. I had to shower and pack the last items in my beauty case so I'd get to the airport on time. *Why would he stay the night? I'd be away for several weeks. We kissed, nothing else happened, right? That's probably why he left. He won't wait for me? Pity, I really thought we had a connection.*

While replaying our evening in my head — in vivid detail — I heard a key unlocking the front door. *Did I give Alex or Jane a key?* To my surprise, it was Patrick, holding two mugs of fresh coffee. He was freshly showered and wearing a dark navy-blue suit with an indigo tie, which looked powerful and strong while still conveying integrity and some sincerity.

Did he stay after all? Or did he go home and come back this morning? Did I give him a key? Oh, I can't remember.

"Hi, you slept well?" he asked.

"Yeah. But way too short. You?" I had to find out if he'd stayed.

"A bit. It's hard to sleep when you're lying next to me." He smiled.

So he stayed. Yes! My inner goddess cheered loudly.

"I snored?"

"No, you didn't," he said with a huge smile. He placed the paper coffee cup on the counter in front of me. "I went out for some coffee and stopped at my place to shower. I have a meeting later this afternoon and wanted to make the most of our time together." He leaned forward and gave me a long, deep kiss. "Mmmmm, I don't want you to go. We'll keep in touch during your trip, right?"

I bit my lip and blushed. "That would be nice."

I stole another look at the clock. I only had a little time left before the cab arrived. "I'm sorry, but my cab will be here in fifteen minutes. I have to get ready. I'm already so late. Sorry."

He put me at ease. "Don't, you have time. When I ran out this morning for some coffee, I asked Sammy to call off the cab."

"But how will I get to the airport? I..." I panicked.

"Take your time getting dressed. My chauffeur is waiting downstairs and will take us to the airport when you're ready. We'll have some time together before you leave. Is that okay?"

I nodded. Patrick was the greatest. But a little voice inside my head asked, *"His chauffeur?"* I was in a good mood — correction, I was walking on air — so I didn't ask for more details. I jumped into the shower, dried my hair quickly, and put it up in a low, sleek knot. Twenty minutes later, I emerged from the bathroom wearing my travel outfit: a navy-blue business suit, a white mousseline blouse with short sleeves, and matching blue wedge heels. The trousers would keep me warm on the plane — after all, it was a long flight — and the shoes were comfortable enough to walk through the airport. I grabbed my grey-and-blue poncho off the coat hanger in my bedroom and headed back to the kitchen.

"I hope that wasn't too long a wait," I said.

"No, it's okay, I checked my mail in the meantime. You look charming, by the way," he added.

"Thanks." I beamed at him. "I'm all set. We can go."

Everything went as planned. Patrick's chauffeur, Darren, was waiting in front of the building next to a black Mercedes-Benz C-Class Sedan. He wore a grey suit, no hat, no gloves, but still oozed stylishness.

"Good morning, miss," he said. "I'll take these for you." He took my suitcase and briefcase, and Patrick opened the door for me. I hesitated at the curb but slipped into the back. Patrick took a seat next to me. I peered out the tinted glass and saw pedestrians looking curiously at the car, trying to see who was inside.

Darren drove us to the airport. Even with the delay I'd caused, I would still be on time. After last night, I didn't want to go to India, but Patrick assured me we would have a proper date when I got back. We exchanged phone numbers in the car and promised to stay in touch for the next three weeks. But I knew if I closed the negotiations quickly, I'd be back in two weeks — tops. After I checked in my luggage, Patrick kissed me goodbye and wished me a good trip. I promised to call him as soon as I checked into the hotel.

And there I was, on a plane to India, smiling widely as I played back the events of the previous night. Lightheaded from a lack of sleep but feeling happy about my Rhett Butler moment. I knew I had to be careful or I'd jinx it. I texted Alex quickly to keep him updated.

He kissed me. Call you once I'm checked into the hotel.

XXX

I switched my phone into airplane mode, turned off the reading light, wrapped my scarf around my shoulders, and reclined my seat. I had a nineteen-hour flight ahead of me, with a three-hour layover in Istanbul. I wouldn't have any contact with Patrick. I didn't know if I could handle it. I was still having flashbacks to last night. I closed my eyes, drifted off to sleep, and dreamed of what might have happened if I'd allowed it. *More self-confidence in that area certainly wouldn't hurt,* I thought in a dreamy haze.

ESPRESSO

My trip in India lasted two weeks and three days to be exact. Patrick and I texted and called whenever we could. At the end of the day — well, for me it was evening and for him midday because there was a ten-hour time difference — we tried to Skype. Every night I waited impatiently to see him, for the beep announcing his call. My breath caught every time the screen switched on and I saw his lovely face. I told him about my day, the work I'd done, how hard it was to do business in India. Luckily, I had Akshita, a Hindu lawyer, who helped me when the translations and customs got tough. I'd been baffled by the way she did business; her name literally meant "without limitations." And indeed she had balls and no clear limits. She wasn't a typical Indian woman. I'd been upset about the poverty and the disparity in New Delhi. I spent whole days negotiating with top companies, sitting in beautifully decorated offices, going out to eat at top restaurants with my clients, and then at night I drove by neighborhoods where people slept outside and barely had food. The contrast made me think about what was valuable in life. As a kid we didn't always have it easy — we had it good, but not like some people in India. It made me grateful for everything. It made me want to make the most out of life. And I shared that with Patrick.

He was extremely open too, talking me through his day, the difficult relationship he had with his father, their constant quarreling, day-to-day stuff. But that was what I enjoyed; it gave me a feeling of normalcy. I showed him my hotel room, and he walked me through his office. We talked for hours and admitted we were looking forward to seeing each other back in New York.

When I finally returned, I stopped in at the office. Kate, my over-worried boss, insisted on seeing us after each foreign trip. Sort of a debriefing. It's a strange habit, I know, but it was her routine. After each trip, small or big, we sat together, went through the details of the trip, the contracts... She wanted to be sure we hadn't overlooked anything. No loose ends, that was one of her mottos.

It was nine o'clock by the time I left the office, and I was tired. The time difference didn't help. After every trip, I needed a few days to reset my body clock, and it was hitting me hard. I'd worked a lot of long hours, so I could wrap up my work quickly and get back to New York to see Patrick as soon as possible. I wanted to see him but not in this condition. For once, I wanted him to see me when I wasn't in pajamas or exhausted, so he just had to wait. I had no energy for a date.

I called Patrick the moment I stepped into the apartment. He answered instantly. "Hey, you're back?" He sounded thrilled.

"Yeah, my plane arrived this afternoon, but I just got home a few minutes ago. I had a meeting with my boss this afternoon, and we just wrapped up."

"Great boss," he said sarcastically.

"I know," I said. "I don't think she can sleep if she doesn't know every single detail of our trips. Kind of a ritual."

"You must be tired."

"I'm exhausted. Would you mind if we moved our get-together back to tomorrow?" I asked. "I've got nothing planned for the whole weekend."

"Sure, no problem. I'm actually still at work, so I'll finish a few tasks I'd planned on doing this weekend. We can have the weekend all to ourselves, no work involved. I promise," he said.

"Sounds great. I'll call you tomorrow morning." I yawned loudly. "Sorry."

"Don't be," he said. I could hear him smiling through the speaker. "Sleep it off so I can enjoy your company tomorrow. Call me when you're awake and we'll make plans."

"Okay, good night," I said.

"Good night, Sophie. I'm counting the hours."

I went straight to bed. I didn't even take time to put on my pajamas. I just undressed and slid underneath the duvet, wearing only my underwear. I fell asleep in no time.

It was ten thirty when I woke up. *Dammit, I slept around the clock.* I wanted to see Patrick and I was wasting valuable time sleeping the day away. I got up quickly, took a refreshing shower, and dressed in a pair of grey jeans, a soft pink silk shirt, and a grey sweater jacket. I grabbed my purse and my cell, slipped on my pink ballerina flats, and dialed Patrick's number while I rode the elevator down to the lobby. *Maybe he'd like to join me for brunch at Alex's Starbucks,* I thought.

The phone rang several times before it went to voicemail. "Hi, you've reached Patrick's voicemail. I'm not available at this time. Please leave a message and I'll get back to you as soon as possible." I left a message and hailed a cab. Alex would be at the coffee shop like every other Saturday, so I could have brunch there.

In the cab, my mind started racing. *Patrick didn't answer his phone. Strange. I hope everything is okay? Or maybe he finally came to his senses and doesn't want to see me. Is this his way of telling me he isn't interested?* I shook my head. *Oh come on, Soph. You heard him on the phone last night. He didn't change his mind overnight. Aaargh, I miss him.* I knew I had to take things slow and not rush into it. I knew it could be over in a heartbeat. But I liked him too much.

Alex saw me coming and opened the door for me with a big-hearted smile. He pulled me into a bear hug. "Hello, sunshine, nice to have you back," he said.

"Hi, it's great to be back. You know," I said, hugging him firmly, "they don't have your coffee and cinnamon buns in India."

"Well, let's do something about that. Hungry?" He towed me toward the bar.

"I'm starving," I admitted, raising my eyebrows.

I sat down at the end of the counter, while Alex made me a latte with caramel and set a tray of fresh cinnamon buns in front of me. They were still a little warm and moist, just the way I liked them. I was enjoying the familiar feeling. Between customers, we talked about India and everything I'd missed in New York, especially Patrick. Alex filled me in on the latest gossip, his favorite topic.

Patrick still hadn't called back, and it was almost noon. I had my chin propped in my palm, checking my phone and my watch every ten minutes, waiting for a message. Or any sign of life.

Alex was serving customers, so I had no one to talk to at the moment. I had made no plans — well, not yet — so I decided to hang around the shop. I ordered another coffee and went to the back to settle in to the comfortable sofa with a novel. I was so caught up in it I hadn't noticed someone entering the room.

"Hi, gorgeous," he whispered in my ear.

I turned my head and smiled. *Patrick.*

"Hi," I said nervously.

"I'm so sorry I didn't return your call and kept you waiting. Something came up at the office last minute, and I had to finish some paperwork. I was hoping you'd still be here. I'm all yours now." He sank into the couch next to me and drank me in with his beautiful blue eyes. He looked bright and happy.

I was relieved. He showed up. I studied him. Patrick wore dark blue jeans, a white V-neck t-shirt, and a smoky grey woolen cardigan. Casual, but he looked handsome as hell. We kept staring at each other for a few minutes, taking our time getting used to being in the same room again. Finally, he leaned in and gave me a lush, wet kiss. I enjoyed the warmth of his lips and the tenderness of his touch. After a few seconds, he deepened the kiss, urging me on and longing for more. We stopped for a second, my heart beating frantically, Patrick breathing deeply. His eyes were all heated. The way he looked at me made my cheeks redden instantly.

"Let's get out of here," he commanded in a raw voice. He grabbed my hand and pulled me off the sofa. I was speechless and followed him outside. I waved quickly at Alex, who was laughing as he watched us. Surely, he had seen Patrick come in and knew what we were up to.

The sun was shining brightly for this time of year and wrapped me in warmth when we stepped out. Patrick held my hand while we walked through the busy streets of New York. It felt strange, holding hands, because we hadn't known each other that long. But it felt fantastic, too, and sent a charge of awareness through me.

"So, where are we going?" I dared to ask after a few blocks.

He jerked to a halt, his gaze darkening and his voice lowering intimately, showing me with his whole body what he was thinking. "We're going to my place." He looked around, held his hand up, and hailed a cab. "We need to get there faster."

"Oh, okay." I didn't ask what we were going to do at his place. I sort of guessed.

The cab ride seemed short. Patrick and I stared at each other the whole time, from the coffee shop to his place. Only our hands were linked. But even that made my inhalations shaky, revved my heartbeat. The cabdriver parked in front of a posh apartment building in Central Park. Patrick hopped out of the car, rounded it, and opened the door for me. He paid the driver and towed me through the lobby, passing his doorman — "Good afternoon, sir, miss." We rode the elevator up to his apartment on the top floor.

Smoothly throwing his keys on the kitchen counter, he turned and watched me while I looked around. I was stunned by the view. His living room had a huge sliding glass door that led to a terrace overlooking Central Park. The place was huge and bathed in sunshine. I stood in front of the window, baffled by the scenery.

"You like it?"

"Patrick, it's breathtaking. What a view! This is yours?" I asked.

"Mmhmm. It's temporary. My new place is still under construction."

"So why did you bring me here? You didn't want coffee?" I smiled provocatively. He didn't respond but closed the gap between us in a few strides.

"I brought you here so we could have some privacy." He slowly caressed the contours of my arms. The sensation was phenomenal, and it was only my arms. The tension between us was building. We didn't need a lot of words to understand each other's needs since we'd been apart for a couple of weeks. I knew if he lost control, like earlier in the coffee shop, he wouldn't stop. And now that we were in the privacy of his apartment, he wasn't worried about being interrupted.

"I had to restrain myself back there in the coffee shop, Sophie," he said.

"Oh." I gasped for air loudly, my nipples hardening instantly. He wanted me, but was I ready? It had been years since I'd been intimate with anyone. What if I didn't meet his standards? Wasn't this too soon? What should I do?

He didn't give me a lot of time to think. He pulled me closer by placing his hand at the back of my neck. He kissed me roughly, rekindling the same intense kiss from earlier at the coffee shop. My mind couldn't reason this time, so I followed the directions my body gave me. I entwined his hair in my fingers, looking for some balance. My knees weren't holding. His hands were cupping my head now, holding it in place. After a few minutes, we were up against the living room wall, his body pressing me tightly against it. His hands were all over me, and he tried to pull my shirt over my head. And I froze. My mind came back online. We'd only met a few weeks ago, and I'd been in India most of that time. *This is too soon, way too soon! This is lust driving us insane,* I thought. I took a step back and held him off.

"Don't, Patrick."

"What? What's wrong?" He acted all surprised and took a step back.

"Look, this is going too fast. I'm not that kind of woman," I said.

He was quiet, taking it in. "Talk about a cold shower..." he said dryly and raised his eyebrows, sighing loudly.

Wow, I didn't expect this from him. Doesn't this mean anything to him? I was right: He wasn't in it for the long run. I tilted my head, so I could make eye contact with him. "I like you, Patrick, but I can't do it. Not right now. We met a few weeks ago, and I was mostly abroad. If you don't want to see me anymore, I understand," I said. I looked down at my toes, waiting for his answer, feeling uncomfortable.

"I'm sorry," he said. "You're right. We'll take it slow." He placed a kiss on my lips. "We're okay?' he asked questioningly. He looked deeply ashamed of his urge.

"Yes." I smiled at him brightly, feeling a bit more at ease. Emotions reeled through me though. I understood his need. After all, he's a man. My body was giving all the signals and I wanted it too, more than anything. But this wasn't me, throwing myself at someone. I wanted to know him a lot better, a lot longer before I gave myself to him. Surely, I asked a lot of him, to restrain himself. I was happy he didn't send me home. Instead, he gave me a guided tour of his place, trying to change the charged atmosphere between us. He passed his bedroom quickly. Maybe he didn't want to be triggered again.

The entire place was too clean and sterile for me, like it was cut out of a glossy magazine. It lacked character and warmth. I missed pictures, cards, mementoes of family and friends. Flowers to brighten up the room. None of that was present. It was only when I walked back into the living room that my eye caught a wooden chessboard. It looked totally out of place on the windowsill, as if there had been a game in progress or maybe the chess pieces had been displaced by someone else. Either way, it caught my attention. I walked toward it and picked up a piece. I traced every curve with my finger.

"Don't touch it!" Patrick snapped loudly, startling me. "Don't touch it!" He grabbed the piece out of my hand and replaced it on the board.

"S-sorry... I thought it had been misplaced," I said.

He registered my reaction. He grabbed my hand and placed a gentle kiss on it. "This was my grandfather's chessboard," he explained. "We played a lot together when I was young."

"Oh, that's nice," I said quietly.

"My grandparents are from England, but my mother moved to the States when she met my father. But her heart is still in England. Whenever we visited my grandparents, I'd play chess with my grandfather in front of the fireplace." Patrick paused. "A few years ago, he suddenly became ill. It started with a lack of appetite, but even when he could eat, he lost weight unexplainably. He was in constant pain. After a few weeks, he was hospitalized. They ran some tests and found out he had stomach cancer, but it was already in an advanced stage. The cancer had spread to his esophagus and his liver. And then it spread everywhere. My mother stayed in England to take care of him and her mother. Once and a while, I flew to England and visited my grandfather in the hospital. My mother had moved this chessboard to his room. It was the only game he loved playing. So when I was there, we played chess together, like old times. Grandfather and grandson together. This was the last game we played. He won…" He rubbed the chess piece gently with his thumb and placed it back on the board. Just as it had been.

I saw the sadness in his eyes, reflecting his deep grief at the loss of his grandfather. "Thanks for sharing that with me," I said, pinching his hand. I loved seeing this more personal side of him.

He smiled sadly and changed the subject. "You want to go for a walk in the park? It's still warm outside."

"Yes, that would be nice."

Patrick literally lived a few steps from Central Park. We walked through the park, no real destination in mind. For the beginning of October, the sun was offering a warm glow, but the wind was a bit chilly. I hugged my grey sweater jacket firmly around me. Patrick noticed and wrapped his arm around me, his hand rubbing some warmth into my arm. I mouthed a thank you. We made some small talk, but you could tell we both wanted to avoid discussing what happened in his apartment. He seemed sad, maybe because he'd been triggered by old memories. It was uncomfortable, and I didn't know how to be there for him. I felt like I had turned our rendezvous into an awkward afternoon.

After our walk, we ordered some Thai food and watched an old James Bond movie. Kneeling on the thick creamy carpet, we ate in silence. Patrick leaned against the couch and took me in his arms, my back pressing against his chest, our heads resting against each other. But after a while, he got up and sat at the opposite end of the couch. I didn't move from my spot. Something was off. I didn't want to ask what was bothering him, afraid it would turn into a discussion. I had already done enough stupid things today, so we watched the rest of the movie in complete silence.

Patrick surprised me by asking, "Do you want to stay the night?"

I had to turn him down politely. I needed the alone time and was overwhelmed by the day's emotions. "Um. I think I'll head back to my place. I... With the jetlag and stuff... We can meet again tomorrow, right?" I was feeling off, so it was better if I left. Still, he was courteous and called me a cab. I grabbed my stuff and stood awkwardly at the front door. He caught my face in his hands and gazed down at me, his expression bleak. "Good night, Sophie," he said, kissing me as if it were the last kiss we'd ever share. At least that's how I interpreted it. I took the cab back home, all alone.

On Sunday, he didn't call, and we didn't meet up. *Should I call him? Or should I wait for him to call?* I worried. I was too stubborn and was waiting for a sign from his side, any possible sign. I wanted him to show me we could have something without diving right into bed. But there was no sign. Maybe it was for the best.

STRESSED, BLESSED, COFFEE OBSESSED

Luckily, Alex invited me to Sunday brunch. Clearly, he wanted details about my night with Patrick. So I hauled myself to the shop.

"Look what the cat dragged in," he said.

"Hi," I mumbled. "Sorry but I'm kind of in a gloomy mood today."

"Wow, you okay?"

"No, not really. I didn't sleep well last night. I was up all night thinking."

"Oh, nasty. Don't do that," Alex advised. "You'll get wrinkles at the age of thirty-five."

"I know," I said, snickering at his response.

"Come on, what's wrong?" He looked troubled as he prepared my coffee.

"I don't know," I said, collapsing into my chair. "I'm having an off day. I'm getting older and I'm feeling alone. I'm not attractive..."

"Wow, wow, wow... Let me stop you right here. No wallowing in my shop," Alex said.

"Sorry." I held up my hands in apology. "Maybe it's better if I call it a day. I'm not in the mood."

"Here," he said, placing my latte on the counter. "Drink up."

I took a sip of the warm latte and settled into the chair. Looking straight into his familiar, blue eyes, I pulled myself together a bit. "Thanks. This helps."

"Listen, darling, you're great just the way you are. Where is this all coming from?" he asked.

"I have a bad feeling about me and Patrick," I said. "I don't know if it will last. I'm not a model, I'm working most of the time, I have nothing interesting to say... He probably has ten other women waiting for him."

"I'll have to stop you right there, Sophie!" Alex interrupted. "So you're not a model. Who cares? You're a real woman with curves. You're not fat or chubby," he said when I started to protest. "I know you don't think highly of yourself, but I've seen men admiring you, turning their heads when you walk by. And trust me. They're not looking at that extra pound you think you're carrying. They see what I see: a lovely, smart, and beautiful woman they want to fuck."

I blushed. "Jesus, I feel like a whore now."

"You know what I mean." He laughed. "Come on. You're smart. You can talk about anything. Even when a conversation starts to die out, you can change the topic, you can sense the mood, you can feel what people need. You worked real hard to get where you are. And yes, some men find it intimidating, but you don't want to date those men. Oh yes," he added, "there's something else. You're fun. I've seen it before. One word, my dear: TE-QUI-LA!"

"Great. I'll be drunk all the time and find the love of my life with my wicked and smart replies. Thanks, Alex."

"Terrific mood, Sophie, really. You're a keeper." He snorted.

I sighed deeply. "Maybe you're right, Alex."

"Maybe? I am right, darling! Just come out a little bit more, do some stuff — with me, for example. You're fun to hang out with, and if Patrick doesn't see that, others will." He grabbed my hand across the bar and pinched it.

"I don't know what I would do without you. Great pep talk," I said.

"You know I'm always here for you." His face lit up. "You know what? Let's do something this week or Friday evening? Just us girls. Let's have some fun. What do you think?"

"Deal." I jumped off my chair and leaned across the bar to hug him. "Thanks."

My talk with Alex had lifted my mood a bit, but back home, I wanted to be alone and wallow in regret. If I had accepted Patrick's advances, I wouldn't be all alone on a Sunday. *What is wrong with me? Really?*

Still, I'm not the kind of person to just jump in the sack at every opportunity. Aaargh! But thinking it through, I would have taken the leap. I would have let him. Everyone needs some affection. I know I do. Was this the end of what we'd started? Could I even call it a relationship? Dammit, I couldn't even pinpoint it. I had to talk it through with Alex and Jane on our girls' night out. They could give me some advice.

Finally. Friday. I had busted my ass at work all week. Patrick hadn't called or texted, but I hadn't tried to reach him either. I was too stubborn. I knew drinks with Alex and Jane would do me good.

I changed into a more suitable outfit and spent a little more time putting on my makeup than usual. I looked chic in my plum-colored sleeveless dress. I finished my look with some glossy black pumps and a black trench.

Jane was already at the bar when I arrived. She waved frantically as soon as she saw me. I quickly dropped my trench at the coat check and took a seat next to her.

"Sophie, how was India?" she asked. "I have so many questions..."

"Hi to you too." I cut her off mid-sentence and gave her a peck on the cheek. We both laughed.

"Sorry, it's one of the countries I'm dying to visit," she said.

"Let me get something to drink first, and I'll give you all the details. By the way," I said, "where's Alex? He didn't forget, did he?"

"Oh no, he's running late. He called ten minutes ago. He'll be here in half an hour."

"Typical Alex." I rolled my eyes. "What are you drinking? Up for some cocktails?"

"Totally!"

I ordered two margaritas and filled Jane in on my trip to India. The people I had met, like Akshita, the few places I had seen and visited in and around New Delhi, the difference in mentality and social ranking. Jane listened attentively. I hoped she could visit the beautiful country one day, but with her busy life and her hardworking husband, I doubted it would happen.

By the time we finished our second round, Alex had arrived. He gave Jane a peck on the cheek and spun toward me.

"So, Miss Sophie, where the hell have you been all week?" he demanded.

I was stunned. Why was he being so rude? "I..."

"I haven't seen you for the last five days. What's going on? I know you weren't out of the country. Is Patrick involved in this? Because he didn't stop in for coffee this week either," he said.

"He didn't?" I asked surprised.

Alex softened when he saw my reaction and sat down next to me. "So, you weren't with him? I thought you were staying at his place and you didn't come in for coffee and an update because you were with him. I thought, after our talk on Sunday, he'd called you and everything was okay again."

"No, I wasn't with him," I said. "I'm sorry, but I just wasn't in the mood. And I didn't want to run into him." I shrugged.

Alex and Jane glanced at each other questioningly, sensing something was off. Alex waved the waiter over and ordered a round of tequila shots. It was a ritual of ours. If one of us hit a rough patch, like a bad day at work or a relationship going down the drain, we always had tequila shots.

"Girl, you need a shot. Go on," he said, nudging the glass toward me.

After a few shots, I was feeling a bit more courageous.

"So what happened, Sophie?" Jane asked cautiously.

"Well, I got back from India last Friday. I was exhausted and asked Patrick if we could meet Saturday instead of Friday evening. In the morning — well, it was already noon — I called him, but he didn't pick up. So I left him a message telling him I was at the coffee shop and if he wanted, he could join me for brunch. Patrick surprised me later on and apologized for being late. We made out, and he kind of got carried away. He literally dragged me out of the coffee shop and took me to his place."

"Yeah, the guy was all over you." Alex suppressed a laugh. "So what happened next? Is he good in bed?"

"Alex! Seriously?" I shot him a dirty look.

"Okay, sorry, go on."

"So we got to his place and we were kissing and he started to take off my clothes and... I froze. I couldn't do it. I asked him to stop," I said.

"You what?" Alex yelled.

Jane intervened. "Alex, let her speak. Come on, Sophie, don't let us stop you."

"I know," I said. "It wasn't my finest moment. But all I could think was what if I was just another conquest, nothing more? What if I slept with him and that was it? What if I didn't meet his standards? I blew it, guys, I really did."

"Why are you even thinking about this?" Jane asked. "If he really liked you, if he was really into you, this wouldn't come between you. He can wait." Jane was so amiable, always looking for the best in people.

"Oh come on," Alex said. "He's a guy. They think with their dicks."

Jane ignored him. "So have you heard from him since Saturday?"

"No, but I stayed and he gave me a tour of his apartment that afternoon. I stupidly misplaced a piece on a chessboard that belonged to his grandfather. He was really mad, but he apologized. So we went for a walk in the park to change the mood, then ordered in and watched a movie. He asked me to stay, but I was so ashamed and didn't feel so great, so I left. I haven't heard from him since."

"And did you call him?" Jane asked.

"Not exactly," I admitted. "Look, I don't know how to say this. I still can't understand why I rejected him. You've seen the guy, right? He's gorgeous. And..." I hesitated. "Well, it's been a while since I've had sex. Maybe I'm not good at it. Maybe that's why I rejected him."

"What? Are you even listening to what you're saying, Sophie?" Alex was exasperated. "You sound ridiculous. You're a wonderful woman with a lot going for you. You're smart, beautiful, curious, and definitely not a quitter. You've never quit something just because you're not good at it. I know you. You take matters into your own hands. Don't get down on yourself. Yeah, okay, you got cold feet because this is all new for you. So what! I'd sleep with you if I dated women."

I rolled my eyes. "Thanks, Alex, really reassuring."

"Do you like him?" he asked.

"Yes, I do."

"Do you want him?"

"YES."

"Well, let's do something about it."

I nodded. Alex was convincing.

We kept drinking as Alex brainstormed different ways to get Patrick and me back together.

Alex knew the bouncer at a nearby club, so we headed there next, cutting the line to get in. I'd already had my fill of alcohol but didn't let that bring my evening to an end. For once, it was exhilarating, the buzz of the booze, the lights flashing everywhere. I got lost in the crowd and moved Patrick to the back of my mind. Just for now.

Earlier that evening, at a pub downtown...

"Patrick, my man. It's been ages. How are you?"

"Hello, David. Great to see you," I said. "Mark, Jonathan, Andrew... Andrew. Wow, you're here!"

"Hey, Patrick, it's been a while, right?" Andrew laughed.

"It sure has." I shook all my old schoolmates' hands. "It's great to see you all. David, you've got to get married a lot more so we can see each other once in a while."

"Not gonna happen, dude," David said. "I'm happy with my fiancée. But it's good to know you want to buy everyone drinks more often." He laughed loudly.

"Hey, first round's on me. But don't think I'm paying for the whole evening," I said. I headed to the bar, and Andrew joined me.

"So, what have you been up to lately?" Andrew asked.

"Well, I've been working with my father in real estate for a few years now," I said.

"And how's that going? The last time I saw you, you weren't too fond of each other."

I snorted. "We still aren't close. Since my parents divorced, he replaced her with me at the firm. Well, replaced is a strong word," I said. "He made me chief operating officer. We have an agreement: If he doesn't bother me, I leave him alone. But I'm finding it hard to connect with him. He changes women like he's changing underwear. Every one of them younger by the day. I see him every day. It's like he's haunting me, harassing me at the office, and I can't handle it. The only way out of this whole mess is if he amends our contract. Or drops dead."

"A contract?" Andrew asked. "What kind of contract? Isn't there a loophole in it?"

"Yeah, I know it's bizarre." I sighed. "To get him to leave my mother alone and not broke, I had to sign a contract binding me to his company, to him. My mum suffered enough, so I didn't think it through and signed it without hesitation. I regret it, but my mother is free. And believe me I've had different lawyers try to revise the contract, hoping to find a way out. But they haven't found one," I said, shaking my head. The bartender came over, and I ordered drinks for the table.

"This is what he wants," I continued. "He enjoys having control over me. There's no way out."

"What does your job even entail?"

"I'm managing the complaints, day-to day-operations. It's not the coolest job, but I'm making the most of it. We're the concierge for all the estates in my father's portfolio."

"Is it that big then?"

"Well, most of the companies in that portfolio are supermarkets, shopping centers, stores on Fifth Avenue, but we've got a few extraordinarily luxurious condos and townhouses around New York too." I took a gulp of the beer the waiter had placed in front of me. "It pays well, so I'm putting up with him and all of his bullshit. But enough of that. It's boring. What are you doing these days?"

"I'm still in finance. I'm working at a small office in Harrisburg, nothing special," Andrew said. "I'm hoping to climb the ladder and take on some more responsibilities, maybe become manager. I'm looking for something in a bigger firm but haven't found the right fit yet. I've thought about getting started on my own, but it's too early."

We took the drinks back to the table. "First round," I announced. "Many more to come, David. I hope you're taking a cab tonight." I raised my glass.

"I hope so, too, guys. To old days and new beginnings," David said, raising his glass.

"To David and his lovely fiancée Renée," I said.

After a few drinks, we quickly got on the subject of women. Since David was getting married, Mark and Jonathan were already married, and Andrew had been in a relationship for three years, I was the only single guy.

"So what about you, Patrick, have you found your match? Or do you still enjoy a different girl every week?" Jonathan asked.

All eyes were on me. I felt awkward. In high school, we'd had a lot of fun, but now, years later, they'd settled down.

"Well, I'm still not settled like you guys. But don't think I'm hooking up with someone every week. I have to work for it, too, you know," I said lightly.

"Oh come on," Mark exclaimed. "Back in high school, you had your pick. Girls threw themselves at you."

"I hate to disappoint you, but those days are long gone," I said. "But I met a woman. She's remarkable. I don't know where things are going. We'll see what happens."

"That's great, man!" I could tell David was sincere.

Not Jonathan. "And is she hot?" he demanded rudely.

Mark cut him off. "Oh man, really? You're not getting it at home?"

I didn't have any juicy stories, so I was glad the questioning ended and the conversation moved on to work, family, and cars. Besides, I didn't want to reveal what had happened last weekend.

As the night went on and we got drunker, David moved onto the dance floor. It was packed with half-naked women and guys trying to woo them, their bodies frantically following the music's rhythm. Like their lives depended on it. The rest of us could only stand by and watch. We didn't have the rhythm David had in his pinky toe alone.

That's why Mark had brought us to this new club. David had always been a fervent dancer. Back in school, girls wanted him to accompany them to dances or an evening out because he was such a good dancer. That's how he scored with the girls.

Foxtrot, salsa, jive, you name it, and he could dance it. Okay, his mother was a dance teacher. As a kid, she had dragged him on the dance floor, teaching him every dance step he knows today. She taught him how to dance with a girl. So yeah, it wasn't hard to see why he could dance so well.

The club was buzzing. I looked around and saw trendy people seated in black leather lounge seats sipping even trendier cocktails.

It was nice to be out with the group of guys I'd grown up with. In high school, we'd been teammates. Some wild years if you ask me. We partied as hard as we played on the field. We scored on the field — and off the field. We were the popular guys.

After high school, we went our separate ways. I studied economics at a business school in New York. It was what my father wanted. Andrew studied finance, but David didn't finish college. His mother homeschooled him because, until a few years ago, he and his mother ran a dance school together. That's where he met his fiancée, his soon-to-be wife. But he had always been interested in art and now owned a gallery. Word got out he's quite famous in New York.

Mark's the only one who kept playing. He got scouted by the Philadelphia Eagles. But he had to quit after just a few years thanks to a severe fracture in his leg. He never played again. Now, he's a scout, looking out for new football talent all over the country. In his free time, he coaches a youth league.

Seeing what my friends had achieved, I could only be proud of them. But I didn't feel like I'd done much. I worked for my father, and it wasn't even my choice. Okay, I made the decision to put my signature on that wretched contract. I was too young and too naïve to believe I could back out of that contract whenever I wanted. Big mistake! Very big mistake. My father enjoyed the "make Patrick's life miserable" game too much and wasn't backing out or releasing control of me. I didn't have a choice either. If I backed out, he'd disinherit me and probably harass my mother again. And that's something I really didn't want. She'd already been through too much. But after so many years, I was getting fed up with the whole situation, I wanted out of it, I wanted to make something of my life, because I wasn't where I wanted to be.

I was happy to be out with my friends and catch up, especially with Andrew. When we were little, he lived across the street. I saw him every day. He was like the brother I never had. We hadn't seen each other in a long time, mainly because he and his girlfriend, Caroline, lived in Harrisburg where she was a pediatrician at The Pinnacle Health Hospital. It was one of the best hospitals to work at in Pennsylvania. Andrew had done Caroline's taxes, so they saw each other on a regular basis and one thing had led to another. I was genuinely happy for him.

"It's terrific to hear you two are doing so well," I said.

"Come on, Patrick," Andrew said, picking up on my despondent tone. "You'll find someone. What about that girl you mentioned?"

I ran a hand through my hair. "I don't think I have another chance with her. I blew it."

"What happened?"

"We'd only kissed once, right before she left for a business trip. We texted and Skyped a lot while she was gone. We had such a good connection, Andrew," I said. "I can talk about everything with her, even the shitty stuff with my father. I've never felt like this before. She's a good listener, smart, and she's so sincere. So, when I saw her on Saturday, I was thrilled and excited and I took her back to my place and made my move..."

"And?" Andrew prompted.

"She rejected me." I sighed. "Well, rejected might not be the right word. It started with a kiss, and I tried to take things further... But she held me off. She thought it was too soon."

"Ouch, that must have hurt." Andrew winced.

"Yeah, it did. I'm not used to getting rejected," I admitted. "Anyway, I asked if she wanted to stay the night, but she refused again."

"So you've seen each other since then?"

I shook my head.

"But you called her, right?" Andrew asked.

"Hell no."

"Why not? You like her. Obviously. Otherwise, you wouldn't have waited for her while she was gone. Give it some time," Andrew advised. "Don't give up. She wouldn't have kissed you if she didn't like you. You have to take the lead, man, but take your time. She probably wants to take things slow. Get to know her. See how it evolves."

"I guess," I said doubtfully. "How did you make it work with Caroline? I'm really struggling to find a decent relationship. You can't imagine the kind of women out there. They're strange, man. I just want to have a good connection with someone. Maybe I'm not cut out for it. I'll probably end up like my father. It's genetic."

"Patrick, stop," Andrew said. "It's the booze talking. You're a catch; you're just not handling it the right way. You have to pamper them, woo them, win them over the old-fashioned way. Don't throw yourself at them or expect sex on the first date. Not if you want a serious relationship."

"So what do I do?"

"Well, do you like this woman?"

"Yes."

"So, what's holding you back? Ask her out. Not just one date. Several. Show her she's special to you. Get to know her, give her a chance to see who you really are. Give it time, man. It'll pay off."

I nodded. "Thanks, Andrew, you're the best."

"Let me know how it goes, okay? And if you need more advice, just call." He smiled. "I don't live on the other side of the world, you know. Harrisburg is still civilization."

I snorted. "Okay, I will."

On that note, Andrew left. He had a four-hour drive, and he wanted to get home to Caroline. I didn't blame him. I'd love to come home to someone I loved every day. Have someone to talk to, to do stuff with. Andrew and I didn't see each other often, but when we did, we had a lot of fun. I could always talk about serious stuff with him. Maybe I had to rekindle our friendship, pick things back up.

I'd had too much to drink, so I headed for the restrooms. I splashed some water on my face, washed my hands, and looked at myself in the mirror. Then, it dawned on me.

"What are you doing, Patrick? Really?" I asked my reflection. I had to take control of my life. Stop playing, achieve something, something I could be proud off. I'd messed up with Sophie, I was stagnant at work, I couldn't even maintain a normal friendship. That had to change.

I had to get out of the club. I couldn't think straight anymore. Too much alcohol. I had to go home. I quickly said goodbye to Mark and David — the last two standing — and grabbed my coat and left before they could convince me to stay.

While I waited for a cab, I recognized the woman talking to the bouncer. What were the odds? It was Sophie. She looked stunning. Her dress and heels showed off her legs, and her black trench, draped over her shoulders, gave her a sophisticated edge. She noticed me and gave a little wave. She ended her conversation with the bouncer and walked over, very poised.

I wasn't sober, and I knew that, after a night out with my friends, I didn't look good. I was sweating, my hair was totally out of place. Hurriedly, I pushed my hair back with my hands, hoping that would make me look a little more decent.

"Patrick, what a surprise." She gave me a huge, sincere smile. "Of all the clubs in New York, somehow we end up at the same one. What a coincidence."

"You were here tonight?" I asked.

"Yep, girls' night out. You?" Her eyes were glistening in the dark. I could see she was a little hazy.

"Bachelor party for a high school friend," I said sheepishly.

"Oh, heavy night?" She raised her eyebrows.

"A bit." She'd taken me completely off guard. I'd been talking about her this evening, and now she was standing in front of me. How many more chances would I get? *Forget your pride, Patrick, and do your best. You can win her back.*

"Look, Sophie, about last week. I'm sorry I didn't call."

"Don't be sorry. I think you did both of us a favor."

Ouch, that hurt. I totally handled things the wrong way. I had to say something, anything, to make amends. If I didn't do it now, it would probably be my last chance with her. Or maybe I already blew it and she wouldn't give me a second chance?

"No, I'm genuinely sorry. I put you in an awkward situation, and it made you uncomfortable," I said. "I like you, Sophie, and I want to get to know you a lot better. If you'll give me another chance, of course."

She paused, hesitating. If she refused, I'd understand. I can be a real douche sometimes. The one-liners and moves I usually relied on wouldn't have an effect on her. She was so different from the women I'd dated before.

"I guess I can give you a second chance." Her face lit up.

"Really?"

"Yeah, really." There was a hint of sarcasm in her voice.

"So, what about dinner? Next Thursday? I'll pick you up around seven?"

"Okay, but let's meet there. You can text me the address."

Sophie's cab arrived, and I opened the door for her and helped her in. "So I'll see you on Thursday," I said.

"See you then. Good night, Patrick."

"Good night, Sophie."

I followed the taxi until it was out of sight. She said yes!

MORNING JOLT

Finally Thursday. I'd counted the endless days since I'd last seen Sophie. She had every reason to ignore me at the club, but she didn't. To my even greater surprise she'd even accepted my invitation. It was karma, luck, I didn't know, but what I did know was that this was my chance to make everything right. And I would do everything within my power to make it a memorable evening. But I had to keep in mind what Andrew told me: No pushing, take it slow, no sex on the first date.

Finding the perfect venue wasn't easy. It had to be a bit serene, calm... Certainly not too crowded or high end. After some research, I found the perfect location for our second first date. Green Garden. A dreamy, overgrown rooftop bar, south of Hell's Kitchen.

I was a bit too early, twenty minutes to be precise. You never know with the traffic in New York, and I'd taken all possible precautions to make this evening as perfect as possible. I found a spot at the outer rim of the bar, so we'd have some privacy. The terrace overlooked the entire city and tonight was exquisite. The sun had started its descent, rays of sunlight peeping through the large skyscrapers, and here and there they reflected beautifully onto the windows of the buildings. In the background, jazz music played softly.

I ordered a Green Garden Mojito to kill time. It had a unique taste, probably the combination of the fresh mint and basil, all grown on the terrace itself, so the bartender told me. Suddenly I spotted Sophie as she entered the bar. She wore an asymmetrical ivory top that showed off a nude shoulder with some navy-blue wide-legged pants. Her hair floated loosely around her shoulders. She looked stunning.

Wow, how will I restrain myself this evening?

Patrick, you have to.

Don't mess this up.

She peered toward the bar. When she spotted me, her face lit up. I couldn't take my eyes off her. I was so happy she was here.

"Hi." She spoke softly and clasped her brown leather clutch with both hands.

I jumped off my stool and kissed her on the cheek. "Hi. You look gorgeous, Sophie."

"Thank you." Blushing instantly, she started to fiddle with her purse.

I could clearly see she was nervous. *Makes two of us.* "Come on, have a seat. What do you want to drink?" I asked.

"What are you having?"

"A Green Garden Mojito. It's their signature cocktail. You want to try it? Here," I said, sliding my glass toward her, "take a sip of mine." I watched as she placed her lips on the glass and took a sip.

"Mmm. It's nice, very particular, but a tasty touch with the basil," she said.

"I know. If you want something else, no problem." I handed her the cocktail menu.

She bit her lip while scanning the menu, making my heart race in no time. I wanted to bite that lip. I wanted to kiss her, right here, right now. Holding back would be enormously challenging tonight. I had to cool myself down. I hastily drank the rest of my cocktail, mainly ice cubes. *Oh, coo-old.*

The bartender came to take our order. "So what can I get you two?"

"I'll take the elderflower cocktail," Sophie said. "Patrick?"

"Another mojito for me please."

"Coming right up." The bartender flipped a bottle of rum in the air, putting on a show. He shuffled some glasses around the bar, filled them with mint and basil, and started making our drinks.

"Patrick, this place is fantastic. How did you find it?" Sophie asked, looking around.

"Online. Just typed top ten rooftop bars in New York. Et voila."

"Splendid."

There was an awkward silence. I thought maybe if I asked her about her job she'd be more at ease. "So, how was work today?"

"Hectic," she said. "This morning I had to be in court and tempers ran real high. The judge transferred our case to a later date. I had to go to the judge and propose a settlement. Wasn't easy at all."

"What's the case about?"

"Sorry, I can't tell you. I'm bound by professional secrecy you know."

"Of course," I said. I should have known that. "No problem. I don't want to pry."

"It's okay. Thanks for being interested."

"You know, I never asked. What's your specialty?"

"Environmental law. But it's a broad topic," Sophie said. "You have waste management, air quality, water quality, wildlife management."

"Wow, I never would have guessed."

"Yeah, a lot of people aren't aware of it. But, you know, the concept of environmental law, as a separate type of law, was only developed in the twentieth century. It's not very old. People recognized that our natural environment was fragile and in need of special legal protections, so this recognition was translated into legal structures in the sixties."

"So what attracted you to law?" I asked.

"Um, I think it's mainly the advising part," she said. "People and companies aren't always aware of their environmental footprint. By advising them we can prevent a lot of lawsuits."

"You're helping make our world a better place."

"Sort of, yes. If you look at it that way," she said. "So do I have the job?" she added.

"What?" I was puzzled by her question.

She snickered loudly. "I'm sorry, but I feel like I'm on a job interview."

"Right." I smiled, and Sophie laughed.

We'd clearly broken the ice, and the rest of the evening went smoothly. We were right where we'd left off last time. Kidding and genuinely having fun. I had a lovely evening, was a gentleman, and accompanied her home before heading back to my place.

Our next few dates were fun and refreshing. Coffee and brunch on Saturday at Chix Lay Eggs, a recommendation from Sophie's boss. A small restaurant in Brooklyn — it had high ceilings and exposed-brick walls and offered breakfasts and lunches made with seasonal and local produce and every egg variety you could think of. Sophie loved Eggs Benedict, and I liked them scrambled.

We went to see a movie at the Sunshine Cinema. I'd never been there before. The cinema was housed in a handsome Yiddish vaudeville theater dating back to 1909. I liked the old classy and glossy atmosphere. And the salted caramel popcorn was finger-licking good. I even went back for a second portion during the movie, so we could share it.

A few weeks later I took Sophie to see David's showing at the Agora Gallery. This was the first time one of my friends would meet my girlfriend.

David's paintings shared the gallery with the work of a French sculptor who did mainly nude statues. Sophie had seen her work in Paris and wanted me to see them too.

The nudes were truly stunning. You could see the artist was inspired by Rodin. The statues each revealed a certain emotion. They weren't rude or provocative, but soft and serene. The lines of their bodies flowed seamlessly into one another.

At the end of the vernissage, I introduced David to Sophie. David instantly adored her. Wasn't that difficult with Sophie. She showed a lot of interest in his work, asked him about the stories behind each painting and the evolution of his technique. I knew he enjoyed being the center of attention, and Sophie listened intently to every word, sensing his need for the spotlight and asking questions from time to time. She was truly fascinated by his work. Because of their passionate conversation, she'd drawn other people over. People were gathering around, eager to hear David's story. By the time we left, David was surrounded by a crowd of potential buyers.

I really got to know Sophie a lot better. She was kind, sociable, and so clever. I could take her everywhere. Even our date at the art gallery showed how intelligent she was. She had her own opinions and knew what was happening in the world. But she also knew her way around a courtroom. Sometimes she hesitated but that was mainly a lack of confidence. I knew she'd grow a pair of balls within a few years and move up the ranks. She just didn't know it yet.

I got to show her more of myself too. It was strange, but with her I wasn't afraid to let my guard down. I was at ease when she was around. I adored her, and I wanted to spend every free minute with her.

But we were taking our time. I didn't want to go too fast. I'd already made that mistake.

We'd been dating for a month and a half and gone on seven dates, and our relationship had reached a new level. We'd just had dinner with Alex and Jane at a small Italian restaurant a half a mile from Sophie's apartment, and we were walking back since the weather was cooperating. It was cold, but it stayed dry.

When we came to a stop in front of her building to say our good-byes, I was hesitant. We still hadn't kissed since the last time at my place — more than two months ago — and the anticipation was killing me. I didn't know if she was ready for the next step, so I'd been waiting to make my move. We gazed at each other for a few minutes. I was rubbing my hands together, warming them, when Sophie took a step forward while saying goodnight. I thought she wanted to kiss me, so I took a step closer and closed the space between us, kissing her fully on the lips.

At first, she didn't respond, but after a split second she threw herself into the kiss. Those eight weeks of anticipation were worth the wait.

Six months later, we were still dating. We saw each other every day, except when Sophie had to travel, of course. Most of the time I stayed at her place because it was closer to her office and our favorite Starbucks. I didn't care where I was, as long as we were together.

We even went away for the weekend, hosted dinners for friends, went clubbing with Alex and Jane... Stuff couples usually do.

I realized Sophie was the woman I wanted to spend the rest of my life with. It didn't mean "getting married right away," but why not take it to the next level? Maybe we could move in together; my new apartment was nearly ready. But with Sophie's job it was hard to get settled. She traveled a lot. Right now it was just a couple weeks at a time, but what if she had to go away for a longer time? She'd already cut back on trips since we'd started dating, refusing some major deals abroad — just for me. I didn't want to hold her back. I didn't want her to miss an opportunity. She always told me to seize the day and the moments we had together. She said if she got another offer, we'd discuss the possibilities together.

CAFFEINE BEFORE CHAOS

I shouted in the bathroom's direction. "Sophie, are you almost ready?" I'd already asked a few times but hadn't gotten an answer from her. I stood up from the sofa and headed to the bathroom, where Sophie was with Jane preparing for this evening's real estate gala. The gala was held every year for the top ten best-selling real estate agencies in New York. This year, it was in Gotham Hall, a perfect venue for a gala. Located in a landmark building, once home to the Greenwich Savings Bank, it was seventeen thousand five hundred square feet. The main hall boasted a hundred-twenty-foot ceiling with an ornate stained-glass skylight. There were some smaller event spaces, but the main hall had always been my favorite spot in the building.

My father owned one of the biggest real estate agencies in New York, so our invitation to the event was never a surprise. Every year I went alone or brought some friends for moral support or to restrain me if my father started to provoke me. Before my parents' divorce, my mother could bring some balance between me and my father. We never really had a good relationship; our opinions differed too much. Plus, he wasn't around much growing up. After their divorce, our bond definitely deteriorated even more. Working for him didn't help either. But this year it would be different. I had Sophie. The moment I asked her to go, she looked up the venue and the event online. She did some research and of course had seen the pictures from last year and how everyone had been dressed. The women wore expensive gowns, their husbands — in their handsome black tuxedos — and their accessories. All this luxury frightened her, and I'd needed a lot of time to persuade her to go with me. At first, I thought I'd have to go alone. She really didn't feel like spending an evening with New York's elite. She already did this enough for work. Luckily, Jane, who'd often had to attend similar events with her husband Gerald, finally convinced her. Jane didn't hesitate and helped Sophie with everything. I knew they'd gone on a shopping spree last week, but I still hadn't seen Sophie's dress.

We really had to go if we didn't want to be late for the opening ceremony. I knocked on the door. "Sophie, honey, I'm sorry to rush you, but we have to get going. Otherwise, we'll be late."

Jane emerged from the bathroom, blocking my way. "Give her a few more minutes," she said. "She's dressed and her hair is done, but she needs a little more time."

"Okay. I can wait a few more minutes," I said, retreating to the living room.

Meanwhile in the bathroom…

Come on, Sophie, you can do this. Patrick always goes to your business events. You can do the same for him. Don't pay too much attention to those other women. It's one night. What's one night?

I inhaled deeply, gave my reflection one last glance, picked up the black beaded clutch Jane had lent me, and slowly walked out of the bathroom, making sure I didn't trip over the hem of my dress. The moment I walked into the room, Jane and Patrick stopped talking.

Patrick stared at me. "Oh my. Honey, you'll turn some heads tonight." He stepped forward to kiss me gently.

Jane went totally overboard on the dress. The bust was black lace, front to back, flowing down from my hips into a long black skirt with a high slit on the left side. Only when I walked could you see the slit; otherwise, the skirt completely covered my legs.

I'd needed a little push from Jane because I thought it showed a bit too much. But once I tried the dress on, I felt sexy. Like a real woman. I'd never worn anything like it.

In the shop, I'd been convinced it was the right dress. But putting it on this evening made me question my decision. Jane had to reassure me a thousand times. She told me how beautiful I looked. She wanted me to have an amazing evening, sort of a Cinderella moment. A night out where Patrick would be bedazzled by my presence. When I asked her why, she admitted that she and Gerald were going in a different direction relationship-wise. His attitude toward her had changed recently and she didn't know why. So she just wanted it for me. How nice of her. Seeing Patrick's reaction just now took every last doubt away.

Patrick handed me my black fur stole, which I carefully wrapped around my shoulders. "Darren is waiting downstairs. You have everything you need?" he asked.

"Yes," I said.

Jane followed us outside, watching and smiling contentedly. She was pleased with the result. I mouthed a thank you before sliding into the back of the car. She mouthed "no problem" back.

Patrick couldn't take his eyes off me. "Sophie, you look stunning in that dress. Thank you for doing this for me. Really!"

"Well, you always go to my dull lawyer events," I said. "It's the least I can do. But you'll have to thank Jane. She chose the dress."

"Oh, I will." He gently stroked my leg with his fingers, making the slit fall completely open. "Still, if you change your mind, I can ask Darren to turn the car around."

I hesitated a split second. We could do that. But then I would have bought the dress for nothing. I rearranged the slit and shot Patrick a reprimanding look. "No. We'll go. You have to show up. It's too important. Besides, you don't want to give your father a reason to argue with you."

"You're right." He placed a small kiss on the back of my hand. He didn't let go until we arrived at the hall.

I immediately got overwhelmed by all the people crowding the entrance. There were two trees guarding the building's entrance, fully lit with small LED lights. We waited in line, but it wasn't until I entered the grand ballroom that I really faltered. The space was magical. The room was large, oval-shaped, striking with inlaid marble floors, granite walls, and soaring solid limestone Corinthian columns at each end. The ceiling was unique with its gilded, stained-glass dome. A massive chandelier hung from its center, lit by hundreds of candles. Smaller chandeliers illuminated the space, making it feel intimate but somewhat mysterious. Large round tables were adorned with long white tablecloths and set with spectacular plates with golden rims and silver cutlery, no small detail overlooked.

As we wove through the tables, Patrick stopped to greet a handful of people and always introduced me as his girlfriend. Which I greatly enjoyed.

I had a hard time getting comfortable surrounded by all that New York elite. I hadn't been raised in these circles like Patrick. I'd defended these types of people's companies before, but I'd never spent a posh evening with them like this. Patrick was completely at ease, like a fish in the sea. He knew the customs, how to greet people, what topics to avoid. He mingled effortlessly, all poise and self-confidence.

Wearing something out of my comfort zone made it even harder. Was my dress showing too much? Was I overdressed? I kept looking down to see if the slit was too explicit and fumbling with the fabric.

As the evening continued, I started to relax. But Patrick stayed by my side all evening. He didn't expect me to insert myself into conversations or do something I wasn't comfortable with. He was pleased that I was there. The rest would follow eventually.

Dinner was remarkable and refined. Between each course there was a speech and an award presentation. We were eating dessert and Patrick was having an intense discussion about the rental market. Since Airbnb, larger city apartment rentals had decreased. And this was a market they had controlled for years. The conversation was relatively heated, and I excused myself to go freshen up. On the way back from the restroom, I stopped at the bar. Something fresh would do me good. I'd had too much wine already.

"So, you're Patrick's date, right?"

I looked up. An elderly man was leaning against the bar next to me. "Um, yes. If you're talking about Patrick Downey, then yes."

The man didn't look at me. He inspected me. He took me in from head to toe. Like he could see through my dress. And that made me feel even more uncomfortable.

"Well, I think introductions are in order. I'm his father. Albert Downey," he said, holding out his hand.

I shook it politely, even if I didn't want to know the man. Patrick had told me enough stories about his father's reputation, how he'd dated quite younger women while married and even more after his divorce. Patrick's mom stayed with him through this betrayal. It was only when his grandfather passed away back in England that his mom had the guts to leave him. Albert Downey was a controlling, manipulative, deceiving man. And losing control over his ex-wife meant he had to regain control elsewhere by binding his son to his company. Patrick agreed to help his mother, but that didn't help loosen their difficult relationship.

He clasped my hand tightly and pulled me closer, then swiftly released my hand and took a step to the side, placing himself right behind me. Without hesitation or embarrassment, he placed his left hand on my back.

I shivered in disgust. I swallowed hard.

He bent forward, his head a few inches above mine.

I closed my eyes in discomfort. An old man's fragrance, combined with a heavy musky perfume, invaded my nose. I was shocked, disgusted by his power, which he abused simply because he was a man. But I couldn't make a scene, not here, not now. And he knew it. That's exactly what he wanted. Attention. He wanted to see how I reacted. I wanted to punch his face, but I couldn't move, even though I wanted to so badly. My throat was entirely blocked. I thought about Patrick. If I did something, acted out, his father would make his life even more complicated than it already was. What could he do to me in a big crowd like this?

His lips were so close to my ear, I could hear him breathing heavily. I heard him swallowing, his tongue gliding over his lips.

"You know, you should call me," he whispered. "You and I could have a lot of fun together. Patrick has no clue how to please a woman like you. I'm a real man and can give you more than he ever could. Think about it."

I saw Patrick emerging from the crowd, clearly looking for me. Not a minute too soon. His father spotted him too, which made him cock his head to the side and step back. "I have to go, but we'll see each other again, beautiful."

Again he looked at me with a dirty, penetrating look. He traced his fingers down my arm, touching the side of my breast.

I turned my face away and waited for him to leave. Patrick spotted me at the bar, coming to my rescue. Father and son crossed each other.

"Patrick." Albert looked at his son victoriously. His look said he could have anything he wanted, that rules didn't apply to him.

Patrick gave him a cold look. You could clearly see these two men didn't have a warm relationship.

As soon as Albert was out of hearing distance and out of sight, I exhaled loudly.

"Sophie. Oh my god, are you okay?" Patrick didn't know what had happened, but he didn't need much explanation. My reaction to meeting his father was all he needed to know. "What did my father say to you?"

He took me in his arms. If he hadn't, I think I would have fainted.

I swallowed deeply. "He... I can't... Patrick, it's too gross for words."

Even though I couldn't see the look on his face, I could feel Patrick's heartbeat accelerating. I could feel his outrage.

He held me at arm's length. "You have to tell me. I know he can be an asshole, but you have to tell me."

I inhaled deeply. I didn't want to repeat the words he'd said, but Patrick had asked. "He emphasized that if I wanted a real man..." I had a hard time saying it out loud. "That I had to give him a call. Because you don't know how to please me."

"What! Oh my god, I'm going to kill him!"

I had to restrain Patrick with all my strength. His expression was feral. If I let him go, he'd make a huge scene. He might even beat up his own father.

"Patrick, don't. Come on, calm down. He isn't worth it! It's my fault," I pleaded. "I should have stopped him as soon as he grabbed me."

"He grabbed you?!" Patrick roared. "He can't get away with this!" He shook his head. "Sophie, no, this isn't on you. It isn't your fault. He has to keep his dirty hands off you!"

He scanned the hall, and I knew he was looking for his father. I knew if we didn't leave right now, this would end badly. I grabbed Patrick's face with both hands and kissed him fiercely. I sensed his surprised. He was too mad. But the longer I kissed him, the more I could feel his anger ebbing away. He kissed me back roughly. I stopped after a few minutes, caressed his face, took his hand in mine, and led him out of the building. While we waited for our coats, I called Darren so he could pull the car around.

Patrick didn't say a word from the moment we left the ballroom. I never wanted to see his father again, that was obvious. We got in the car, the silence between us deafening. Patrick stared blankly out the window. Maybe after a good night's rest we could discuss it. But right now, we weren't in the mood. I focused on the song on the radio to clear other thoughts from my head and looked at the illuminated streets of New York. When I really listened, I recognized the song. Frank Sinatra, "The Way You Look Tonight." One of my favorites. It made me feel a bit calmer.

The moment we entered my apartment, I hurried to the bathroom, leaving Patrick confused in the hallway. I couldn't move fast enough. I wanted to shake off the vile memory of his father's touch, remove the encounter from my memory, starting by scrubbing it off. Unzipping my dress, I stepped out of it and quickly threw it over the stool in the corner, not wanting to waste time hanging it properly. Stripped down to my black lace underwear, I took a long look at my complexion. I touched my face, pressed my hands to my neck, traced the places where he'd invaded my space. I took a washcloth from the drawer under the sink, turned on the faucet, and let the cool water run before wetting the cloth completely. Testing the water's temperature with my finger, I felt the cold against my skin. It was refreshing but woke me instantly. I didn't want hot water. It had to stay cold, ice cold. Because if I wanted to remove that memory, I had to make this as unpleasant as possible.

The washcloth was entirely soaked in ice cold water, dripping. I brought it to my face. I rubbed hard, and the water ran down my face and trickled into my cleavage. A chill ran up my spine. I rinsed the washcloth, turning the water black from my mascara, wet it again, and started the process all over. I washed away the memory of his touch on my face, my neck, my ears, my breasts.

It wasn't enough, so I undressed completely, throwing my wet underwear on top of the pile of dirty laundry, and turned the shower on. Naked, I stepped into the cold stream of water. It hit me instantly, taking my breath away and making me gasp for air. I rubbed my arms with both hands, warming myself up a bit. But nothing would change my mind and give me enough strength to turn on the warm water.

After ten minutes, I'd submerged myself long enough. I turned the faucet off, stepped out of the shower, and dried off with a thick fluffy towel. Feeling a bit more like myself, I put on my purple flannel pajama bottoms and a grey t-shirt. Leaning on the sink, I studied my complexion again. My cheeks were red, flushed by the blood once again streaming through my veins. This was the effect the cold water had on me. My mascara was running, smeared across my eyes. I removed it carefully. I brushed my teeth and rubbed myself from head to toe with lavender oil, making his smell disappear completely. Exhausted from the long night, I crawled into bed next to Patrick, avoiding eye contact. Patrick shot me a worried look but didn't say a word. He'd already said enough. Deep down I knew this wasn't the last time we would talk about his father. Patrick wouldn't leave it this way. This story would play out eventually.

I turned on my side. Patrick followed suit, switching off his bedside lamp and wrapping himself around me, holding me close. I could feel his heartbeat and hear his breath slowing down as he fell asleep. I fell asleep listening to it.

BLACK EYE

A week had passed and Patrick hadn't mentioned that notorious evening once. I didn't have the courage to bring it up. He was already struggling enough, working under the tyranny of his father. I wisely kept my mouth shut, hoping it would vanish. Disappear completely.

But nothing could be less true. I should have known better. I knew, sooner or later, he'd do something about it. Little did I know it would happen so fast.

On rainy days, like today, Darren picked me up after work because Patrick didn't want me walking home in the rain. Patrick wasn't with him, so I took my time catching up with Darren as I got seated in the car.

"How are you doing today, Darren?" I asked.

"I'm fine, madam. Thank you for asking."

"And the kids? If I remember correctly, Anne-Marie started kindergarten in February."

"Yes," he said. "She likes going to school. And it's easier having Anne-Marie and Jordan at the same school. Saves me from driving all over the city every morning."

"I understand." I smiled at him warmly.

"So how is Mr. Downey's hand today? I noticed he was still in pain."

I had no idea what Darren was talking about. "His hand?"

"Yes, his hand. From the punch he threw yesterday?"

"Oh yes, his hand," I said slowly. "I'll take a look at it again this evening. Thank you for taking such good care of him."

"It's what I do, madam." Darren directed his attention to the road.

Staring out the window, I was lost in thought. He did it anyway. He fought his father, he confronted him. I wasn't surprised.

"Honey, I'm home," Patrick called as he entered the apartment a few hours later. He sounded upbeat.

I was making spaghetti for dinner and was at the stove, stirring the sauce. "Hi."

He kissed me eagerly but quickly returned to the hallway to remove his wet coat.

"Is it still raining?" I asked. "I am so looking forward to spring."

"Yeah, me too."

Patrick took a seat at the other end of the bar. "Mmm, spaghetti. Will definitely taste good with this cold weather."

"You want a glass of wine? I've got some pinot left."

"Sure. Can I help?"

"Nope. Dinner is almost ready." I poured him a glass of pinot blanc.

I watched as he took a sip. He lifted his glass with his right hand. He was left-handed. I looked down at his hand and saw a discoloration on the back. It was slightly swollen too. I grabbed his hand and he squirmed. He was in pain, that was for sure.

"Patrick, what happened?" I demanded. "What happened to your hand?"

"Nothing. I just bruised it a little."

"A little!?" I cried. "Patrick, your hand is swollen. Look at this mark. Come on, tell me what happened."

"Okay, okay." He removed his hand from my grip. "I hit my father yesterday. I ran into him in the hallway before a meeting, and he was provoking me. He insinuated he had you on speed dial... And I... I lost it."

"How bad is it?"

"He's got one black eye... Look, he had it coming!" he added, edgy when he clocked my reaction.

"Hey, don't take this out on me. It's not like I'm taking his side, you know."

He sighed. "Sorry, but you know he brings out the worst in me."

"And now he can feel that. Come here," I said, wrapping him up in a bear hug. "I'll check your hand after dinner. And if it isn't better in a few days, you're going to the hospital. It could be broken." I kissed him on the cheek.

"Yes, ma'am," he teased.

"Don't 'yes, ma'am' me. I'm not your mother," I said. "At least try to ignore him or just quit. If it was me, I would've resigned a long time ago. How much more shit can you put up with?"

Patrick was silent for a few minutes and then blurted, "Really?! Sophie, are you really saying that? You know I can't quit that job."

"Yes, you told me, but you didn't tell me what's in the contract. So in my eyes it's that simple. Leave. You have so much more potential."

"I don't want you to get involved," he said. "End of discussion."

"I'm a lawyer, for god's sake! You know I can help you or a colleague of mine can help. Don't be such a stubborn ass!" I cried, exasperated. "Or maybe you don't wanna leave because of the money." The moment I said it, I regretted my words. I was mad because of his attitude, because of the fight with his father, because he still didn't trust me to review that contract.

Patrick stood up and swept everything off the bar in a rage. Glasses, cutlery, plates. Everything fell to the ground and broke into a thousand pieces. I was glued to the spot. I had never seen him this furious. This was a sensitive subject.

"That money isn't my father's!" he yelled. "Every dime I've earned was because of my hard work. I've put everything in shares, investments, savings... Yeah, it's not the ideal working situation, and believe me, I really wish it were different. I don't have to explain myself to you. But thanks, Soph, now I know what you think of me. You've opened my eyes."

"No, Patrick, I'm sorry. I didn't mean it! I just..." I felt tears rolling down my cheeks, my voice starting to crack. I swallowed hard, trying to get the lump out of my throat, but it didn't work. It just got worse. I was losing control of the situation, of my emotions, and that couldn't happen. I needed to be in control. I needed to get out of my apartment. "I'm sorry, but you're shutting me out... I can't do this..." I brushed the tears away with the back of my hand and turned around to grab my keys and purse. I left the apartment, slamming the door with a loud thud before he could leave. I had to stay in control and leaving was for the better.

I heard Patrick cursing loudly and shouting for me, but I didn't care. I just needed to get out of there, and instead of waiting for the elevator, I took the staircase down to the lobby, walked by Sammy, and gave him a quick nod. Once outside, I sped up my pace, not noticing that the rain was pouring harder and harder. By the time I reached the corner, I was soaked. I knew there was a deli a few blocks further, so I ran and waited there until the rain had stopped. One coffee and a whiskey later — the first to warm myself up and the second to calm myself down — the sky had cleared. I was feeling more in control. I had said some nasty things to Patrick, but I didn't mean them. But why was he keeping me in the dark? Why couldn't he trust me to help him? I hated confrontations, I always went out of my way to avoid them. We'd been dating more than six months, and he was always complaining about his father and dreaming about the things he really wanted to do. So why wasn't he leaving? *There must be something he could do,* I thought. *Or I can do. If only he'd share this with me.* It really made me insecure not knowing what he was thinking or that he didn't want to share stuff with me.

I didn't care if he lived in a huge condo in Central Park or in a shabby apartment in the Bronx. I didn't care that it was daddy's money. All I wanted was for him to be happy. That he had a job that challenged him. That he could be Patrick.

Okay, Soph, time for action, I told myself. *You can't just hide in the deli. Just tell him how you feel about all this secrecy stuff. If he doesn't want to share, fine.* I couldn't push him. I could only be there for him and hope that one day he would involve me.

LIQUID ENERGY

I grabbed my phone and dialed Alex's number, hoping he'd pick up immediately. I had to talk to him.

"Hello, dear." He sounded upbeat.

"Hi, Alex. Can you meet for a drink?" I asked quickly. I had to see him. He would know what to do.

"Hello to you, too, Miss Urgent. What's going on?"

"I can't tell you over the phone. I'm at the office, but I really need to talk to you. Something happened last night," I added.

"Sure. I'm always up for a drink. You okay, dear? Do I have to worry?"

"No, yes. No! I don't know. When can you meet me?"

"Well, I'm alone at the shop right now. Besides Carmella, of course, but I can't let her run the register or I'd go bankrupt overnight. Howard had a half day, but he'll be here in an hour," Alex said. "Can you wait until then? You can always come by. You know that."

I smiled despite myself. "I know, Alex, but we need to go somewhere else. Meet me at Garibaldi's in an hour. I'll reserve a table so we can have lunch and drinks, a lot of drinks."

"Sophie, you sure I don't have to worry? You aren't making any sense at all."

"No, you don't need to worry," I reassured him. "I just need to talk to you. I need you, okay?"

"Sure. I'll be there, I promise. Don't do anything stupid in the meantime."

"I won't." I hung up. Was I being too dramatic? Alex would understand. He was a great listener and would know if what I was feeling was okay. I finished answering my email, turned on my out-of-office for the afternoon, and switched off my laptop. I called Garibaldi's and asked for a table in the back at noon. I didn't want anyone overhearing us. I put on my double-breasted pea coat from Oasis, the one I bought online at Asos. A real catch. Alex called it the centerpiece of my office wardrobe. And he was right. I loved that coat. I grabbed my purse and the empty coffee mug from my desk and stopped in the kitchen before I went downstairs to hail a cab. My mind wasn't right for working today, so half a day with Alex would do me good.

Ten minutes after I was seated, Alex arrived. I'd already ordered a pinot blanc and the waiter was pouring it when Alex sat down across from me.

"Sir, can I bring you something as well?" the waiter asked.

Alex took a measured sip from my glass, nodded, and ordered the same. The moment the waiter was beyond hearing distance, he reached across the table, wrapped me in a bear hug, and patted my back as he said, "P left you, right? I'm so sorry, Sophie. I..."

I had to stop him midsentence. That wasn't the reason I wanted to talk to him. "No, no he didn't. We're fine, we are more than fine — well, except for the fight we had last night, but we made up!" I pulled away and sat down.

"Okay," he said slowly. "I don't follow. What's the crisis? We never come here — at noon — for drinks and lunch. You wanted me here as soon as possible. I'm sorry, but I assumed he'd ditched you." He looked around. "This isn't *Candid Camera*, right? Is Jane coming?"

"Alex, STOP," I cried. "Really STOP. Patrick and I are still together. This isn't *Candid Camera* or a joke. Jane isn't coming. I just wanted to talk to you." I took a deep breath. "I've been having a problem since I moved to New York. And you've always been there for me, offering good advice, listening, helping me out. I don't know where to start, it's a bit... I don't know how to say it. It's out of my comfort zone."

"You're speaking Chinese to me, dear. We need reinforcements." He waved the waiter over and ordered four tequila shots and some appetizers. He called Howard, told him he had an emergency and wouldn't be back.

The waiter placed the tequila shots on the table and I quickly downed one.

Alex studied me. "I have time. Whatever it is, I'm here for you. I cleared my schedule, I have nowhere to be, so drink up and tell me what's bugging you."

I took my second tequila shot. Feeling a little more courageous, I said, "Well, it's about sex." The instant I said it, I turned red as a tomato.

Alex snorted. "What? You asked me to come here to talk about sex?" He pulled himself together when he saw my reaction, rearranging his face into a wide grin. "Sophie, I'm sorry, I didn't mean to offend you. But it sounds strange coming from you. I know you're not a virgin. Sorry." He stretched out his arm and took my hand. "I'm sorry, dear, I cut you off midsentence. Tell me what it is."

I polished off the rest of my pinot blanc, inhaled deeply, and laid it all on the table. "Patrick and I have already had sex. It's unbelievable. We're all over the place, but I've never had this experience before. I..."

"You never had an orgasm? You faked it with the other guys?" Alex's eyes were wide.

"Oh come on, Alex, I'm not all dust down there, you know." I rolled my eyes. "I've had orgasms," I added quieter. "Before."

"Okay, we cleared that up." He held his hands up as a sign of peace.

"I don't know how to say it. But... Patrick takes his time. He really takes his time." When I repeated "time," I smiled full-mouthed, reliving the moment. Patrick's fingers tracing a path over my thighs, his hands cupping my breasts firmly, and oh my god his mouth exploring my body. *Hmmm.*

Alex pulled me out of my daydream. "Oooh, I see. He pleases you damn good. Your eyes are all twinkly."

"Yes. He does. And he's so good at it. Oh, Alex, I've never felt this before. He's doing this for me. Every time, over and over again, with his hands, his mouth. It makes me crazy. In the beginning, we had great sex, but you know what happened at the gala with his father and then the fight..."

Alex nodded.

"And I don't know. But since then he's really taken things up a notch and now it's — it's wow — mind-blowing. It's like he has to prove himself. Prove his father wrong. That he can keep me. I don't really know what's going on, but it's great sex!"

"I'm sensing a but?" Alex said.

"Well... I don't know how to please him. Properly," I admitted. "I don't have any experience at all. I know a few positions, but I want to do something just for him and I don't want to blow it because I don't know what I'm doing. You know what I mean, right?"

"I hear you..."

"You're a guy, you date guys, you have sex with them. I was thinking..." I hesitated. "You're my best option. You can teach me some skills, so I'm not scouring the internet for pornographic DIY stuff."

"Yeah, I wouldn't recommend that." He wrinkled his nose. "I get why you came to me about this. Drink up." He pushed the last tequila shot toward me. "We have some shopping to do. Then, we'll head to my place so I can teach you some tricks and you can keep this man of yours satisfied."

"Oh, Alex, you're the greatest." I jumped up and threw my arms around his neck. "I knew you'd understand."

"I know. That's why we're friends," he said. "And I'd like to see how you handle a banana," he added with a raised eyebrow.

I looked at him in surprise. A banana?

We took a cab to SoHo for some me-shopping. Well, if you saw what I bought, you'd understand Patrick was in for a treat. We stopped at Agent Provocateur and Kiki de Montparnasse, but those pieces were a bit too provocative for my taste. Maybe some other time, when my paycheck arrived, because those bras and undies were expensive. Alex took me to La Petite Cocinelle, a small lingerie shop selling the finest Parisian lingerie. Delicate lacework, good construction, fair prices. I bought two sets. The first was a lacy, gold-and-black see-through bra from Chantelle with delicate lace flowers stitched on the sides, surrounding the cup. I bought the matching underwear.

The second set was a bit more provocative. Alex pushed me, so I gave in. At first, I wasn't into the whole corset thing. But after trying on a few more with stockings and garters, it won me over. So I bought a deep purple and black one with black string and black garters, all in a luxurious satin and tulle. Extremely soft, smooth, and "sexy as hell," as Alex said when I came out of the dressing room.

From there, we went to the supermarket. I still had no idea what Alex was planning. He left me in the dark, and I grew more curious by the minute, especially after buying a dozen bananas, a bag of grapes, and a bottle of champagne.

"Thanks for coming with me. I love what I got." I gave his hand a small pinch.

"The pleasure is all mine," Alex said. "You know I like going shopping with you. And what you bought is worth every dollar."

We got out of the cab, carrying all our bags, and took the elevator up to the tenth floor. I went to the kitchen and placed the bananas and grapes on a plate and set it on the huge marble bar. I knew my way around this place. Before Patrick and I were dating seriously, I had crashed on Alex's couch on several occasions.

Alex opened the bottle of champagne with a small pop, poured two glasses, and put the bottle in the fridge. He handed me a glass, clinked his against mine, and said, "To your training, dear," as he picked up a banana.

I'd needed a few more glasses before I could pretend the banana was a certain male body part, but Alex taught me everything I needed to know so I wouldn't choke on it, mash it, or even bite it into pieces. I was a good student, and after practicing the whole afternoon, I got an A- on my oral exam and went home tipsy. I would have gotten an A+ if I hadn't needed so much alcohol. And now I had to put it into practice and test my skills on Patrick. Still, I kept 911 on speed dial.

YOU MOCHA ME SO HAPPY

I'd been toying with the idea of the two women who meant the most to me meeting. My mother must have read my mind because she invited us to Sunday brunch. This was a first. I'd never introduced a girlfriend to my mother or brought a girl home.

It was already May, days were lasting longer, and good weather was now more of a guarantee. It was a beautiful, sunny day, so there was a good chance we'd eat outside on the terrace.

My mother had moved to a house in Forest Hill Gardens in Queens after she divorced my father. Forest Hill is a private community dating back to 1910. It's very typical and structured, with private roads, green spaces, and houses mostly built in a characteristic red brick. She loved it there because it was a tranquil family area.

We were only a few miles from the house, and I could feel the tension oozing from Sophie as we got closer. She was tapping her fingers on her upper thigh while she looked out the window. I put my hand on hers. "She'll love you instantly. You'll see." I smiled at her warmly.

"You think?"

"I'm positive. Don't worry. Look, there it is." I pointed toward the large red brick house at the end of the street. I parked behind my mother's Jeep. The moment we stepped out of the car, my mother emerged from the house wearing a blue A-line dress dotted with white roses. Her silky grey hair floated loosely over her shoulders. I knew she'd been on the lookout.

"Darling, finally you're here." She hugged me firmly.

"Hello, mum."

She turned her attention to Sophie. "And you must be Sophie."

"Hello, Mrs. Downey," Sophie said. "It's lovely to meet you."

"Nice to finally meet you, Sophie. But away with Downey. It's my ex's name. You can call me Madeleine. Just Madeleine."

"Sorry. I didn't mean to offend you."

"Oh, dear, you didn't. He and I just aren't on good terms. But enough of that." She waved her hand. "Welcome to our house," she said, taking Sophie in her arms.

That was my mother, a real hugger. Sophie was clearly struggling; she wasn't used to that kind of attention. I stepped between them and handed my mother a bouquet of yellow and white tulips.

"Patrick, you shouldn't have. They're marvelous!"

"But I did. Go put them in a vase. We'll be right behind you," I said.

"Come on in," she said, stepping into the house. "George is already in the garden."

As I moved to follow her, I glanced in Sophie's direction, making sure she was holding up. She nodded, slightly over-whelmed. And she hadn't even met George, my mother's new husband.

My mother took the flowers to the kitchen while we walked through the house toward the garden. In the garden, it felt like you were in England. Big hydrangea bushes — in different varie-ties and colors —were scattered throughout. Some were already in bloom, while others would only brighten up the garden later in the year. There were flowers as far as the eye could see. Roses, lavender bushes, parterres filled with astilbe, geraniums, daffodils, hyacinths. Most of them were only starting to bloom. But the wisteria and the clematis, wrapped around the wooden frame on the terrace, were in full bloom. On summer evenings, when the sun went down, they filled the air with a delicious but sweet smell. With this garden, my mum had brought a piece of home, of England, with her.

My stepfather George appeared from the back of the garden, his salt-and-pepper hair covered by a cream Panama hat. I wasn't surprised to find him there; he spent most of his time in the garden, picking weeds, breathing in the scent of the flowers.

George and my mother had married a few years after she divorced my father. George was about ten years older than my mother and had been a successful businessman. Last year he sold his firm, making quite a profit. But he couldn't sit still, so after just a few weeks he returned to his old firm as a consultant three days a week. He spent the rest of his time traveling with my mother and gardening.

I must admit, George was more of a father to me than my real father. Mainly because of his charisma and, of course, he was incredibly clever. The world kept no secrets from him, and he'd seen most of it. He spoke six languages. Conversations with George could get quite animated, especially when the right amount of wine was served. As soon as he got going with a story, the whole evening was gone, believe me.

He greeted me with a kiss on the cheek and a hug as usual. Sophie flanked me in silence, surprised by the warm welcome my stepfather gave me. As soon as he noticed her, he pushed me away.

"Ah, you must be the remarkable Sophie. Patrick did you justice." He held her at arm's length, taking her in. "You are indeed a fine-looking lady, if I may say so."

Sophie blushed instantly. She still didn't know how to handle a compliment.

George enveloped her in a bear hug. "It's okay, you're in good hands. Welcome, my dear."

All she could manage was "Thank you, sir."

"Come on, kids," George said. "Let's have a drink on the terrace. It's such a beautiful day today, and I could use a glass."

As always, my mother had set the table festively, with a luxurious linen tablecloth, my grandmother's silver cutlery, and her finest china. Lovely flower arrangements brightened the scene.

My mother could be a tad overwhelming. Whenever she hosted something, she put in a lot of effort, some called it extravagant. This could be a bit much for Sophie, but I hoped it wouldn't be the last time I'd bring her home.

George took a seat at the head of the table. He sat Sophie at his right and me at his left, so my mum could be across from him. I couldn't read Sophie's mind, but I was hoping she wouldn't take off. She was very quiet. I knew my mum and George — and their enthusiasm and affection — could be a bit overwhelming.

"Sophie," George said, picking up a decanter filled with red, velvety wine. "I hope you enjoy a good glass of wine because here it's well appreciated."

"I do, sir. I've savored some marvelous bottles on my travels," she said. "Can I ask what we're drinking?"

"It's a Brunello di Montalcino. Go on, taste it." He served her a glass.

She smelled the wine, twirled it around in her glass, and took a small sip. George and I watched her expectantly.

"Wow, that's delicious. It's rich and full of flavor," she said, taking another sip. "Tuscany is such a beautiful region," she went on. "Did you know the word "Brunello," if you translate it roughly, means little dark one?"

"No, I didn't," George said.

"Well, it's the local name for the Sangiovese Grosso, the large, berried form of the Sangiovese grape, which grows in the area..."

Sophie was starting to ramble. That meant she was at ease. I enjoyed watching Sophie taste wines with such pleasure. And I loved how she always brought something new to the table.

"You're impressing me, dear. You have impeccable taste."

"You too, sir. 2008?" she asked.

"Actually no, it's a 2006. But close. And, Sophie," George said with a wink, "enough with the 'sir.' You can call me George."

I could tell George was thrilled by her presence. Not only was Sophie easy on the eyes, but she was smart, and he liked intelligent woman. He was already growing fond of her.

"Of course, sir… Um, George," she quickly corrected.

George smiled. "We'll let the wine open a bit more so it's at temperature when Madeleine serves the main dish. For now I have some champagne."

As my mother brought out some appetizers — artichokes, sundried tomatoes, a homemade pesto made from black olives, and some crackers — George took the opportunity to make a toast. He stood up and raised his glass.

"Sophie, it's a pleasure to finally meet you and to have you with us." He turned to me. "Patrick, you fool. I don't know why you kept her from us all this time, but we're happy you're sharing her with us now. To a lovely afternoon and many more to come, I hope. Cheers."

We all clinked our glasses.

Sophie helped my mum serve the main dish, even though my mother insisted she stay seated because she was a guest. But that was how Sophie was raised, always a helping hand.

The wine was perfection with the roasted beef, plum tomatoes, and green beans mum presented for lunch. I didn't just savor the wine — I enjoyed the scenery. Sophie fit in perfectly with my family. She needed time to loosen up, but now she was having an animated conversation with George about wine. It warmed my heart, filled my day with joy. I had truly found my match and under no circumstances would I give any of this up. My mother looked at her in adoration. I knew she approved of her without hesitation. The small pinch on the shoulder as she passed on her way to the kitchen was a hint.

After dinner, we strolled through the different parts of the garden, each with a different theme. The air was heavy with the scent of lilac and honeysuckle. The bees were humming freely throughout the flower beds and the birds chirped happily. I took Sophie's hand in mine and entwined our fingers.

She looked at me, her eyes twinkling. I could lose myself in those big, warm, dark brown eyes. Correction. I was already lost, but she saved me and had lit up my life entirely. I'd been alone and lost for a long time, had become a bit bitter to be honest. My horrible relationship with my father, the constant quarreling, him pushing me to my limits, didn't do me any good either. But now, with Sophie, everything seemed brighter and better, went easier.

"Are you okay?" I asked quietly.

"I am now." She gazed at me in utter adoration.

"I know they can be a bit overwhelming."

"They're amazing, Patrick. I'm so happy you brought me here today. You're letting me into your life, and that means a lot to me." She paused. "Patrick, you're lucky to have them in your life. Your mother is affectionate, sweet, caring, and George is... I don't know where to start. He's great, intelligent, and so proud of you. Seeing you with them is a little hard. It reminds me of my parents. My mother was social, open, she wore her heart on her sleeve. Nothing was ever too much for her. She put everyone's needs before hers..."

"She must have been a remarkable woman," I said gently.

"She was..." A small tear was creeping from underneath her eyelashes, revealing her deep, unresolved grief. She quickly stopped the tear from running down her cheek, wiping it away with the back of her hand. She turned her head so I wouldn't see her tears. "Sorry, I'm being gloomy."

"Don't be sorry. I understand this grief isn't easy to bear. I want you to be part of my life, Sophie, and that includes my family too. So I want you to feel at home with them. What's mine is yours." I cupped her head with my hands so I could take a long, deep look into her eyes, put some strength behind my words. I wanted her to understand she was my everything and that she was part of me, part of my life.

She smiled at me happily. "That means a lot to me, Patrick, thank you."

"And don't you forget it," I said, softly kissing her lips.

I took her hand and steered her toward the garage so I could show her the old Aston Martin D4 I was restoring.

"What a beauty. Is this your grandfather's car?" She rounded the car in admiration, gently stroking the dark green hood.

"Yes, this was the car he bought on his sixtieth birthday. He always wanted an Aston Martin, and by his sixtieth birthday, he'd saved enough. Whenever we visited my grandparents in England — my mum was born in Essex — he drove me around the countryside. Just me and him. And when I got my permit, I took it out for a spin. Some great memories." I smiled, remembering. "He left me the car when he died a few years ago. We had it shipped to the States. George and I are fixing the engine. When we find the time, of course. But it reminds me of him, and I enjoy being busy with my hands, fiddling with the small pieces, taking everything apart and putting it back together. I'm on another planet when I'm working on the car. It helps clear my head."

The rest of the afternoon flew by. After our stroll, we ate fresh cinnamon apple cake with coffee and tea on the patio at the rear of the garden. The sun was setting, illuminating the whole patio with its warm glow. Around six o'clock, we said goodbye and drove back to the city, saturated by the sun, the food, and a lot of wine.

MORE ESPRESSO, LESS DEPRESSO

I was working on a presentation when my phone rang. Caller ID unknown — *strange.* I picked up anyway. "Sophie Smith."

"Hello, Sophie, this is Dr. Ashton. Sorry for interrupting, but it's an emergency. It's about your sister Carol."

I knew Carol was prone to relapse. When I was in India, she had told me she'd found a counselor in New York, someone to talk to, just in case. Dr. Ashton had recommended a support group where women could share their stories and support each other when things got tough. Personally, I thought this was a super idea. Especially since I didn't know how to help her. So professional help was always good. The group met every two weeks or so. I guess I hadn't been involved in that part of her life, but she had a group of people she could fall back on. I'd seen her a few months ago, a few weeks after the gala. She'd gifted me a one-day massage workshop at a beauty academy for my birthday. We had a blast. Never thought I'd enjoy giving someone a massage so much.

Carol had seemed fine back then. *She was fine, right?* I doubted myself now and replayed that day in my head. We never had deep conversations. I just wanted to see her, keep in touch, have a bit of fun together. And that was when I had the time. It wasn't easy with my work schedule.

"What's wrong? Is she okay?"

"Carol has been hospitalized. Her neighbor found her unconscious in her apartment this morning. Can you come?"

"Of course," I said without hesitation. "Is she at St. John's?"

"Yes. But before you see her, please stop by my office first. We need to talk."

"Oh, okay. I'll take the first cab I can get."

I was a bit panicked. They found her unconscious? What if no one had found her? What did she do? I closed my laptop, grabbed my purse from under my desk, and rushed toward Kate's office, entering without knocking.

"Kate, sorry to bother you, but can I take the day off? My sister has been hospitalized, and I need to go there right away." I knew I sounded agitated.

"She's okay?" Kate asked.

"I don't know yet."

Kate nodded. "Go. And if you need more time off, just call me."

"Thank you," I said. "Look, I have my cell and I'm taking my laptop. I'll send you the details for the voluntary conservation case. It has all the deals we worked out for the private land-owners."

"Sophie, you don't have to, but I appreciate it. Go now."

I sprinted out of the office without another word.

I was in deep thought on my way to the hospital. *What if she wasn't doing better? Maybe she could stay with me, so I could keep an eye on her. This is all my fault. We haven't seen each other a lot lately. Maybe if we'd spent more time together, this wouldn't have happened?*

I decided to call Patrick. I needed him to be there. I started dialing his office number but pressed the cancel button immediately. I couldn't. Carol didn't know we were dating. I couldn't take him with me. How would she react? Oh, but I wanted to share everything with her. I wanted to scream it from the rooftop. I wanted to tell her that I was happy and madly in love with Patrick. Perhaps she'd forgotten the incident at Starbucks. It had been seven months, so what were the odds?

I found Dr. Ashton talking to a nurse in reception. He greeted me and led me to his office on the fourth floor.

"How is she?" I felt anguished. Like I couldn't make the walk from the elevator to his office at the end of the hallway.

"Not good," Dr. Ashton said. "She starved herself and she's dehydrated. We had to put her on an IV. But she keeps pulling them out, so we had to strap her to the bed. She's not happy."

I halted and looked up at him, my lower lip trembling, my hands shaking. I hadn't known. How couldn't I have known? "Oh my, how long has this been going on? I thought she was doing fine?"

Dr. Ashton took my arm to steady me. "Sophie, are you okay? Come on, let's sit down in my office. You'll be more at ease there." He let me lean on him until we reached his office, where he settled me in a petrol-colored armchair in front of his desk. He handed me a glass of water and watched as I drank, waiting for me to regain some color. Then, he took a seat in the opposite armchair, his hands tucked into his armpits.

I managed a smile and mouthed a thank you.

"I see this comes as a shock to you," he said gently. "She was doing better. But something happened. We don't know what. She started to miss some of her counseling sessions, coming in irregularly. And when she did show up, she didn't say a word. She just sat there quietly."

"Did she lose weight? No one noticed?"

"We didn't notice." He shook his head. "She seemed fine. The last session she attended was a month ago. Last week she didn't show up. A friend of hers, Alice — she attends the same support group — lives on her block. She tried to contact her, but Carol didn't answer her calls. So she went to her place, but Carol didn't open the door. Alice knew something was wrong, so she forced the door open and found Carol on the floor in the bathroom. When I examined her, I could tell she'd been starving herself for a few days. She probably fainted and hit her head on the sink."

I clasped my hands in front of my mouth and swallowed hard, tears welling up in my eyes. What kind of horrible sister was I? The tears started to roll down my cheeks.

"Sophie, we'll do our best to help her. But we need your help," Dr. Ashton said. "Maybe you know why she did this? Did anything change recently? Did she move? New boyfriend? Something work-related?"

I sniffed. "Well, we don't see each other often. I've been out of town for work," I rushed to explain. "When I called, she didn't mention anything. I don't even know if she's dating or who her friends are." I wiped a tear away. "Look, we hadn't seen each other for years. Not until I moved to New York. Is that it? Is it because I'm in her life again?"

Dr. Ashton shook his head. "I don't think so. But it's a possibility we'll keep in mind. Maybe we can get to the bottom of this during family therapy."

I nodded. Was I the reason for all this misery? Did I jog her memory? Was it because I was back and I reminded her about everything: mom and dad, our family back then, the crash, our loss? Oh, I hope not. Carol was the only family member I had left. I had to make amends, reconnect again on a deeper level with her. I felt gloomy.

"So, what do we do?" I asked.

"Well, she needs to regain some strength. Then we'll start with some therapy." He looked at me pointedly. "Carol, you, and a counselor. Are you up for that?"

"Sure. If I can help, I will. When do we start?"

"In a few weeks. She needs time to get stronger." He stood up. "I'll call if there are any changes at all. She's in room 404, down the hall on your right."

I stood up and shook his hand. "Thank you, Dr. Ashton."

It had been months since I'd seen Carol. *She couldn't have changed that much,* I told myself. I gave a small knock on the door and waited for an answer. But it didn't come, so I let myself in.

Carol was on her back, facing the window. Her bare arms, lying on top of the covers, were covered in bruises. The bruises were probably from pulling out the IVs. She looked extremely fragile and thin. Was this woman Carol? My sister? How could someone change so much in so little time? She didn't look up when I entered the room.

"Carol, hi, it's Sophie," I said, trying to sound upbeat.

She turned her head at my name. Tears rolled down her face. I kissed her on the cheek. It was only then I noticed her arms strapped to the bed.

"Carol, what happened?" I whispered.

"I'm fine, Sophie," she said. "I tell them all the time. But they won't listen."

"But you've lost a lot of weight. Why are you doing this to yourself?"

She pulled at the straps. She wanted to sit up, and she looked to me for help. "Sophie, could you loosen them a bit? They're so tight."

I felt sorry for her. I wanted to help, but I couldn't. It was for her own safety. "I can't. Sorry. They're doing this to help you."

"Sophie, come on. You know me. I'm fine." Her voice was getting louder. "What kind of sister are you? Why won't you help me? What good are you?"

I was pinned to the floor. This wasn't Carol. What had happened to her?

Carol shouted, louder and louder. A cry for help. Witnessing this was the worst kind of pain. And I couldn't do a thing to help her.

"Sophie," she screamed. "You have to help me! I want to get out of here! Take me home. I'll do better. I'll eat again. Please don't leave me here." She pleaded over and over, raising her voice in anger, in despair.

And I could only stare, feeling more miserable by the minute. I didn't know what to say.

Two nurses rushed into the room. They'd heard Carol's outburst. One was trying to calm her down, the other shot a sedative into Carol's IV. It took only a few minutes before Carol calmed down and fell back onto the bed.

Dr. Ashton stepped into the room a few minutes after she dozed off. He guided me into the hallway.

I didn't know what to say. I couldn't move.

"Sophie, go home," he urged gently. "She's not herself. I'll call you as soon as she's doing better. It's for the best. Let her get some strength back."

Outside, I hailed a cab and sat in the back, numb. Exhaustion overwhelmed me, and my head ached badly. I dragged myself out of the cab and into my apartment.

I took a painkiller and sat down on the sofa. I needed to rest my head a bit.

The doorbell woke me. A quick glance at the kitchen clock told me it was already ten o'clock at night. Did I sleep the entire afternoon? I stumbled to the door and opened it halfway.

Patrick was standing in the hallway, concern on his face. "Are you okay?" he asked.

I nodded, ushered him in, and closed the door behind him, staggering back to the sofa.

"Sophie, what's wrong?" He took his hand in mine. "I called a dozen times. You didn't answer, so I came over."

I couldn't manage a single word.

"What happened? Tell me. Say something, Sophie!"

I started to cry, unleashing the afternoon's emotions. In between my sobs, I told him about Carol, that she had been hospitalized. I told him about the screaming and how she thought I didn't want to help her.

Patrick listened intently. When I finished my story, he gathered me in his arms, hugging me tightly. "She's going to be okay, Sophie. She's in good hands."

"I know," I said. "But still. She's all I have left. I can't lose her. I could've prevented this. If only I'd spent more time with her these last few months..."

"Don't be so hard on yourself. We'll work it out."

Patrick was kind and thoughtful. He ordered food, but I had no appetite at all. He cleaned the kitchen, helped me into bed, laid down next to me, and held me tight.

When I woke up, Patrick was gone. Maybe he had left after I fell asleep or maybe he had left early that morning and I hadn't heard him go. I found breakfast on the kitchen counter. Fruit, granola, and coffee in a Thermos. Patrick had left a little note with it.

> *Everything is going to be fine. Eat this. Call me if you need me. I'll drop everything.*
> *Love you, Patrick*

I just had to wait it out. I had to trust Dr. Ashton. He knew what was best for Carol.

I DON'T GIVE A FRAPPE ANYMORE

I had an appointment at St. John's Hospital. Carol had gained strength over the last three weeks, so we'd started group sessions with Dr. Ashton. The main goal was to figure out the reason behind Carol's relapse. Three times a week, I sat with Carol for one-hour sessions to talk about our past. We talked about her work, her friends, her life in New York. And the harder parts of our past, the car crash, my move to Paris...

Carol admitted she missed me all those years I'd been abroad. But she said she didn't mind because we kept in touch. She understood why I'd gone to Paris and why I liked to travel. But she was happy I'd moved to New York. She thought we'd finally do stuff together as sisters — when I was in town, of course.

I thought she gave me too much credit. In the months I'd lived in New York, Carol and I had only gotten together a few times. And now that Patrick and I were dating seriously, I hadn't seen her much at all. I was oddly grateful to have some us time. And I couldn't help but wonder if maybe now was the right time to re-establish our sisterly bond. After all, she was the only family member I had left.

But we still didn't know why Carol wasn't eating. So Dr. Ashton tried a different approach. He asked about dating and her relationship history. Who had she dated? For how long? Why did they break up?

It was clearly a difficult subject for Carol. But she made it through those sessions. She talked about high school and how she needed attention after our parents passed away. And then Patrick came into the picture. How they'd had met after a game, how they'd dated briefly, how devastated she was when she caught him making out with a cheerleader. He broke up with her without explanation. He just stopped calling one day.

No! That must have been the trigger, I thought. I had to ask. "Carol, when we met at Starbucks. You ran out of there when you saw Patrick Downey. Did you start paying attention to your body weight after that?"

Dr. Ashton quickly turned toward me, a question in his eyes.

I explained my theory. "Well, eight, no, almost nine months ago now, I moved back to New York for work. Carol and I hadn't seen each other in years, so we agreed to meet for coffee."

Carol picked up the story, and I let her. "We were waiting in line, chit chatting, when I saw that dog Patrick Downey, the guy who'd betrayed me with that bitch Chelsea, the captain of the cheerleading squad. I kind of made a scene when we broke up. Anyway, when I saw him at the coffee shop, I couldn't stand being near him. So I ran out and left Sophie behind."

I was shocked by Carol's hatred for Patrick. Was he the cause of all her issues? It couldn't be. What if she found out I was dating him? She'd never speak to me again. That wouldn't happen... Right?

Dr. Ashton interrupted my thoughts. "Are you okay, Sophie? You look so distant all of a sudden."

I gave my head a little shake and forced a smile. "Oh no, I'm fine. I was lost in thought for a moment. I was trying to recall a memory from that day. But I'm all ears now."

After the session, Dr. Ashton thanked me for helping Carol make progress. He was certain he'd found the root of the issue and could go deeper with her, work on her self-esteem, eating habits, and relationship issues. Without me. It was something Carol had to work on.

On the way home, I replayed the session in my mind. If Carol and I hadn't seen Patrick at the coffee shop that day, she would've been healthy now. If she found out I was dating Patrick or even saw him, it would trigger her. I had to make sure she didn't fall back into her old habits. And I was the only one who could make sure she avoided him.

I couldn't lose her. We were getting close again. But what about Patrick? We had it good. He was kind and tender. We had a lot of fun. He was my soulmate, a friend, a man I loved deeply. I had to make a decision, the hardest one I'd ever have to make.

Patrick was staying at his new apartment in Brooklyn. After months, he'd finally gotten the keys. He'd been anticipating that moment. It was a brand-new apartment, one that belonged only to him, and he'd invested all his savings in it. It was an achievement — and a clear sign to his father that he owned something his father hadn't had a hand in.

We visited the apartment a few times when it was under construction. It was in an exquisite new building in the heart of Boerum Hill that combined sophisticated minimalism with superior craftsmanship, all situated in Brooklyn's most charming neighborhood.

Patrick owned a penthouse, four bedrooms and twenty-five hundred square feet, not counting the terrace. One of the bedrooms was downstairs, and Patrick planned to use it as an office. The apartment was open concept, with a huge kitchen, a cozy dining area, and a large sitting room. The living room looked out over the area's historic brownstones. The whole place, upstairs and downstairs, had hardwood floors, ten-foot ceilings, and over eight-foot windows that bathed it in light.

Admittedly, there was still a lot to do, but the kitchen and the bathroom were complete. He was working with an interior designer on the finishing touches, and within a few months, all the furniture would be delivered and then he could finally call it home. But that hadn't stopped him from moving in.

I called his cell phone. I was too much of a coward to confront him face-to-face.

He answered immediately. "Hey, sweetie, I missed you this week." He sounded upbeat and so pleased to hear from me.

"Hi," I said. "I'm not interrupting anything?"

"You? Never. You had a busy week I presume? I haven't heard from you in days. Everything okay with your sister?" he asked.

"Yes, she's fine. It was a hell of a week." I paused and gathered all my courage. I had to go through with it. "Look, Patrick, it's not working."

"What isn't? The sessions with your sister? You want Darren to drive you to the hospital?" He had no clue what I was trying to say.

"No, it's us. I don't think we have a future together. It's better to stop it right here than to waste each other's time."

I didn't want to do this. It felt so wrong and in conflict with my feelings for him. But I had to do it. I couldn't be with him and not involve him entirely in my life. There would undoubtedly be a day when he'd have to meet my sister, and I didn't know how Carol would handle that. Patrick was silent on the other end of the line.

"Patrick?" I asked carefully.

"I thought we had it good. What happened? Did I do something wrong? I don't understand." He sounded confused.

"It's not you, Patrick, it's me," I said. "It's better if we just stop seeing each other. I'll bring your stuff back tomorrow."

"Sophie, we can work it out. Whatever it is. Give me a chance. Please," he said. "Tell me what I've done wrong. I'll make up for it. Come on, we've been together for months."

I didn't know what to do with his pleas. "I'm sorry, Patrick, but I can't." I ended the call before I could change my mind.

Tears instantly welled up in my eyes. What had I done? I loved him, I did. But it was for Carol's sake.

Maybe Kate has a project abroad, I thought. The firm operated around the world, so maybe I could get out of the city. It wouldn't be a problem since Carol was still under Dr. Ashton's supervision. She was in good hands. And a change of scenery would do me good.

Afraid that Patrick might come over, I called Sammy and asked him not to transfer any of his calls. I instructed him to deny Patrick access to the building. Sammy didn't ask why, just confirmed my wishes and told me if there was anything else he could do, I only had to ask.

The next morning I begged Kate to send me abroad. She wasn't surprised. She knew how much I loved traveling, and it had been a while since my last trip. We'd cut down my trips because I'd wanted to spend more time with Patrick, and Kate had been flexible. Luckily, there was a case in London. The lawyer who was assigned to the case, Dean, couldn't go because his wife had given birth to a son over the weekend. I could be there in less than a week.

So I grabbed the opportunity with both hands. Two days later I was on a plane to London. Far away from New York. Far away from Patrick. And there was a chance the case could get prolonged. I could stay for a month. Even a year. But no matter what, I wouldn't forget about Carol. Maybe she could move to London when she got better. Start over there. But I swore no guy would ever come between us again.

Patrick had tried to call me countless times before I left. I didn't call him back. I didn't answer his messages. I knew if I talked to him, I'd change my mind in a heartbeat. Some of his messages were friendly, others were cold or pleading, asking me to take him back.

I was too scared to take his things back to his place, so Sammy had ordered a courier. I changed my cell number and my apartment was sublet to another expat. Technically, I didn't live in New York anymore. London was my new home.

When I arrived in London, I called Sammy to make sure my personal belongings had been shipped to my new apartment. And I couldn't hold back and told him what happened with Patrick.

"Did he call, Sammy?"

"Yes, several times," Sammy said. "Friday night he even came to see you. He thought you were out for the evening. I had to tell him, Sophie. Poor guy. Always so polite. I really felt sorry for him."

"What did you tell him?"

"Well, I told him you moved abroad for a new project. I didn't mention London." He hesitated. "I understand why you don't want to tell him, but still, Sophie. If I can be honest, you two were great as a couple."

I sighed. "I know, Sammy. But I had to end it. I didn't want to waste any more of his time. You know, with all the traveling," I lied. "It was too much to handle."

"After Friday, he hasn't been around, so I think he got the message."

"Thanks again for everything, Sammy. I owe you big time."

"You sure do."

We laughed and wished each other all the best. Sammy hoped I could stay in the same apartment — or at least the building — when I returned to New York. I hoped so, too, but hopefully under different circumstances.

After a few weeks in London, I was eager to make some space for my new life. I decided to start by cleaning out my purse. I threw out everything from New York. I wouldn't return — well, not in the near future. So what was the point of keeping all those membership cards, tickets, vouchers, discount coupons?

I dumped my purse out on the kitchen table. To my surprise, I found my old SIM card. I don't know why I'd kept it. I rubbed it between my fingers. I couldn't just throw it in the garbage. I had to take a look. Didn't I? Maybe I'd missed some messages from work.

I carefully removed the new SIM card from my phone and replaced it with the old one. I waited a few minutes for my phone to restart. I stared at it blankly. What was I afraid of? *Really, Sophie, it's just a phone,* I scolded myself.

I dialed the voicemail number, expecting to hear I had no new messages.

"You have twenty-six new messages," the automated voice informed me.

Damn, that's too much. Don't tell me they're all from work. Please.

"Message received on Wednesday, July 17 at 9:30 p.m."

"Sophie, it's Patrick. Call me back. I guess the connection got interrupted."

It dawned on me. These were from the day I'd broken up with him. I'd ignored his calls and texts, and totally forgotten about these messages. Never took the time to listen to them. Because I knew I'd reverse my decision if I listened to his pleas. What if all the messages were from Patrick?

"Message received on Wednesday, July 17 at 9:46 p.m."

"Hi, me again. You won't call me back, huh? Please, Sophie, talk to me. Tell me what I did wrong. We can work it out, but don't end it like this. Call me. I'll be waiting for your call."

"Message received on Wednesday, July 17 at 10:30 p.m."

"I spoke to Sammy. He told me you were out for the evening. Call me when you get back. Doesn't matter the hour. I can come back over if you want."

"Message received on Thursday, July 18 at 8:25 a.m."

"Sophie, Alex here. What the fuck happened last night? Patrick was here this morning asking for you. Fill me in, girl, because I hope it's not true. Tell me you didn't break up with him. Call me."

Oops, missed that message from Alex. But he knew I was in London. And he knew the whole story. But I reminded myself to come up with a good excuse for not taking Alex's call.

"Message received on Thursday, July 18 at 8:34 p.m."

"Sophie, Patrick here. This is ridiculous. Why aren't you answering? Everything okay?"

"Message received on Thursday, July 18 at 9:02 p.m."

"Hi, it's Jane. Alex told me about you and Patrick. Are you okay? We're here if you want to talk or hang out. Don't forget that. I'll try calling again later this week. Keep safe. Big hug from me in the meantime."

Dear Jane, always caring for others. I could ask her to come for a visit. That would be fantastic. I decided I'd ask her later that week.

OMG... Still twenty messages left. Come on, Soph, get it over with.

I pressed the end call button. It was too much. I'd left New York in a rush, ended my relationship with Patrick like a coward, left my friends in the dark about what had really happened...

I moved into the living room, taking a seat on the leather sofa. I gathered all my courage and dialed my voicemail again. Jane had called once more, a few calls from the office, five more messages from Patrick. The last one was the hardest one to listen to.

"Message received on Friday, July 19 at 10:48 p.m."

"Sophie, me again. Thank you for returning my stuff. The courier brought everything today. Pity you couldn't do it. I really wanted to see you. I stopped by your place again this evening. Sammy told me you moved abroad. Something about a new case? But he didn't know what country. Is that the real reason you broke up with me? How long will you be gone? We can keep dating. I don't mind the distance. I love you. You know that." He paused, altering his tone. "Look, I'm having a hard time with this. It was so sudden. We used to talk about everything. Why didn't you talk to me this time? Dammit, Sophie,

TALK TO ME. SAY SOMETHING!!! Look, this is the last time I'll call. It's up to you now. We had it good. I deserve to know what happened. I hope to hear from you. Bye."

I got goosebumps. He loved me, he cared for me. And what did I do when things got hard? Nothing. I fled the country. Even if I wanted to be with him, even if I wanted to consider a long-distance relationship, I had to keep Carol in mind. I didn't know how she'd react. She was already so fragile. No, it was over. I had made a decision, and I wouldn't change my mind. I ripped the card out of my cell and threw it in the garbage.

I stayed in London for a year. The months flew by because I worked seven days a week. I didn't have much time to think about Patrick or New York. The fact that an ocean separated us did enough.

I have to admit, the first few months were hell. I missed him, I missed the life we had, I missed his company, having a person to talk to, someone to do stuff with, our morning coffee at our favorite Starbucks. I missed my sister and evenings out with Alex and Jane. I missed tequila shots. I missed the apartment. I missed the roar of the city...

But I couldn't go back. It would never be the same. The feeling eventually faded.

I woke up to work, went to bed with it. And it paid off. Kate put me on one of her biggest accounts. I went to Dubai for two months, Cape Town for five, then three in Singapore. Nearly two years had passed before I returned to New York.

While I was gone, Carol transformed into her old self — with the help of Dr. Ashton, a lot of counseling and online support from me of course, and a few trips to visit me. I wasn't in New York often. But when I was in town, I wanted to spend my time with her and my two best friends. Alex and Jane were the hardest to please. After my sudden departure, I had to make it up to them. But we worked it out.

Carol had grown more confident and even met a guy during her recovery process. She was madly in love with him. I had met Dennis a couple times when I visited. He looked a bit gruff but took good care of her. She'd confided in him, and I could tell they had an open and loving relationship. That was all I needed to know.

After two years of traveling and working around the world, I landed a position managing a small team of new recruits at the firm's headquarters. I was their guide and tutor. I got another apartment and started over again in New York. Still glued to my job.

DEAD EYE

It had been months since Sophie left me without any explanation. I replayed those last months over and over again, every word, every moment, but I couldn't find a clue. She disappeared so suddenly and I hadn't gotten any news since then. Not even a single call.

At first, I thought something horrible had happened because it was so sudden. She had broken off our relationship and left the country a few days later. Sammy had told me it was because of work, which was a bit comforting. He didn't know where she'd gone. Or maybe he wouldn't tell me. So I tried my luck with Alex and Jane. But they were ignorant as well. Maybe to protect her, maybe they really didn't know. I couldn't ask her employer, far too direct.

So, after a while, I stopped looking for her. She clearly didn't want to be found. I concentrated on my job and furnishing my new apartment, hoping to find some distraction. I practically lived at the office now. I didn't have a cozy home to share with someone or a loving partner to go home to at night.

The day started like any other, but that would quickly change. It began with a rapid knock on the door, pulling my attention from my meeting.

"Yes?" I looked up, annoyed. My secretary, Anne, came in, quietly coming to a halt next to me. She seemed discomforted.

"What is it, Anne?" I asked loudly, so everyone could hear.

"I'm sorry, sir. But we have a situation outside." She was calm, but I heard an underlying tremor in her voice.

"Can't it wait until after this meeting?" I demanded.

"I'm afraid not, sir."

She was dead serious. We'd been working together since I'd started at my father's firm, so I knew her quite well. She wouldn't interrupt if it was nothing. I got up, told my team to take a ten-minute break, and left the meeting room. Once out of earshot, I turned toward Anne.

"What is it? What's so important?" I hissed. But then I heard someone crying loudly. I didn't need more information because even from a distance I could tell it was Cora, my father's newest addition. His twenty-five-year-old girlfriend.

I glanced at Anne. "Really? This is the situation?" I rolled my eyes and headed toward the lobby.

Cora was a beautiful girl, if you liked them blonde and stupid of course. I didn't know what my father saw in her. She was a complete and utter moron. I'd only seen two sides of her — all mushy and "oh, honey, you're the greatest, you're the best" or going on shopping sprees — but I bet there was more drama I hadn't witnessed.

Sometimes she was a total emotional wreck. Like now. She was the cherry on top, making my living hell even worse. I exhaled loudly. *What would it be this time?* I wondered.

She was making a scene in the lobby. People were turning to stare at her as they passed. As soon as she caught sight of me, she ran toward me and threw herself into my arms. I peeled her off, dragged her into my office, and sat her in the Eames chair in front of my desk.

"Shhh, Cora, what is it?" I asked rudely. She didn't notice my cold tone and started telling me what had happened. I didn't understand a word because she was sobbing constantly.

"He turned...blue...collapsed... The doc...to hospital..."

"What?" I handed her a tissue and tried to calm her down. "Cora, rewind. What's going on? Why are you here? Can't you go to my father?"

She looked up at me, with her exotic blue eyes and thick eyelashes coated in mascara. I didn't know how it was possible, but even with all the crying, her makeup didn't move an inch. She looked immaculate. "He's gone, Patrick. Dead. Your father had a heart attack."

I sat down abruptly, shocked. But I still found the words to address her. "Where is he?"

"The Presbyterian." She dabbed at her eyes.

"Why aren't you with him?"

She scoffed at me. "Really, Patrick. He's dead. What do you want me to do? Hospitals are so gross. I could've easily caught something. I took the first cab out of there. Blech. I already called Valerie. I told her I needed an appointment today. It's an attack on my complexion. I really need a spa treatment. Look, I've got a photoshoot in two days. And him dying right now isn't ideal. This could ruin my career." She crumpled the tissue in her fist. "Well, I have to go. I'll be late for my appointment. Ta-ta." She was gone, as if nothing had happened. Her life went on.

I sat down to compose myself. Maybe we weren't on good terms, but he was still my father. I pushed my hate for the man aside, stood up, and headed toward the elevators.

"Call Darren. I need to leave now," I called to Anne as I stepped on the elevator. "Cancel all my meetings. I'll call you later." I disappeared behind the closing doors.

Darren was waiting out front, ready to drive me to the Presbyterian, so I could see my father one last time.

A few hours later, after signing what felt like hundreds of declarations and papers, I left the hospital and gazed up at the clouded sky. He was gone, for good. As I settled in the back seat of the car, I dialed my mum's number.

She picked up right away, excited to hear from me. "Darling, what a surprise. Are you okay?"

"Hi, Mum. Well, I've got some time this afternoon. Care for some lunch?" I asked.

"Sure. I'm in town. Where do you want to meet?"

"What about Romarin?"

"Okay. I'll be there in 20 minutes."

I couldn't tell her about my father's passing over the phone. She'd been married to him for over twenty years. Okay, their divorce didn't go so smooth. They'd hated each other for years. But still. She had to hear the news from me, not Cora.

I was already seated when my mother arrived. Romarin was a small French restaurant where my mum and I often met for lunch. I enjoyed being there. They served baguette and bread, all freshly baked on site. They offered a selection of bread with walnuts, honey, rosemary, and raisins, all accompanied by a plate of assorted cheeses. The selections changed seasonally, but you always got a piece of goat cheese, some brie, Reblochon, and a piece of bleu cheese. Nothing special, but it was succulent. For me, comfort food.

My mother swept into the restaurant gracefully, wearing a pale-blue trench coat over a vintage black dress. "Dear, great idea to meet for lunch." She gave me a quick peck on the cheek and sat down as she shrugged out of her trench.

"Mum, I ordered a Scotch. Care for the same?" I asked as the waiter approached.

"Oh no, too heavy. A glass of pinot grigio, please," she told the waiter as she hung her trench over the back of her seat. "So, it's been a while. What's new?"

"Can't I invite you to have lunch with me?"

"Sure you can. But something tells me that's not the case. I've known you a long time, my dear Patrick."

I waited for our drinks to be served before getting to the serious stuff. "Mum, you're right. There's another reason I called. I didn't want you to hear it from someone else."

"What is it? What did you do?" she demanded.

"Why do you think I'm in trouble? It's not about me." I hesitated. "It's about Dad."

"He's going to marry that bimbo Cora, am I right?" She sighed. "Oh, honey, we're divorced. I've got George. I can handle it. But it's sweet that you're so worried."

"It's not that." I inhaled deeply and said calmly, "Mum, Dad had a heart attack this afternoon. He passed away."

My mother turned white, took a large gulp of her pinot, and exhaled loudly.

"Are you okay?" I asked carefully.

"Yes. Actually — and I'm sorry for saying this out loud but — FINALLY. He had it coming, that bastard."

Alright, not the reaction I had in mind. She's taking it rather well, I must say, I thought.

"How are you handling it, my dear?" she asked.

"I'm still trying to grasp the fact that he's gone. No more tyranny, no more ordering me around. It's a huge weight off my shoulders. It's not polite, but I'm relieved," I admitted. "It's over. It's finally over. Isn't it strange I'm feeling this way?"

My mother took my hand. We stared at each other for a few minutes without saying a word. "I know," she said finally. "He wasn't the easiest man to live with. And you worked with him every day. You stuck with him for a long time, dear."

"Yeah, wasn't easy."

"But you are a free man now, Patrick. If I remember correctly," she said, taking a sip of her wine, "the contract ended the moment he terminated it. And he's dead, so it ends here."

I looked at her questioningly. "You knew about the contract?"

"Of course I did." She laughed bitterly. "Your father rubbed it in my face every chance he got."

"Why didn't you say anything? Why didn't you help me out of this mess?"

"It's called growing up, dear. You shouldn't have signed it in the first place," she added. "And I can take care of myself, you know."

"Quite a lesson, Mum, thanks."

"Well, it's over now." She sat back. "You know, I'm still human, and I hope he didn't suffer too much."

"Oh, right. I asked the coroner. He had a pleasant ending." I shrugged.

"How so?"

"Well, he and Cora were in the bedroom. And his heart just stopped. From all the excitement I guess."

"No, you're kidding!" My mum started to giggle.

"I'm not." I chuckled. And then we were both laughing out loud, imagining the situation.

She composed herself after a few minutes. "So, what can I do to help, Patrick? You want me to arrange the funeral? Or is Cora helping you?"

"I don't think we'll be seeing much more of Cora," I said. "She apparently has a photoshoot in two days, and it was too much for her to handle. I wouldn't be surprised if she already has a new boyfriend. So I'd appreciate your help. Thanks, Mum."

"What else? Did you tell the board of directors?"

"No, not yet. How quickly do I have to inform them?"

"We'll call Mr. Hundsham first," she said. "Perhaps I can arrange an appointment for this afternoon. He handles the family's legal paperwork — and the firm's. I don't know what your father had in his will, so Mr. Hundsham will have to give us the details. And first thing tomorrow, you'll have to call a meeting with the board of directors so they can make arrangements and decide who will take over."

I nodded, grateful for her support. "I'll call Anne. She'll schedule it."

Later that week we buried my father. Mum and I decided to keep it small and simple. Just a ceremony with a few family members and some of his closest friends, no colleagues or board members.

Everything changed after that. My father had been so concerned with making my mum's life miserable that he overlooked a small — but critical — detail in the contract that had bound me to him: his own death. So, legally, I inherited everything, not Cora. They weren't married, so she had no claim. I inherited his entire estate, including the company.

I thought I'd be a free man, but I was wrong. He still had control over me. I inherited his entire life, the life he'd been leading, the life I'd hated so much. The board made me his successor. At the age of twenty-eight, I became a multimillionaire and the CEO of a large real estate firm. Not on my merit. I hadn't run the company. I hadn't made it successful. I felt trapped in a life that wasn't mine. The more I tried to untangle myself from him, from his life, the more I became him. Everything reminded me of him. His house, his office, his car... I couldn't handle it and sought comfort in women and booze, to my mother's great displeasure. She tried to get me back on track, but I refused. I was too far gone.

BRAIN JUICE

For the last few weeks, I'd been crashing at my mother's house. I couldn't bear staying at my father's house anymore. Since he'd passed, I'd inherited his company, his house in Staten Island, his condo at 57 Bond Street in NoHo, and his villa in the Hamptons. At first, I stayed in the Hamptons to manage the sale of it, but it went agonizingly slow. I still had my own apartment in Brooklyn, but I didn't have time to oversee the sale of my father's estates and go back and forth every night.

But his energy was everywhere in those houses, and it just depleted me more every day. I gave up and found my consolation in booze and meaningless sex and started to crash at my mum's house. I knew my mother was fed up with me. But she couldn't find it in her heart to throw me out, so she just tolerated my behavior. Thought it would pass. But it didn't.

I came home in the middle of the night, wasted, and each time with a different girl. I'd grown conceited, immoral, and egotistical, if I must say so myself. And I didn't care. For once, everything revolved around my needs. I decided how I wanted to live my life and no one had a say in it. It was ten o'clock in the morning and I was still in bed. There was nothing waiting for me anyway.

A hard knock on my bedroom door pulled me out of my thoughts.

"Mum, get lost. It's only ten a.m.," I growled loudly. Turning around to get some extra sleep wasn't an option because Andrew — not my mum — barged into the room.

"Mate, it's me, Andrew." Andrew switched the lights on and opened the thick, light-blue curtains, bathing the room in light.

I covered my eyes reflexively.

"Man, you look like shit! Just like your mom told me."

Dark circles surrounded my eyes. The distinctive smell of alcohol mixed with perspiration and smoke, probably from some bar, filled the entire room. I hadn't shaved in days; thick stubble covered my chin and cheeks. I'd even gained a few pounds.

"Andrew? What the hell are you doing here?" I grumbled, only half awake.

"It's an intervention," Andrew said. "This has to stop. Get up, get your ass into the shower, get dressed. We're leaving in fifteen minutes."

"What? I'm not going anywhere..."

"Don't argue with me. If you aren't dressed in fifteen minutes, I'll drag you out of the house in your pajamas," Andrew threatened.

My jaw tightened but then relaxed. I knew I couldn't argue with my best friend. "Alright, alright. Dammit, Andrew." Hauling myself out of bed, I lumbered to the bathroom, completely ignoring my friend. Didn't matter to Andrew; I was out of bed.

Twenty minutes later, I came downstairs, freshly showered and dressed in a pair of casual blue jeans, grey sneakers, and a grey hoodie. I hadn't shaved, but the vile odor was gone.

My mother looked impressed and nodded her thanks at Andrew.

"Do I at least have time for some coffee?" I asked politely.

"Nope. We'll stop on the way. Come on, we're leaving." Andrew stood up, kissed my mother on the cheek, and dragged me outside, where his pickup was waiting.

"Man, you're bossy. I'd be afraid if I were your kid," I said.

Andrew laughed. "Good to know you haven't lost your sense of humor." He glanced at me. "You look like you could really use some coffee."

"Hell yeah." I rubbed my eyes and yawned loudly. "My mother called you, didn't she?"

"Yep. She's worried, Patrick. And when I saw you this morning, she has every reason to be. Have you taken a look at yourself lately?"

"Don't start, Andrew..." My jaw tightened.

"Not gonna happen. I'm dragging you out of this," Andrew said. "You're one of my closest friends, and I can't let you destroy yourself like this."

Andrew pulled into a local diner, and we found a seat in the back. I ordered a black coffee, an omelet with tomato and mushrooms, and some brown toast. Andrew ordered the same except he asked for scrambled eggs.

"You've changed since the last time I saw you. What happened?" Andrew asked.

"I don't know, I'm fine," I said, taking a big sip of coffee.

"I don't buy a word of what you're saying. Come on, spill it."

I sighed loudly. "What do you want me to say, Andrew? I'm losing it!" It all tumbled out in a rush. "It's been a lot, you know, with my father's passing. He's gone, and I'm happy it's over. He made my life a living hell. But I still feel haunted by him. It's like he's back from the dead. I see him everywhere and in everything. At home, at work. The people I talk to or meet with. They all tell me how he would have done something. They question me. I'm sitting in his office, on his chair, at the desk where he worked and probably had sex. I shouldn't think about that too much. It makes me sick." I shook my head fiercely to chase away the image. "He trapped me in his fortune. You know, people only want to be around me because I'm rich now. People are only interested in me because of my father's wealth. Everyone wants a piece. I never wanted this. I mean, I'd wished he would just vanish. But I didn't want this."

"Is that why you're drinking so much?" Andrew held up his hand at my sharp look. "Your mother told me. She said you go out every night."

"When I'm drinking, clubbing, hooking up with random women, he's out of my mind for a while. It's the only way I can stop thinking," I admitted. "The high from the booze, the music, the sex — it makes my brain numb. I can escape from all this. But when I wake up, whether I'm alone or there's a girl whose name I forgot next to me, he's there again. And then I'm him. Repeating the same patterns. The circle is round. I'm not better than him. My life has no meaning anymore."

Andrew frowned. "Oh come on. Are you listening to yourself? It's gibberish, Patrick. You're nothing like him. I understand you don't want the money. It was his, and it's bringing you down. So do something about it! Get yourself out of this loop. Sell his stuff, get rid of his life. What do you want? Because, right now, you're just making yourself miserable."

I took a sip of my coffee. "You're right. I'm not handling this the right way. I have to get out of this vicious cycle."

"Look," Andrew said, "you've got the money. You own the firm. So you can do whatever you want. No one is going to make the decision for you. But I promise. If you keep doing what you're doing, the board is going to fire you."

"And that wouldn't be wise." I took a bite of my omelet, munching on it slowly while thinking through my options. "Okay. I can sell all his houses. I can sell the firm. I can donate his stuff. You know what?" I smiled, my voice upbeat. "I can do whatever I want with his money!"

"Okay, now we're getting somewhere!" Andrew said. "I remember you wanted to start an organization that helped companies in need. What happened to that idea?"

I snorted. "Nothing. It got locked away. I was bound to my father and his firm, so everything else, every idea, went up in smoke. Maybe I can figure something out, but I have to think it through."

"If you need help with a business plan or want to brainstorm ideas, just call, okay? We live in the same country, you know." Andrew patted me on the shoulder. "I can always hop on a plane."

"Thanks. You're a good friend," I said genuinely.

"But first, get your ass back in the gym and shave your face. This isn't you." Andrew paused. "One other thing. Get Sophie out of your head. She's not coming back."

I sat back. "It's hard, Andrew. I still don't know the real reason she broke up with me or fled the country... I don't know. I can't get any closure. She had — still has — a special place in my heart. I need someone to support me, to love me, now more than ever. And I'm trying. But all these other women, they aren't Sophie. Maybe it'll fade, but I'm not ready to forget her." I chuckled self-consciously. "Maybe I'm an old romantic sucker, but this will do for now."

"As long as it remains a memory, I'm fine with it. You were a total wreck when she left. I don't want you to go through that again," Andrew said. "Look, I've got a proposition for you." He leaned forward and tapped the table. "Maybe it's better if you stay at my place. Get yourself together. I can keep an eye on you, we can hang out... Caroline won't mind."

"You sure? I don't want to be a burden. With her being pregnant..."

"Yeah, I'm sure. She's not due for another few months. Come on," Andrew said, finishing his coffee. "We'll pick up some of your stuff on the way. Caroline can make dinner and we can watch a game. Sunday we can talk about your plans. And on Monday you'll be back in New York."

"Thanks, mate." I took one last bite of my omelet.

"I know you'd do the same for me," Andrew said, sliding out of the booth.

My mother was waiting for us. The second we walked into the house, she called, "Already back? Andrew, you want to stay for lunch?"

"No thanks. We grabbed a bite," he said. "I'm taking Patrick with me for a few days."

My mother shot us a worried look.

"Mum, it's going to be okay," I assured her.

She sighed and looked away. I couldn't expect her to keep an eye on me forever. And I knew she knew, in her heart, a couple days away would do me good.

"I know," she said. "You want some dinner for tonight?"

"No, that's not necessary," Andrew said. "Caroline will make dinner when she gets home from work."

"You sure?" My mother looked doubtful. "She's pregnant. And now the poor woman has to prepare dinner for you guys? Come on."

I nodded. "You know, Andrew, Mum is right. Let's make a steak or something on the grill?"

"Yeah, maybe." Andrew shrugged. "She's been walking around rather moodily these last few months, so it won't make much difference if I cook or not. I can't do anything right. But yeah, she was like this before she got pregnant, so..." He ran a hand through his hair.

"Just help her out a bit, okay? It's not easy being pregnant," my mother said, quickly kissing Andrew on the cheek. She gazed at him warmly, like he was her son. Then she hugged me firmly, like it would be the last time she'd ever see me. But that was my mother, overreacting and caring too much.

I grabbed my toothbrush, pajamas, fresh clothes, and my suit for Monday morning, and threw them into my weekend bag. As soon as we started driving down the street, I felt a bit better. Andrew wanted the best for me. I'd get through this. I didn't know how or how long it would take, but I would get there. Eventually.

After a few hours, Andrew pulled into the parking lot of a grocery store a few blocks from where he and Caroline lived.

"So, what are we making for Caroline? Is there a list of food she isn't allowed to eat?" I asked, jumping out of the truck.

"Well, lots of stuff she can't eat. And she only wants the finest, healthiest food these days. That's why I told your mom she would cook. I can't do it right. It's like I can't do anything right. She's gotten rather controlling," Andrew said.

"We can try, right? Besides, I'm crashing your house. It's the least we can do."

"Okay, we'll cook. What do you have in mind?" Andrew asked as the store's automatic doors opened for us.

I scratched behind my ear. "I don't know." I took a quick glance around the store. "My mother! She's a wonderful cook. She'll know a simple dish a pregnant woman would like!" I pulled my phone out of my pocket and dialed my mother. It rang a few times before she picked up.

"Yes, dear?" she answered. "Forget something?"

"Hi, Mum. No, but we're at the grocery store. We're going to make dinner tonight, like you suggested. But we don't know what to make. Can you help us out?" I'd already sunken pretty low by crashing at my mum's house, bothering her and George, so I was hoping she wouldn't mind one more favor. And I admit, I still needed her sometimes.

"Oh, dear, I'm so happy to hear that! She'll feel so blessed!"

"Okay, don't overdo it, Mum. You're on speaker," I warned her.

"Right. Here's a simple dish you can make: cod with cherry tomatoes cooked in tinfoil in the oven. Andrew, Caroline likes cod, right?"

Andrew leaned toward the phone and said, "Yes, she does."

"Good." My mother sounded pleased. "Listen carefully, you two. You'll need a piece of cod for three. Not too thick, otherwise it'll take forever to bake. Ask someone at the store for the right piece. Get some cherry tomatoes, some small potatoes, and a branch of rosemary too."

We nodded and listened carefully while my mother walked us through the recipe. It was so simple, even a five-year-old could make it. In twenty minutes, we were out of the store. Andrew had even rented a few movies for Caroline.

When we told Caroline we would be cooking and she didn't have to do anything, only watch a movie and relax, she was delighted.

Take note, I thought. *Don't overcomplicate things. And call Mum for advice if you get stuck.*

We kept my mother on speed dial, but without too much trouble we made, in our opinion, a great meal. The potatoes could have used a few more minutes — they needed a bit more bite — but Caroline loved it. She didn't even mind I was staying for the weekend and prepared the guest room for me. I was lucky to have such good friends.

The weekend passed in no time. Andrew and I watched a football game, drank some beer, went out for a walk, and talked a lot about the future. A few good ideas come out of our talks. I'd have to make some huge, life-altering decisions, but I had a goal. Deep down, I knew what I wanted to do. It was coming from the heart. Now I had to take matters into my own hands and make some changes.

BULLETPROOF

I was in a rush. Glenn, one of the firm's new interns, had called me at six thirty in the morning to request an urgent meeting. He didn't say what he wanted to talk about and I was too tired to ask, but I agreed to meet him at seven thirty.

In hindsight, that was a mistake. I miscalculated the time, but before I could think it through and maybe move the meeting to later in the day, I'd already ended the call.

The night before I'd gone out with Alex, and as usual, it was rather intense. I could have used some extra sleep, but Glenn's call had woken me before my alarm, so I didn't feel fully rested. All I could remember from his call was him mentioning a huge problem with one of the accounts he was handling. Since I was his coach and mentor, he could ask me anything at any time of the day. I was responsible for him and for making sure his work was done properly.

I wanted to get it over as soon as possible. I got dressed in no time, called downstairs, and asked my doorman, Dillan, to hail me a cab. I took my breakfast to go. I could eat on the way to the office to save a couple of minutes.

The cab was waiting in front of the building. Two minutes before seven. *Okay, next stop, coffee.*

The cab stopped in front of Alex's Starbucks. I hurried to the counter, kissed Alex good morning, grabbed my latte, and apologized for skipping out on our usual chat. I was in desperate need of some morning gossip. But to be frank, it had been months since I'd chit-chatted with Alex. He'd been complaining a lot. And last night he brought it up again. I was becoming a workaholic, I needed to find work-life balance again. What he meant was I should go out a lot more and date or I'd end up all alone. I'd be an old spinster. And for once he was right.

After my breakup with Patrick, I'd thrown myself into my job. I traveled a lot and worked extremely long days. I usually wasn't home before ten. It was all I ever did. I breathed work.

But I tried to follow Alex's advice. I certainly didn't want to end up alone. Drinks and dinner with clients — that was going out, right?

But Alex was fed up with the whole situation, with me. He took me out at every possible opportunity. The first few times were awful. He dragged me to every new bar and club in town. I tried to fit in, have some fun, loosen up. But I just wanted to go home, to be in a quiet place.

I tried to tell him that this wasn't how I wanted to get to know someone. This wasn't me, going to clubs, talking to complete strangers, ending up in bed with someone and having a one-night stand. No thank you. Eventually Alex gave up. But Alex wouldn't be Alex if he didn't find another way to get me out of the house.

Lately, everyone was throwing dinner parties. It was the latest trend. So of course Alex threw some dinner parties. We dined with some of his friends, and then he'd invite a guy he'd met at the coffee shop or in a club. His friends quickly figured out what he was up to and started searching for new single men to hook me up with.

Alex was desperately hoping I'd meet someone. I hated the way they pushed me, but I did my best not to show it. Alex cared about me, like a big brother would. He was a marvelously good friend, and he just wanted me to be happy. So I went on a couple dates with some of the dinner party guys. We'd usually go on a few dates, get lunch or dinner, sometimes there was casual sex, but I didn't fall in love or even have a strong connection with any of them. I always compared them to Patrick. They couldn't compare. They were mediocre.

I came to a point where I didn't want to put more energy into looking for a boyfriend or a lifetime partner, as Alex called it. So, most of the time, you'd find me at work. If I didn't accomplish anything in my love life, at least I could achieve something at work. Once in a while, I went for a massage so I had some physical contact. I chuckled thinking about my last deep tissue massage. *Gosh, I loved those.* Maybe I could learn how to give them some day. That would be nice.

I was waiting for Glenn to arrive. It was already nine o'clock. I'd hurried into the office, only to wait. I'd been foolish to set an early meeting. But I hated tardiness, and an hour and a half late was inexcusable. I hoped Glenn had a good explanation for being late. The more I thought about it, the more I realized Glenn wasn't just perpetually late. He was disorganized and never prepared. Two things I hated.

A quick knock announced his arrival. I couldn't wait to hear his excuse. "Yes, come in," I said shortly.

Glenn was red-faced and sweaty. *Ugh, gross.* His curly black hair hung in his face, and his shirt wasn't tucked in. Dark circles of sweat were clearly visible under his arms. What the hell had he been doing?

"Sorry, Miss Smith. The subway was behind, and when I arrived, I realized I'd left my papers at my apartment, so I had to go to get them." He didn't look up. Clearly, he was embarrassed by his tardiness.

I sniffed. "Don't let it happen again, Glenn. Next time, call to say you'll be late."

"Yes, Miss Smith."

"So, tell me, what was so urgent that you had to call me at six thirty this morning?" I asked, obviously irritated.

"Well, Devon & Sons called last night. They weren't happy with the contract. Mr. Fernando, the CEO, shouted at me," he said.

"Hmm. What wasn't he happy with?"

"I don't know," Glenn admitted. "He didn't say."

"You asked him, right?" I cracked my neck and took a deep breath. *Soph, calm down.*

"Well, no, not exactly."

I had to control myself or else I'd lose it. How could he not ask? That was basic stuff. *Relax, Soph, stay calm,* I told myself. *You can handle this. You just have to guide him in the right direction.*

I spun my chair away from Glenn and took another deep breath. My lack of sleep was speaking, not me. I had to walk Glenn through this, step by step. I inhaled and exhaled a few times, finding myself a bit more relaxed. "Okay, Glenn, what contract did he mention? We've sent over several contracts."

"I think the last version."

"You think?" I asked. "Or you know?"

Glenn still wasn't looking at me. He was studying his shoes, like a child being punished. "I don't know."

Throwing my head back, I turned in my chair and managed a smile. "Glenn, here's what you're going to do. Call Mr. Fernando, apologize for calling, and ask him for more details."

Glenn nodded.

"Shouldn't you write this down?" I asked. *Aargh.* I felt like I was going to explode before he got this right. I handed him a piece of paper and a pen.

"Yes, call Mr. Fernando," he repeated, scribbling my instructions furiously.

"Ask him to highlight the part of the contract he wants revised. Ask him which sentences need to be rephrased. Knowing him, it will be something like that. Got it?"

Glenn nodded uncertainly.

"I want this info and the contract on my desk by six o'clock this evening, okay? Devon & Sons is one of our oldest clients, so I'll check the paperwork before you send it back to them."

"Thank you, Miss Smith." Glenn hurried out of my office.

I have to admit, he was always polite. I leaned back in my chair and looked out the window. He had to learn — quick. We could lose clients over his bungling. If his performance didn't improve, I'd have to fire him. I was lost in my thoughts, and my phone's ring startled me out of them.

"Sophie Smith," I said.

"Sophie, can you come to my office please?"

My boss, Kate. I recognized her voice. "Okay, I'll be there in five," I said.

Kate was an amazing woman and a real inspiration to me. She had worked hard to get where she was, but sometimes she could be a real bitch. I guess once you reach her level you have to put your emotions aside so people follow your orders. You couldn't expect everyone to be your friend.

Kate had a huge corner office, with a superb view of the city. I knocked once and she told me to come in.

"Good morning, Kate," I said cheerfully.

"Good morning, Sophie. How was your weekend?"

"Fine, thank you!" I sat down in the brown Chesterfield in front of her desk. She had cut her long brown hair into a bob over the weekend and was wearing a short-sleeved black top. It made her look older than she actually was, but it suited her.

"Okay. I'll get to the point, Sophie. As you know, Brian left the firm last week." She paused.

Hallelujah! Brian managed the other team of interns. I hated him. He thought he always knew better, but he didn't do anything and never knew what was going on. He was great at putting on a show, impressing you with deals he'd closed. But if there was actual work to do, he was the first to bail. No one really liked him. Especially me, because I did all the work and he got all the credit.

"Sophie, I'm dividing his client portfolio. I know it's short notice, but I want you to take over a few of his clients and delegate some of your cases to your team. I won't take no for an answer. I won't look for a new manager for now, so his team will fall under your supervision," she said.

"Uh, okay..." I was surprised. He wouldn't be replaced? What Kate wanted, Kate got. And this was a great opportunity. Besides, I was always doing his work, covering for him, even though I never got recognition for it.

Kate's voice shook me out of my daydream. "As you know we have a major deal with Copco coming up. I remember you helped Brian with it?"

I'd done everything for that client. "Yes, I know the deal," I said. "I'll have to review the details again, but it won't be a problem, Kate."

Typical. Brian presented my work as his own. Silly me. Why hadn't I told Kate I did all the work? Maybe it was just my nature. I wasn't direct. But this was an opportunity to take the lead and show Kate I was worthy.

"Well, get ready, Sophie, because you're going to Milan to close the deal on Monday. There's a huge meeting next week. I've already planned everything; you'll just present our deal and handle the closing. Sophie," Kate said, "you only have one chance to close this deal. There's a lot at stake. Millions if we land this. I trust you."

Okay, that's some pressure! Why do bosses do this? I wondered. Two minutes ago I got the news my team had doubled, I got a new client portfolio, and now I had to close this deal or... Or what? Would she fire me?

"Kate, you won't regret this!" I said. Inside, I was screaming, *How will I manage all this?* I knew I'd find a way. I always did.

"Okay, it's settled. You can go. Irene will send you your itinerary. Work hard, and I expect a call from you next week telling me we got a signature." She waved me out of her office.

"Kate, thanks again. I…"

But she wasn't listening. Discussion over. I went straight to Irene's glass cubicle opposite Kate's office. Irene was a real doll. Of all my colleagues, she was the one I had the most fun with at work. She'd became a good friend over the years. She knew how I worked, what I needed when I was out of the country, and she didn't need a ton of instructions or explanations. She got things done.

"Hi, Irene," I said, leaning into her cubicle.

She smiled broadly. "Hi, Sophie. So she told you?"

"Yep. I don't know what to think," I confessed. "Should I be excited for the opportunity or afraid? Afraid they'll show me the door if it doesn't go well? Like Brian?"

"Oh, I don't think so," Irene said. "Kate wouldn't give you this opportunity if she didn't believe in you. Brian was a real ass. You're so much better than him!" She smiled again. "Enjoy what's coming. You'll do great."

"Thanks. I don't know what I'll do without you," I said. "To be honest, though, I've missed traveling. And I really need it right now."

She frowned. "Still having a hard time?"

"Yeah. I just haven't found the right guy. Oh well." I shrugged.

"Come on, girl, head up. Enjoy the trip, the wine, maybe some Italian guys." She laughed. "Hey, if you close this deal, maybe a big promotion will come your way. You're working so hard."

"Yeah, you're probably right."

"I am," she said with a wink. "Let's talk business. Everything is booked." She handed me a stack of papers. "This is your hotel confirmation. These are your plane tickets. I've already arranged a cab. It will pick you up Monday at eight and take you to the airport. The hotel will send a car to pick you up when you land in Milan. You'll stay at the Rosa Grand in Milan. It's a beauty! It's in the middle of the historic district. The Duomo and the Via Napoleone are in walking distance. I think you'll love it."

"Wow, sounds great." I shuffled through the papers quickly.

"You'll have to thank Kate. She wanted something special, something with class. To suit the opportunity. Oh," she said, handing me an envelope. "This is your schedule. One last detail. Miss Parizzi will be your point of contact. If you need anything or want to know something, call her. She sounds charming."

"Thanks," I said. "So there's nothing left for me to do?"

"Nope, this is what I do!" She laughed. "Oh yes, there's one thing you can do. It's crucial. Enjoy yourself. I know it's work, but I hope you can relax and take a little time for yourself."

"Thanks again for everything. I mean it."

"Not a problem. Call me when you're back. We'll get lunch."

"Sounds great." I turned to go. "Oh, Irene," I said. "I forgot to ask Kate. Who will coach Glenn and the other trainees while I'm in Italy?"

"Don't worry. Kate will manage them."

Kate would manage my team? Strange, I thought to myself. But I'd take it if it meant I wasn't behind on other work due to this trip. She really was making an effort here.

I took the papers back to my desk. There was still a lot to do before my departure on Monday.

It was eight p.m. by the time I was leaving the office. Harold from finance was walking by while I waited for the elevator.

"Hello, Sophie, you're working late today." He stopped and stood beside me.

"Harold." I nodded at him. "I had to finish some work because I'm leaving for Italy on Monday."

"Italy? Great. Holiday or work?" he asked.

"Oh no. Work. Always work. You know me," I said with a little smile.

"Well, have a good trip."

The elevator arrived, so I thanked him and wished him a good evening. As the doors were closing, he added: "Good to know you're on Tinder, by the way."

What? Before I could say anything, the doors closed. What was he talking about? Tinder? Did I have a subscription to a business magazine called Tinder? I couldn't remember. I was too tired. Whatever.

On Saturday morning, I slept in. It was already late, so I decided to get brunch at my favorite Starbucks. I changed into fitted soft-pink jeans, a blue shirt, my favorite comfy blue Abercrombie sweater, and grey sneakers and walked to City Hall Park.

Alex opened the door when he saw me. "Hi, beautiful. What a surprise." He kissed me on the cheek. "Lazy Saturday?" he asked, gesturing at my comfy outfit.

"Yes, as a matter of fact. It's a total relax weekend. I'm leaving for Italy on Monday. Work-related, of course."

"Of course." He rolled his eyes.

"Milan this time. I've got a deal to close."

"Posh, Milano. Well, let's have a leisurely brunch then. The usual I presume?" he asked, already walking away to prepare my latte.

"Yep."

While Alex made brunch, I took our coffees to the back and settled near the fireplace.

"So, what's this deal about?" Alex asked, handing me a plate. "It's short notice, or have you known about this trip for a while?"

I took the plate from him, "Nope. Only a few days ago. Kate asked me to take over one of Brian's accounts. They fired him last week."

"Brian, Brian..." he said as he sat down. "Oh yeah, that douche who was always taking credit for your hard work. He had it coming. Good for you, dear."

"Thanks, it's a great opportunity. It'll be a huge account if they sign. And it's been a while since I've traveled. So what's up with you?" I asked, changing the subject. I knew Alex was tired of hearing about my job.

"Nothing special. Mark and I are thinking of taking a trip to Turkey or Greece. We haven't decided yet."

I touched his arm in support. "So things are going great between you two? You deserve it, Alex."

"Yeah, we've decided to date each other exclusively. Quite a step for me." He smiled broadly.

"I know! You've resisted settling down. And look at you now. Oh, Alex! I'm so happy for you two."

"Thanks."

"Let me know when you book your trip. I can take care of your place, your plants, your mail while you're gone."

"Great! I'll do that," he said.

"Right, before I forget. There's something I need to ask you." I took a sip of my latte. "A colleague said it was good to know I was on Tinder. You know it?"

Alex's eyes twinkled and he suppressed a smile. "Sophie, it's a dating site. Well, sort of a dating site. It's hugely popular. You've never heard of it?"

"Oh yeah," I said, wrinkling my nose. "But I'm not on it. Maybe he confused me with someone with the same name?"

"I don't think so. I..." He hesitated a bit. "I made a profile for you. I linked it to your Facebook account."

I glared at him. "You did what? Alex, I'm not looking and certainly not through a dating site. I'm not that desperate, you know."

"Oh, come on, Sophie. I'm doing you a favor. Sorry to offend you," he said, not sounding sorry at all, "but you're going to end up as an old spinster. There's more to life than work. What do you have to lose? Give me your phone." He held his hand out.

I quickly dug my phone out of my bag and gave it to him.

"Here, this is the app," he said, tapping on the screen. "And this is your login and password. Last time I checked, you had quite a few interested guys."

I snatched the phone away from him. I was surprised. I hadn't noticed the app. "You're kidding, Alex. Come on! What kind of men are interested in dating me?" I glanced doubtfully at the screen and closed the app. "Alex, we're talking about ME. I don't have anything special to talk about. I'm a workaholic, remember?"

"Well, I know you don't think so, Sophie, but you're quite the catch. Here." He grabbed the phone again and opened the app. "Scroll through the profiles. Take a look for yourself. If you hate it, I'll take your profile down. If not, embrace it with open arms. Have a drink, go out to dinner, or use it like everyone else — for a booty call. Your choice." He leaned closer. "Here, if you're not interested in someone, you swipe left. You swipe right and you can start a conversation if the other person is interested too." He noticed my empty cup. "More coffee? Something stronger maybe? Be back in a few."

I stared blankly at my phone. I can't do anything wrong, right? I started scrolling. Left, left, oh no, left, left...

"And?"

I looked up as Alex handed me a fresh cup of coffee. He'd added a hint of amaretto. I could smell it. *Hmmm, delicious.* "It's crazy how many men are available?"

"Yep, and this is only New York. Come on, move over," he said, sitting down and nudging me. "We can go through them together. It's fun."

"Okay."

I was skeptical, but for the next half hour, we reviewed profiles together. It was fun. It gave me a little boost. But a conversation was maybe a step too far. For now. Maybe later.

"Jane should see this too. She's been a bit off these last few days," Alex said.

My phone vibrated and I picked up immediately. "Well, speak of the devil. Alex and I were just talking about you."

Jane burst into tears. "Gerald filed for divorce. He met someone else, and I don't know what to do."

"Oh, Jane, I'm so sorry. You want us to come over?" I knew they'd been growing apart. That Gerald was absent. And a week ago she found out he'd betrayed her. So that fling was probably the reason he wanted to leave her. Poor Jane.

"No, it's fine. I don't want to bother." She sniffled.

Alex grabbed the phone and confidently said, "Stay right where you are. We'll be there in half an hour. Don't do anything reckless. Love you." He hung up.

"Alex, come on. She doesn't want to see us."

He looked at me with his boyish grin "Oh, come on, she can handle it. Let's make a stop at the liquor store on the way. Go hail a cab. I'll ask Jennifer to close up. It's been quiet today."

I quickly grabbed my things and hustled outside to wait for a cab.

Alex joined me a few minutes later, struggling with his brown leather jacket. A cab stopped, and I jumped from the curb, opening the door for Alex so he could slide in.

"East Village, please," I said. "Corner of Avenue A and Tenth Avenue."

"Oh," Alex chimed in, "if you see a liquor store on the way, please make a stop."

Thirty-five minutes later, armed with a bottle of tequila, we arrived at Jane's. We couldn't leave her in that state, so we packed her suitcase and took a cab back to my new apartment. She could stay at my place while she sorted things out.

MILANO BLEND

The intercom beeped, distracting me from my work. As soon as I heard the pilot say we'd be arriving shortly, I stopped listening. *Ouch, I'm a wreck,* I thought. I stretched my legs. A twelve-hour flight. I'd done longer flights, but I'd only managed to sleep for a few hours on this one. My mind had just kept going. I was under so much pressure with this deal. Did I forget something? Did I have all the papers? What if they didn't sign? Would it be the end of me at Leaf?

With those thoughts swirling, I'd worked most of the flight, rereading the proposal a hundred times and rewriting my presentation. I wanted it to be perfect. Feeling exhausted, I was happy tomorrow morning's meeting was already planned. Tonight I would grab a quick bite to eat and go to bed early.

After landing and a thirty-minute cab ride, I arrived at the Rosa Grand. I had looked it up yesterday and learned it was revered as an excellent example of Italian design. With one glance, I could tell it was the finest hotel I'd ever stayed in. Kate had spared no expense.

I checked in and went directly to my room, where I freshened up and changed into something more casual before heading to dinner. I always ate at local restaurants when I traveled. I only ate breakfast at the hotel — and sometimes a quick business dinner.

On my way out, I stopped by the front desk. "Excuse me, sir. Can you tell me where I might find a good local restaurant that serves genuine Italian food?"

"Scuzi, signora. Non parlo che un po' d'inglese. Speak a little English but not so good," he said apologetically.

Think, Soph, think. My Italian wasn't good at all. Damn. "Restaurante? Manggia? Pizza, pasta... " I tried every Italian word I knew, hoping he would understand what I was asking.

"Pedro, puoi venire qui un momento? La signora cerca qualcosa per mangiare." He waved at a slender man with black hair slicked back with a lot of gel. He had a golden tan, which I guessed wasn't from the sun but from lying in the tanning bed too long.

"Good evening, miss, I'm Pedro. Sorry for my colleague. His English isn't good."

"Trying, trying, signora," the receptionist said.

I had to grin. He was trying.

Pedro smiled kindly and pulled a city map from under the counter. "So for dinner, you can go to the market square. There are a lot of fine restaurants. The locals love this one," he said, highlighting it. "All Forno. It's located in the via Borgospesso. The Nona cooks in the back. It's a tiny kitchen, but it's tasteful and authentic. I think this is what you're looking for."

"Yes. Thank you so much for your help."

"Non c'è di che. You are welcome," Pedro replied.

I made a note to myself: Learn Italian. *My god, I sucked.*

Rise and shine, Sophie! Today is your day, I told myself in the mirror. *You have to persuade everyone you're the best in the business. I'm the best. I'll do great. They will sign. I hope they'll sign.*

Just as I was putting the finishing touches on my makeup the phone rang.

"Good morning, Miss Smith. This is the front desk. Your car is waiting. When you are ready."

"Thank you," I said and hung up.

I packed my briefcase, triple checking I had the presentation and all the paperwork I needed. Last night I'd double checked everything. This deal had to work out. It would work out. I was sure of it.

A metallic grey Bentley was parked in front of the hotel. The chauffeur — wearing shiny black shoes and grey gloves and a hat to match his grey suit — waited next to the car. I'd never experienced this level of posh and elegance. There was definitely a lot of money involved in this deal.

I sank into the back seat and enjoyed the fancy car ride. I went through my words, my strategy, even gave myself a little pep talk. Couldn't hurt, right?

The car pulled up to a sizeable Victorian house. It sat on a casual, cobblestoned street, which was flanked by marvelous old sycamores on every side. The chauffeur opened the door for me, and I saw a woman waiting at the front door. Her long black hair was pulled back in a tight knot, and she was dressed in a black pencil skirt and a white top. Her shoes — I guessed Prada — were fabulous.

"Hello, Miss Smith. I'm Miss Parizzi." She shook my hand firmly. "I'll take you to the conference room. Please follow me."

The house was magnificent. High ceilings were divided by wooden beams and large windows looked out on a garden. The rooms were decorated minimally but were welcoming. Leaf's New York office wasn't cozy at all. We had dim lights, the typical upholstered office chairs, horrible paintings that you couldn't really call art. Nothing special in comparison to this superb space.

We entered a small hallway where a tall guy was waiting for us. I guessed he was forty years old, maybe a few years older.

"Good morning, Miss Smith," he said, extending his hand. "I'm Thomas Maxionis, the head of engineering at Copco. We talked earlier on the phone."

"Yes, lovely to meet you, sir." I shook his hand.

"You'll have one hour for the presentation. There will be some time for questions afterward. But we have a tight schedule. This won't be a problem for you?" he asked.

Well, he didn't ask, merely demanded. I had no choice but to answer: "Yes, not a problem."

Eighteen people were sitting around the conference room's large, egg-shaped marble table. They were all staring at me as I walked in. This was my moment. I straightened my back and put on my brightest smile.

This would be one of the biggest deals I'd ever closed. I might even get my own team of lawyers if I landed this. Copco was building several new offices in different countries. As the environmental lawyer, my job would be to closely monitor construction, ensuring no local laws were broken, and keep an eye on building regulations. If any issues arose, Leaf would represent Copco in court. It was a complex matter because every country, every town had different building restrictions. I would work at a high level with several engineers. But I'd be in touch with the CEO too.

Mr. Maxionis introduced me to everyone and then it was all me. I did the best I could. The presentation went well, and they looked interested. They only asked a few questions before dismissing me. Mr. Maxionis informed me that Mr. Knowles, the majority shareholder, and the engineering department would make the final decision. Mr. Maxionis would call me later with the decision.

Strangely, Mr. Knowles hadn't attended the meeting. How could a shareholder make a decision if he hadn't even heard about the project?

I was walking to the parking lot when I heard someone screaming my name.

"Miss Smith, Miss Smith!"

Miss Parizzi was running toward me. "Miss, you'll have a meeting with Mr. Knowles this evening. A car will pick you up at the hotel at six."

What a twist. This could go way faster than I'd imagined. I couldn't believe it.

And I couldn't help but wonder about Mr. Knowles. Copco's leading man. What would he look like? Handsome like Richard Gere? *Silly, Soph, this guy runs a huge engineering company.* Young? I didn't think so. Handsome? Please, men don't have to be handsome to run a company. He would probably be fat, bald, and sweaty. I shivered at the thought.

WAKE UP AND SMELL THE COFFEE

Last check. Makeup — on. Eyes — done. Hair — straight. Pencil skirt, white blouse, black blazer, killer heels for killer legs. I was READY.

The front desk had called a few minutes ago to let me know my ride had arrived. I took the elevator down and walked out of the hotel resolutely.

This time, a black Mercedes coupe was waiting. A true Italian, the chauffeur was dressed to perfection. Well-tailored black suit and — again — the gloves. Black ones. The gloves must have been a signature Copco chauffeur accessory. Or was it something distinctly Italian? No hat this time, but a stylish pair of Armani sunglasses completed the chauffeur's outfit.

As soon as the car pulled away from the curb, my mind wandered off. Strangely, I thought of Patrick. I missed him. He would've loved Italy. I could easily imagine us here. Drinking a glass of wine in the market square, riding a Vespa through the streets. I should call him when I get back to New York. I knew I didn't end our relationship the best way. I owed him that much. Or maybe I wouldn't call him.

Focus, Soph, I told myself. *In a few minutes, you have an important meeting with Mr. Knowles. It's your last chance to pull out all the stops.*

We'd already been driving for an hour when I saw signs for Como. *It couldn't be much further, right?*

I wasn't wrong. Fifteen minutes later, we drove into the hills surrounding Lake Como. With the lake on the right, we drove through a small but elegant town called Cernobbio. I didn't want to pry, so I didn't ask the driver if we were close. I peered out the window and soaked up the nonpareil blue of the lake and the bright-green meadows surrounding it.

The chauffeur glanced at me in the rearview mirror. "Miss Smith, we've arrived."

The car wound up a large seemingly endless driveway surrounded by majestic cypresses. A luxurious mansion flanked by an Italian-style park stood at the end of the driveway. The whole mansion was lit up — you could see every corner of the house. *Wow, this guy is loaded,* I thought.

Hundreds of cars were parked in front of the house and along the driveway. I didn't understand what was happening. Butlers? Valet service? What was going on?

The chauffeur opened the door for me, and I noticed a butler in the doorway. "Welcome to Villa San Michele, Miss Smith," he said. "If you would be so kind as to follow me."

Damn, I'm nervous. But why? I thought. I fidgeted. I was happy to have my briefcase in one hand, keeping me in balance. Something was going on, but I still had no idea.

The butler knocked on a door at the end of the hall. "Miss Smith is here, sir." He gestured for me to enter a bright, creamy waiting room.

Oh god, it's just like I thought. It was Mr. Knowles — bald, overweight... I took a deep breath as I tentatively stepped into the room.

"Miss Smith. Welcome. I'm Mr. Knowles's right hand, Tim Carter. I hope the ride wasn't too long?" He extended his hand expectantly.

Pull yourself together, Sophie! This isn't Mr. Knowles, I told myself.

"Hello, Mr. Carter," I said with a genuine smile as I shook his hand. "It was quite comfortable, thank you."

Okay, where is Mr. Knowles? Why isn't he here? I was thrown off, but I could hide my confusion. I was a professional.

"Let's talk business, shall we?" Mr. Carter led me into a small adjacent office. The walls were covered in wooden panels, painted the same creamy shade as the waiting room. When I took a closer look, I realized we were in a library. Books covered every available space, hundreds of them. There was a fireplace surrounded by some brown leather Chesterfields and a matching two-seater couch in the center of the room. The library was stunning.

Instead of sitting at the oak desk, we settled in front of the fireplace. I summarized the morning's presentation and answered Mr. Carter's questions. It was a strange situation. Why was everyone telling me Mr. Knowles would make the decision? Every time I had a meeting, he wasn't there. He was probably too busy to waste his time in such small meetings. Pity, I would have loved to meet him.

"Miss Smith, I've heard and seen enough," Mr. Carter interjected. But before he said another word, a sudden knock on the door interrupted us.

"Yes. Come in," he called.

"Sorry to interrupt you, sir," the butler said, sticking his head in the room. "But Mr. Knowles would like to speak with you right now."

"I'll be there in a minute." He stood up. "Miss Smith, if you would excuse me."

I nodded. *What an odd way to do business,* I thought. The first meeting seemed just as useless as this one. Why did he say "I've heard and seen enough"? Maybe he wasn't pleased with our deal? I hoped I'd have an answer by the end of the evening. Kate was counting on me, and I wasn't going back home without a signed deal.

"Miss Smith. My apologies for the interruption," Mr. Carter said, returning to the library. "Where was I? Right." He settled back into his chair by the fireplace. "I'm interested in your proposal but not at this price. We want fifteen percent off and then we have a deal."

"Hmm, fifteen percent." I swallowed. "I can offer a five percent discount if we start our collaboration before the end of the month."

"Ten percent," he countered.

"Eight percent!" I could see him hesitate. *Soph, come on! You can drop to fifteen and it's still a good price for this deal. If you agree to ten percent, you're coming out on top.* "Okay, ten percent," I said, "but that's our final offer. If you sign now and we set everything up for the end of the month."

"Then I think we have a deal, Miss Smith." He smiled.

Oh my, did he say we had a deal? Sophie, let him sign first and then you can jump for joy, I reminded myself.

We worked through the paperwork, page by page. He scanned the contract carefully and signed every page with a firm and jaunty signature. He handed the contract back to me, and I placed the original in my briefcase.

I shook his hand again. I was thrilled. Kate would be ecstatic.

"Miss Smith, I want to invite you for a drink. We both deserve it," he said.

"Thank you," I said. "That's an offer I can't refuse." I smiled. I could use a drink after the day I'd had.

Walking into the garden, I was taken by the panoramic view of the lake. It was breathtaking. Everywhere I looked, I saw people in suits and cocktail dresses, sipping champagne and wine. But what were they all doing there?

Mr. Carter noticed my confusion. "It's the annual Copco drink. It's a tradition to encourage and reward the staff," he said conspiratorially.

"Oh, I see..." I said, still a little lost.

"At Copco, we are of the opinion that support, positive feedback, and recognition create a sense of happiness for staff. And that equates to better efforts on their part — and superb year-end results for us."

I whirled at the sound of a microphone squealing and someone clearing their throat to draw the crowd's attention. Everyone turned toward the sound. We were at the back of the garden, so I couldn't see who had the microphone and was about to speak.

Mr. Carter leaned in and whispered, "It's Mr. Knowles. I'll be right back." He sprinted across the grass.

And there I stood, alone, at a business party where I didn't know a soul. Mr. Knowles began his speech. "Good evening, everyone. As you know, we're here to celebrate you, the best of our global team. On behalf of Copco, I want to thank you all for a wonderful year."

His voice sounded familiar to me. Again I wondered who he was. I'd closed a huge deal today, so it would mean a lot to see Mr. Knowles, even if he was short, fat, and bald. At least so I could tell Kate I'd spoken to him in person. I listened carefully, trying to connect the voice with a face. But I couldn't match it with anyone I knew.

"We're happy to announce this year's objectives have been achieved," he continued. "Higher than expected. Due, of course, to your efforts and hard work every day. So I'm pleased to say you'll all be getting large bonuses!" He chuckled as the crowd screamed and burst into applause.

As the cheers faded out, he said, "Every year, our tradition is to enjoy a drink together. But this year we wanted to do something extra special. This evening we've prepared a wonderful dinner. So please enjoy a good glass of wine, some delicious Italian delicacies, and, of course, music. Relax and have a good time with your colleagues! And one last surprise," he added. "When you leave this evening, you'll receive a gift bag as a little extra." He raised his glass. "Cheers to you and your hard work. Enjoy, everyone, and thank you!"

Everyone clapped and cheered enthusiastically, then slowly resumed their conversations.

Wow, why doesn't Leaf have events like this? I thought. Maybe I could bring it up to Kate. But tomorrow I'd be leaving Milan, so I decided I'd better enjoy the moment.

I saw Mr. Carter weaving through the crowd. "Sorry to have left you here," he said, stopping next to me. "But these events require quite a bit of organization."

"Of course. It's a fantastic event," I said. I was so close to meeting Mr. Knowles, I had to ask. "Is there any possibility I could meet Mr. Knowles?"

He frowned. "Well, that might be difficult. He's headed to the airport as we speak. But he wanted you to have this." He handed me a small white envelope. "Go on, open it. It won't bite." He grinned like a little boy. "Read it. I'll get you something to drink." And off he went again, disappearing into the crowd.

It felt so weird. A surprise? What was going on here? In all the years I'd worked for Leaf, no other negotiation compared to this. Not even close. I opened the envelope to reveal a card the size of a credit card. A short note was written on it in curly, elegant handwriting.

Dear Miss Smith,

Today we're headed toward a new future in our cooperation. We haven't had time to get acquainted, so I want to invite you on a trip. Mr. Carter will provide you with all the details. It would mean a lot to us if you could spend more of your valuable time with Copco.
With kind regards,

Knowles P.

I was astounded. This was a personal invite from Mr. Knowles himself. I didn't know how to respond. Was this because we'd closed the deal and this was their way of saying thanks? Or did they want more from the deal?

I had mixed feelings. I'd never been in a situation like this in my career. But I chose to look at it in a positive way. This could grow my network — and give me a few days off. Kate wouldn't mind, and I could use my corporate Visa for the extra expenses.

What the hell, I thought, *I'm going for it.*

Mr. Carter reappeared, holding two champagne flutes. "So, Miss Smith. Does this offer entice you?"

"Yes," I said, accepting the glass. "I just have to confirm I can delay my flight to another date."

"Of course." He nodded. "But let me share the details of the trip with you." He gestured toward a patio surrounded by white and pink magnolias and lavender bushes. It was decorated with large white benches, stacked with fluffy soft-pink and egg-colored linen pillows. Mr. Knowles had exquisite taste — or his wife did. If he was married, of course.

We made ourselves comfortable on the benches, and I took a sip of my champagne. "If I may ask, what's the reason for this trip?"

"Well, Mr. Knowles likes to know the people he works with. When he bought the firm a few years ago, he started organizing a little get-together for employees from all Copco's offices around the world. It's a great opportunity to get everyone together in one location. A bit like today but on a higher level," he said.

He continued to tell me about the retreat. They would discuss the company's annual report, objectives and goals for the next year, and upcoming projects. There would be workshops and plenty of opportunities to relax — a holiday mixing business and pleasure, Mr. Carter said.

Mr. Knowles saw the retreat as an opportunity to speak with people when they were at ease — not under stress. Mr. Carter described the activities, dinners, and cocktail parties for the upcoming five days.

"Our staff is thrilled to go on this trip," he said.

"Why's that?" I asked.

"Well, Copco was nearly bankrupt when Mr. Knowles bought the company. Hundreds, maybe thousands, of people would have lost their job if he hadn't stepped in," Mr. Carter said. "He's only been the owner for two years now, but he's put an enormous effort and lots of money into the company. And now we're listed on the stock market again. What he's doing at his age, it's unthinkable."

I was fascinated. And curious. "How old is he, if I may ask?"

"He's only thirty. At first, no one gave him any credit. But now, well, you'll see for yourself." He smiled and sipped from his flute.

"So what's expected of me?"

"We'll introduce you tomorrow afternoon when the projects are being discussed. The people you meet will be your contacts."

I nodded, trying to process all this information.

"So you'll arrive at noon tomorrow," he continued. "At two o'clock you'll give your presentation. The same one you did earlier today. Then you'll be free to take part in the festivities scheduled for the next five days. You'll also have the opportunity to get acquainted with Mr. Knowles. We'll cover everything, of course. Oh," he added, "about your plane tickets. They've already been changed."

My mouth fell open. "So Mr. Knowles knew I'd commit to this?"

"Yes, he did." He had the same look on his face, the same boyish grin as when he'd handed me the invitation.

I was getting more and more interested in Mr. Knowles. I got the feeling he knew me well, but I knew nothing about him.

He was a mystery to me. I knew that he was thirty, that he'd achieved a lot in his life, had a lot of money. But that was it. "What else do I need to know?" I fought to keep the eagerness out of my voice.

"A chauffeur will pick you up at seven fifteen tomorrow morning. The plane leaves at eight o'clock."

"Isn't that a little late?" I asked. "Check-in, security...?"

"Oh no." Mr. Carter smirked. "You'll be taking Mr. Knowles's private jet."

"Right." I could only nod. I was overwhelmed. I was living a fairytale. Chauffeurs with gloves, luxurious hotels, huge mansions, private jets — I had to be dreaming. *Someone pinch me.*

"Miss Parizzi — you met her earlier — is Mr. Knowles's secretary here in Italy. She prepared a suitcase for you. If you would like anything added, you can call her anytime. Everything, including the itinerary and the luggage, is at your hotel."

I nodded again. A thought occurred to me. "Can I ask what the destination is?"

"Of course. It's Capri, a small island in the Mediterranean Sea," he said. "If you don't have any other questions, the car will take you back to your hotel."

He walked me to the car, where I thanked him again before climbing in. Knowing we'd be driving for an hour, I called Kate.

"Hello, Kate Ford," she answered shortly.

"Kate, hello, it's Sophie. I'm not interrupting?"

"Sophie, not at all. You're still in Italy? What time is it?"

"Almost ten o'clock. I'm heading back to the hotel," I said.

"Tell me. Any good news?"

I smiled. "Yes, they signed. And at the price we discussed."

"Marvelous, Sophie, great work. I knew you were the right person for the job. You're flying back tomorrow?"

"Well, that's the reason for my call," I said slowly. "They invited me to a meeting in Capri. It's a five-day retreat. It's a meet and greet with everyone I'll be working with — and a one-on-one with Mr. Knowles. I won't be back before Monday. And before you say anything," I said in a rush, "it's at their expense."

"Go. This is our biggest deal at the moment. Lots of potential for the firm. Do what you have to do. And when you're back, I want to discuss your future with the company. Well done, Sophie," she said again.

This deal was my ticket up the ladder. All my hard work, the traveling, would finally pay off. I just had to get through the next five days. Maybe I could take a few days off then. It had been years since I'd taken a real vacation.

By the time I got back to the hotel, I was exhausted. It had been a long — but successful — day.

I was so eager to meet Mr. Knowles. I was looking forward to finally connecting a face with the name. I googled him but didn't find any pictures. A lot of articles promising how great he was. But not a single picture. So weird.

I was too tired to think it through. I needed to sleep. But before I got into bed, my curiosity got the best of me. I peeked into the suitcase Miss Parizzi had prepared. She definitely understood my taste. Satisfied and exhausted, I fell into a deep sleep.

BREW-TIFUL

Everything kicked into high gear. Miss Parizzi had planned the entire trip, down to the smallest detail. I flew alone, in a small but luxurious jet. It was extravagant, over the top — a plane only for me — but that didn't stop me from enjoying the experience. Miss Parizzi was waiting on the tarmac of the Naples airport. From there, we took the company helicopter to the island of Capri.

"I'm sorry to spring this on you, but we have a tight schedule," she said, shouting over the helicopter's whirling rotors. "Once we arrive at the hotel, you will have thirty minutes to freshen up. I'll be waiting for you in the lobby and then take you to the meeting room where you will give your presentation. Mr. Knowles won't be attending; he has other engagements. But you'll certainly have the opportunity to meet him." She handed me the trip's program, typed in detail, a map, and a brochure highlighting the hotel accommodations.

I checked into my room and took a quick glance around. I didn't have much time to soak in all the details, but the room was gorgeous, decorated and painted in white and blue nautical shades. I even had a private balcony overlooking the Bay of Naples. The white marbled bathroom was the same size as the bedroom. Oh, how I loved my job!

I was on a schedule and knew I'd have more time to enjoy it later. I changed into a white pencil skirt and a grey V-neck top with short, ruched sleeves. I topped it off with a white blazer. I piled my hair into a bun and slipped my feet into a pair of white stilettos. They perfectly complemented the outfit. No one would notice my nervousness.

I was more at ease when I got through my presentation's introduction. Everyone was so kind, and I was surprised how well informed they were about my role. Made it even easier for me. Turns out, it was more of a social gathering than a high-level meeting, but I was looking forward to our collaboration.

Mr. Knowles didn't attend, like Miss Parizzi had said, but I didn't mind. I was getting used to the idea that he didn't attend meetings. He still knew what happened and made the right decisions.

I scanned the plan Miss Parizzi had handed me earlier. The evening would begin with a cocktail hour, followed by a four-course dinner on the outdoor terrace. I still had time, so I went to my room to change into a more suitable outfit. I found a note from Miss Parizzi.

Dear Miss Smith,
I took the liberty of unpacking your suitcase for you.
You will find everything in the closet.
For this evening I prepared some suitable outfits.
Enjoy.
Best regards,

Sylvia Parizzi

She really had thought of everything. I could see why Mr. Knowles had hired her. Still, it felt weird having someone else choose your clothes.

Three outfits were hanging in the closet adjacent to the bathroom. There was a little black dress with short sleeves, a V-neck in the front, an open back. It was made out of lace and draped around the body. Quite sexy. It would show off my curves but was still elegant. The second outfit was a long pair of white linen trousers and a Prada brown sleeveless mousseline blouse that tied around the waist. The last choice was a knee-length coral linen skirt with an eggshell top that closed at the neck with a pearl button and a blazer in the same warm coral shade. A bit too classic for my taste. I went for the little black dress and added a rose gold shawl to top it off. It was the first evening and if I happened to meet Mr. Knowles, I wanted to make a smashing impression.

I took a seat at the outdoor bar overlooking the bay. The hotel was built on top of a cliff one thousand feet above the sea. Guests enjoyed views of the entire Bay of Naples from their rooms and the ground floor of this marvelous luxury hotel. I'd already enjoyed the panoramic view of the gulf from my private balcony. It was so peaceful.

At the end of the terrace, there was a stone wall completely overgrown with various climbing plants, including a stunning bougainvillea. I loved bougainvillea. They're magnificent plants, so intense and colorful. And then their fragrance. They have such a light scent, it follows you everywhere. Tonight a strong floral breeze, mixed with the saltiness of the sea, infused the whole area. *I could definitely stay here forever,* I thought dreamily.

The sun was slowly setting, leaving a deep orangey glaze in the sky. You could tell it was going to be a wonderful evening. My mind wandered off. It would have been nice to share this moment with someone. I'd worked like crazy over the last few years. I hadn't taken a vacation, let alone a weekend off. I worked seven days a week. Patrick and I used to talk about going on vacation for a few weeks. But I never found the time. I always had something going on. I wasn't going abroad as often, but that didn't mean I wasn't working hard. I made up for it by working late into the evening or on the weekend. We'd gone away for the weekend but never longer than three days in a row.

I missed him. It was still hard to get Patrick out of my head, even after all those years. But after the way I broke up with him, I didn't think he would take me back. Moving on was my only option.

A nearby voice shook me out of my thoughts.

"May I join you while overlooking all this beauty?"

I turned around to make sure the voice was talking to me and saw a remarkable man standing in front of me. His thick, dark brown, curly hair was combed back into perfection. Soft hazelnut eyes and a killer smile brightened up his whole face. Confused by his directness, I gaped at him.

"Something tells me my company wouldn't be appreciated?" he asked.

"No, no, it's okay. I, I... Why would you...?" I stuttered, stumbling over my words.

"Well, you're sitting alone, and the view is breathtaking." He gestured to the bay. "It's better with two, right?"

"Hmmm, I guess so." *Oh my god, I'm terrible. This guy — this gorgeous guy — wants to admire the sunset with me and I have nothing to say. Sophie, come on, get a grip.* I smiled. "I'm sorry, sir, but..."

"Sir?!" He placed his hand over his heart. "Aww, sounds old. Really?"

My eyes widened. "Oh no. No, I didn't mean it that way. I was raised to be polite."

He smiled and I wanted to crawl under my chair and hide. This guy was really enjoying my awkward attempt at conversation.

"I'm Andrew, by the way. So you can drop the 'sir.'"

"Sophie, lovely to meet you. Please have a seat." I gestured at the chair next to me.

"Sophie, hmmm..." He looked at me thoughtfully. "Help me out. I'm guessing you're either here for pleasure or you're with the Copco party?"

"Which one do you think?" I took a sip of my spritzer.

"I guess pleasure. I would've seen you or met you if you were with Copco. So you must be here with someone. On a holiday? Honeymoon? Am I right?"

"Wouldn't I fit in at Copco?" It was my turn to make him feel uncomfortable. He definitely worked for Copco. It was so obvious.

"Um... Now I'm questioning myself. Well, if I were here with you, I wouldn't leave you alone at the bar. Far too risky." He rolled his eyes.

I giggled and stared down into my glass. I felt a blush warming my cheeks. His lines were cheesy, but I was still flattered that a guy like him wanted to talk to me. But I had to come up with a witty answer. What did I have to lose?

"I can tell you work for Copco," I said. "The fact that you can't place me means you're probably pretty high up, otherwise you wouldn't dare make assumptions like that. And you seem like a calculated man, so I'm guessing you do something with numbers, figures... Got it." I snapped my fingers. "You work in the finance department, right?"

He looked at me, puzzled. "How did you know?"

Bingo. If there was one thing I was good at, it was reading people. "I figured it out. You mentioned Copco, so I made the connection. And your first line was kind of cheesy, so I guessed you weren't in sales. And the rest?" I laughed. "Wild guess."

"Absolutely right, wow." He swallowed hard. "I'm Copco's chief finance officer. You got me there." He raked his hand through his thick brown hair.

"Thanks." I smiled happily. I was hoping he'd stay and chat a bit more. My inner goddess was already cheering loudly.

"By the way, I still don't know what you're doing here?" he asked.

"Oh, I'm being rude. I work for Leaf. I'm a lawyer. But you were right. I don't work for Copco, but I'll be working with

Copco as the in-house environmental lawyer. So you were partially correct."

"Right. I wasn't at the presentation this afternoon, but I'm familiar with your firm. You'll be supporting and advising us on our newest project. So, in a way, you are part of the group." He smiled broadly.

"In a way, yes."

"Damn, I'll have to watch my words around you."

"You will. Everything you say may be used against you in a court of law," I said, smiling cunningly.

He grinned back at me.

"Andrew, Andrew, can you come over here?"

Andrew turned in the direction of the call, before spinning to face me again. "I'm sorry, Sophie, but could you excuse me for a moment? Work." He rolled his eyes.

"Sure." I tried to hide my disappointment.

"I'm pleased to have made your acquaintance," he said quickly before heading toward the group of men standing at the edge of the terrace, near the entrance to the lobby.

"You too," I finally managed to say, but he was already out of hearing distance.

So there I sat, alone again at the bar. I didn't know a soul, only Andrew and the few people I'd met at the meeting, but I hadn't spotted them yet. Dinner wouldn't be served until eight o'clock, so I still had an hour. *Aargh, what can I do to pass time?* I asked myself. Checking my email was too much and going back to the room wasn't an option either. I'd be alone there too.

Andrew had made an impression on me. I couldn't help myself and snuck a peek in his direction. He was resting one hand on the back of a wooden armchair and gesticulating heavily with the other. It looked highly entertaining. He was speaking to an older man, who was sitting with his back to me. Andrew put both hands on the chair and leaned forward. Suddenly, he straightened his back, raised his head, and looked straight at me. There was a little sparkle in his eyes and a genuine, gracious smile on his lips. He nodded in response to the older man but kept smiling at me.

I swiftly averted my eyes and turned my head the other way, blushing again. We'd only talked for a few minutes, but it felt like it had been much longer. Curious if he was still watching me, I quickly glanced in his direction. He was looking, without a doubt. Our eyes met for a few minutes. A smile spread across my lips, and he beamed back at me. He turned his attention back to the group. But the attraction was growing, and I looked again. Andrew did the same. We played this hide-and-seek eye game several times. And every time our eyes met, we both smiled. It was like we were completely alone, like there was nobody else around. Everything else faded into the background.

A waiter drew me back to reality. "Miss, would you like another drink?"

I tore myself away from Andrew and ordered something stronger, a cocktail with a hint of holiday, a mojito. Why not enjoy this trip a little bit?

When I spun around to find Andrew again, I saw he'd disappeared. The group of men he'd been talking to were in the same spot but he was gone. I scanned the main entrance to the lobby and the whole terrace, but he was nowhere to be found. Disappointed, I turned toward the bar. But then I detected some movement to my left, not far from the stone wall dividing the terrace and the ocean. I noticed someone at the end of the bar. Andrew. He was sitting a few seats away from me, holding a mojito. How did he pass by without me noticing? How long had he been sitting there? Hopefully, I didn't seem desperate, looking around crazily. He watched me, perfectly at ease, a playful smile wrapping around his lips. Standing up, he walked, composed and confident, toward me.

"Hi," he said. "I see we're drinking the same thing. You know, great minds think alike."

I snorted. His one-liners were kind of old-fashioned. Did men really say that these days? I had two options. I could leave him at the bar in search of some more intelligent conversation, although I was hoping his silly one-liners didn't define him. Or I could stay and talk to him and find out if there was more to him than his stunning features and hazelnut eyes. The eye game earlier made the decision for me. I chose to stay and chat with him. Give the guy a chance, you know.

"Are you looking for someone?" He chuckled.

"Oh, you noticed? Well, there was a remarkable man standing over there." I pointed to where he had stood a few minutes ago.

"And did you find him?"

"Sadly no. I think he left. But you could keep me company."

He laughed out loud and so did I because this was the strangest conversation I'd ever had with a man.

"So tell me," I said, "what were they all laughing about? Don't tell me numbers are that exciting."

"Why? What did I do?"

"Well, you were waving your arms around. It was quite entertaining to look at."

"I was telling a joke. Yep, us financial guys aren't all dull, you know. Everyone's got this impression of us. Don't know where they get it from."

This was so not me, hitting on him in an odd way. My one-liners were also cheesy. But it didn't matter. I had nothing to lose. I was in control, and I loved it.

"So those guys weren't very interesting?" I asked.

"How do you mean?"

"Well, you seemed a bit distracted. I don't know, but something had your attention." I looked at him through my eyelashes. I didn't hold back and flirted openly. It was the mojito kicking in. It felt fantastic, being a bit reckless and self-assured. It wasn't me, totally out of my comfort zone, but it was refreshing. And it worked on him.

"I confess. Something did have my attention."

Why isn't he denying it? I thought. *He's just going along with it.* Andrew leaned forward so he could whisper in my ear. "You know what it was?"

His warm breath tickled my ear. I could smell his woody cologne. It was divine, being so close to someone after all this time.

He straightened, sitting back and creating space between us. "But I don't have to tell you what you already know."

I didn't know how to respond, but my body showed what I was thinking. My inner goddess was lying on the ground. She had fainted.

A microphone squealed to life as a waiter announced dinner was served. I got up to head to the other side of the lobby, but Andrew didn't move. He offered me his arm.

"Sophie, it would be an honor if you could join me for dinner. There's no assigned seating tonight."

"The pleasure is all mine," I said, slowly placing my hand on his arm and letting him lead me to the table.

"Guys, I know, I know," he said. "It's unconventional to have a lady at our nerdy table, but she's worth it." He smiled at me. "This is Sophie. We recently closed a deal with her law firm, so she'll be working with us. We'll be seeing a lot of her. Sophie," he gestured around the table, "the finance dudes."

Everyone laughed and greeted me with a chorus of "Hi, Sophie." Someone even said, "I hope you'll give us some credit."

I looked at Andrew, confused.

"Yep, that's our sense of humor." We both chuckled and sat down, Andrew on my left and a guy named Ferdinand from the Australian office on my right.

The evening was over before I knew it. Most of our table companions had already gone to bed. I hadn't had that much fun in a long time. It was like an evening out with friends — lots of laughter, terrible jokes, and a huge amount of wine.

I was lightheaded. Was it the temperature? The wine? Or the tension between me and Andrew? I didn't want to stay up too late because tomorrow was a busy day. So, I stood up, thanked the rest of the table for the wonderful evening, and smiled eagerly at Andrew. He stayed seated and picked up his conversation as soon as I left. Pity.

I was halfway across the lobby when Andrew called, "Sophie, wait up."

I stopped and turned around, happy he had come after me. "Yes?" I said, keeping my voice light.

"I'm going for a walk on the beach. Would you like to join me?"

"Uh, sure." I followed him through the lobby and down the stairs leading to the beach, where I leaned into him to remove my shoes before stepping onto the sand. It's really annoying to find sand in your shoes the next day. Plus, walking in the sand with high heels isn't elegant.

There was a light breeze, which felt refreshing after dinner. It was what I needed to clear my head. We walked side by side. I walked in the water, letting the sand dip between my toes and enjoying the freshness of the water splashing on my legs. Andrew stayed on the sand, trying to keep his pants from getting soaked by the waves. We didn't need to say much, I just enjoyed being in his company.

On our way back, Andrew spotted some beach chairs. The sky was entirely lit by stars. There was a half-moon, and we had a marvelous view of the coastline. Small fishing boats bobbed peacefully. It was so quiet you could only hear the roar of the surf, followed by the waves crashing on the sand, before slowly reclaiming their place in the ocean. It was a beautiful relaxing sound.

We settled into a white beach chair, and I felt Andrew's hand sliding into mine, his fingers stroking mine softly. I turned my head and looked straight into his eyes. He rubbed his thumb gently over the palm of my hand, leaning forward. I did the same. I licked my lips, closed my eyes, and waited for him to kiss me.

"Mr. Andrew, Mr. Andrew. Are you Mr. Andrew?"

Our eyes flew open and our entwined hands unknotted. The front desk clerk was standing in front of us with a phone in his hand.

"Are you Mr. Andrew?" he asked again, his English broken.

"Yes," Andrew said, a note of irritation in his voice. He was not happy with the interruption. "Who is it?" He took the phone and covered the speaker. "Excuse me, but who is it?" he repeated.

"It's your wife, sir." The clerk scurried back toward the lobby.

I stared at Andrew, confused about what I'd just heard. He was married? We almost kissed and he has a wife waiting at home for him? What was I even thinking? I felt like I'd stepped into a cold shower. I wanted to run, but something stopped me.

Andrew had already taken the call. I could only hear his side of the conversation, but I could follow it easily.

"Hi, Caroline. Yes, I know I promised to call in the evening. Can I call you back? No, oh, she's there. Okay, put her on. Hi, sweetheart, yes, this is daddy. How was school?"

Did he just say "daddy"? He's married and has a kid? *Sophie, get the hell out of here.* I stood up, gathered my shoes, and quickly went back to my room, leaving Andrew on the beach with the phone still in hand.

Sophie, you're here for business and nothing else, I reminded my-self. *How could you have been so stupid?*

I got undressed, put on the white cotton bathrobe hanging in the bathroom, poured myself a glass of whisky from the mini bar, and replayed the evening.

Hadn't I seen any signs? Any? I was sure he wasn't wearing a ring... Or was he?

Aaargh, forget him, Sophie. He wanted to cheat on his wife. I knew being the mistress would only end badly, that I'd always be second place. He would never leave his wife and kid for me. Oh, I was so glad I'd found out now, before anything else happened. To be honest, he played it good. He hadn't mentioned his family, not even to his colleagues. And he wasn't wearing a ring, the bastard! Why was I always falling for the wrong guys?

Sitting on the balcony, I was starting to calm down. The whisky probably sedated me a bit. I closed my eyes and listened to the waves crashing on the shore. *Was that someone knocking on the door? No, it couldn't be. Probably another room.*

Again, a knock on the door, this time a bit louder and harder. *Jesus, it is my door!*

I hopped out of my chair. Maybe it was a message from Mr. Knowles or Kate. Maybe she was calling from New York. What time was it over there? I unbolted the door and opened it halfway. Andrew was standing in the hallway, holding my shawl. Damn, I must have left it on the beach.

"You left so suddenly but forgot your scarf. So I thought I'd bring it back," he said, holding it out.

Stay polite, Soph, I told myself. "Thank you," I said. I held the doorknob with my left hand and grabbed the shawl out of his hands with my right.

"Sophie..." He hesitated.

I wanted to close the door on him. So I could shut him out. "Good night, Andrew." I moved to close the door slowly. But he held the door with one hand and pushed it back open. I stepped backward, not knowing what he was up to. He was quicker than me and stepped into the room. Before I knew it, he was clasping my head between both hands and pressing his lips firmly against mine. I swatted at his hands and turned my face away.

"Andrew, don't. You're married. You have a kid! I'm not that kind of woman," I said.

"But..." He took my hands in his. "Listen, Sophie. I'm divorced. For two years now. Yes, I have a daughter, she's four. I'm co-parenting. I can only see her every other weekend. Because of this trip I had to reschedule her stay. That's why my ex-wife called. I can assure you, my intentions are noble and sincere. I'm not that kind of man, you know."

I stood there with my mouth hanging open. Not knowing what to say. I was probably wrong and too quick to judge. "Sure?" I asked in confirmation, a little bit hesitant.

"Yes, I'm a free man," he exclaimed, loud and clear.

My chest relaxed as I took a deep breath. He wasn't married. Not anymore. I must have looked relieved because he stepped forward and pulled me toward him, placing one hand on my hip and pushing my hair back in place with the other.

"Sophie, I'm sorry I didn't tell you about my daughter or my ex this evening. It was a mistake. I had a wonderful evening, and I don't know. I didn't want to ruin the mood."

He was sincere. I could tell by the way he looked at me. *What the hell,* I thought, *we can talk about this for hours, but I don't want to. I have needs too!*

Reckless and totally out of my comfort zone, I threw myself at him, kissing him without hesitation. Andrew responded eagerly. At first it was chaotic. I turned my head right and he did the same, so our heads bumped against each other. I wasn't sure where to put my hands, so they were hanging purposelessly against my body. Should I hold his waist? Should I start to undress him? Could I go this fast? We'd only met that evening.

I wanted him badly. My body was aching for him in ways I hadn't felt in a long time. My heart was pounding, my breath quickening, my nipples hardening. I opened my eyes and took a step back, remembering the door was still open. I stared at it. Andrew followed my gaze and took a step toward the door. I followed him, feeling naughty, the alcohol taking over. I let my hand slip through his arm while I hung the "Do Not Disturb" sign on the door.

Andrew spun around and kicked the door closed with his heel. "What do you have in mind?"

"Me? Nothing." I grinned playfully. "You never know if someone will bother us while we're deep in a business conversation." I knew it was quick, but I needed it. My inner goddess was cheering for me. Deafeningly. She needed it too.

"Can we be deep in other things too?" He grabbed me by the waist to pull me closer.

"Hmmm." Resting my head against his chest, I could feel his heart pounding. He wanted this too. It was obvious. I unbuttoned his shirt slowly, button by button, taking my time, while he watched. He didn't hesitate, so I placed my hands on his bare chest and slid his shirt off his muscled shoulders. I looked into his deep brown eyes, waiting for his next move.

He kissed me on the neck, which made me throw my head back in pleasure. He slowly undid my bathrobe and returned his hands to my waist. They were warm and soft. Without hesitation he moved them slowly upward. A tingling went up my spine as his fingers arrived at their destination, caressing the edge of my breasts softly. His hands continued upward until he finally whipped the robe off my shoulders. I was standing in the middle of the room wearing only my lacy pink-and-black underwear. *Thank god I chose this today, and thank you, Miss Parizzi.*

He took me in from head to toe. The pleased look in his eyes made me feel more at ease. He didn't notice my imperfections, the dimples on my thighs or the obvious stretchmarks on my waist. He made me feel, in one glance, like I was a wonderful sexual being. His dark stare motivated me to explore him even further. Andrew laughed as he toed off his shoes.

Undoing his pants, I got a better view of his spectacular body. I let my fingers trace the lines of his stomach. He was in good shape, there wasn't an ounce of excess fat on him anywhere. He had washboard abs with that super sexy V of muscle. I stared at him unabashedly and kissed him again, not holding back this time.

With a strong grip he scooped me up, and while we kissed fiercely, he carried me to the bed. We lost our balance and toppled onto the bed, making us both laugh. He pushed himself up onto his elbows so he could float above me. Pinning me down with his torso and grinding his hips, I could feel his erection.

"You're so beautiful, Sophie." He kissed me everywhere, leaving traces of fire behind, spurring my desire for him even more.

It was unbelievable. We made love like ferocious beasts. My inner goddess needed fanning afterward. She'd fainted after one glimpse of his sculpted body.

When I woke up the next morning, Andrew was lying on his side, facing me, still sleeping peacefully. His perfect hair was now a chaotic mess, a few strands covering his face. I'd pulled at his hair last night, messing it up while he made me come. I'd held his head in place as I kissed him. I watched his body move rhythmically with every breath he took. Would it be too much if I woke him for some morning sex? I could maybe start with a small Swedish massage? A good way to put what I'd learned in that weekend course to use. Pleasure rippled through me at the thought of having him inside me or being on top of him. *Sophie, let the guy sleep,* I admonished myself. He probably had some meetings to get to and would need to be well rested. I watched him a couple minutes more, admiring him, devouring him slowly with my eyes.

What the heck, I wanted to wake him! I slid underneath the sheets and stretched my arm out to touch him. He reacted instantly. He didn't open his eyes, but a huge smile lit up his stubbled face. He pulled me closer into the hollow of his body, where it was comfortable and warm.

"Good morning," he murmured.

"Hi."

He kissed me on the neck and then on the lips. "It's too early. Let's stay in bed." He wrapped himself around me.

"Don't you have any meetings today?" I asked.

"Nope, no meetings. I only have one thing on my agenda today. Relaxing and enjoying your company."

"Oh well, we have plenty of time then." I turned on my side to spoon. He wrapped his arm over mine and held me tight, his head resting on my shoulder. We fell fast asleep. We needed a little rest after last night. We'd have plenty of time to play later.

By the time we got up, showered, and dressed, it was noon. We played a game of tennis after a late lunch and took a refreshing dip in the sea. Andrew dozed off in the sun while I read a book. It gave me a holiday feeling, even if there was a little work involved. In all the years I'd worked for Leaf, I'd never taken the time to sit down and enjoy the moment. And now that I was, I didn't want to move an inch. I was enjoying the sun, the beach, Andrew's company — even if it was just for the day or until the end of my stay in Capri. Nothing else mattered right now. I was relishing the moment, enjoying every second. Okay, it was a bit reckless of me. I hardly knew the man, but I didn't give a damn. It felt extraordinarily good. In a few days, I'd head back to New York. I could take a week off and book a real holiday. Kate couldn't say no; I'd just signed a huge deal.

Andrew got called to an unplanned meeting later in the afternoon. I sulked. He'd said he had nothing on his agenda, but he promised to make it up to me. He told me the meeting would be over before dinner, so we'd have time for a drink at the bar before eating together. We arranged to meet at the bar at seven o'clock.

HOT DAY, COLD BREW

Punctual as ever, I arrived at the bar early. I ordered a cosmopolitan and studied it intently. Andrew shouldn't be much longer. I glanced up to see a waiter approaching me.

"Miss Smith?"

"Yes," I said.

"I have a message for you." He handed me a piece of A4 paper folded in four.

"Thank you," I said, opening it to find a note from Andrew.

Hi,
The meeting is running a little late.
I'll be there in 20 minutes.
Andrew

Damn, another twenty minutes! What was I supposed to do? I'd already changed for the evening, so I didn't want to go back to my room. And drinking another cocktail wasn't a good idea either. I wanted to be sober when Andrew arrived; we could get drunk later. I wet my lips and smiled at the thought of what I would do to him tonight. My daydreaming got interrupted by a familiar voice.

"Hello, Sophie."

I turned around on the stool and stared into two beautiful, clear, familiar blue eyes. The eyes of the man I once loved. "Pa... Patrick... What are you doing here?"

Dazed, I got shot back into the past. *How could he be here? In Capri? Hundreds of miles from New York? I haven't seen him in ages and now he's standing right in front of me. Oh, and he's still looking so fine.* The thoughts swirled through my mind.

"Well, hi to you too," he said, with an edge to his voice. "I'm here for some business and saw you sitting at the bar, so I thought I'd say hello. It's been a while, right?' He paused.

I was still shocked and couldn't muster up a response.

"You look amazing. Really, Sophie." His words were genuine. His gaze sparked a scintillation inside me I hadn't felt in a long time. A feeling only he could give me. A feeling so familiar. I blushed. He still had that *je ne sais quoi* that got my heart beating faster.

"Thank you" was all I could mutter. I wanted to ask him so much. But was it the right moment? What were the odds? Both of us staying at the same hotel, in the same country? I hadn't foreseen this at all.

Out of the corner of my eye, I noticed a receptionist looking around. He was saying a name. As he came closer, I could hear him saying, "Mr. Knowles? Is there a Mr. Knowles here?"

Patrick turned toward him, while I craned my neck to scan the area. "The" Mr. Knowles, the man I'd never seen before. Was he here at the bar? Who was he? I quickly assessed the other man sitting at the bar.

"Yes?"

To my astonishment, Patrick was speaking. I stared at him, a questioning look in my eyes.

"Sir, there is a call for you in the lobby. It's urgent," the receptionist said.

"Thank you." Turning halfway, he smiled at me and held a finger up. He'd only be away for a moment.

I was shell-shocked. How could he be Mr. Knowles? Patrick is Mr. Knowles? It was him the whole time? I'd pictured someone else. Not him.

It was as if I'd been thrown into a cold bath. Was this why I was here? Did he know it was me? *Oh my god, there's more to this,* I thought. Was there a connection to the deal?

Everything got blurry. I felt nauseous. I couldn't stay there. I had to go somewhere else, somewhere far away from the bar. I stood up and stumbled away from the bar, completely baffled.

I took the path down to the beach and followed it straight to the frothing water. Deeply inhaling the late afternoon breeze, I tried to pull myself together.

A few gulls flew by and cried loudly. I could easily lose it, but more and more questions popped into my mind. I had to keep my head straight. Did Copco only sign because Patrick knew me? Or was it all a game? Did he want me back?

Oh my god, I hope not, I thought in a panic. That would be horrible. I could lose the deal, even my job! Everything I'd worked so hard for. I had to leave, I had to go back to New York. This couldn't be happening. I ran back to the main building, up the stairs to the lobby — and straight into Miss Parizzi.

"Good evening, Miss Smith." She smiled, then saw my face. "Everything okay? How is your stay?"

Thank god I ran into her. She was my ticket out of there.

"Miss Parizzi, could you get me on the first plane back to New York? Something urgent came up." My lower lip trembled. I bit it to keep it under control.

"I don't think there are any flights this evening, but give me a minute." She took her cell phone out of her jacket pocket.

I saw the look on her face. It wasn't possible to get me on a plane before tomorrow. I couldn't wait that long. What if Patrick found me and I had to confront him?

Miss Parizzi glanced at me again — probably seeing my desperation — and called one last number. As she spoke, a huge smile lit up her face. She said thank you and slid her phone back in her pocket. "You can take Mr. Knowles's jet. He won't need it for the next two days. The captain is willing to fly you back to New York tonight. He can leave in two hours. Is that quick enough for you?"

"Yes, that's great. Thank you so much." I had to stop myself from hugging her. "I'll go pack."

She nodded. "Can you be ready in half an hour? The helicopter can take you to the airport."

"Sure, that's more than enough time," I said, turning to leave in a rush.

I packed everything in a heartbeat. Maybe I was a coward, but I had to leave. I didn't give a shit if it was Patrick's plane taking me back to New York. I had to leave and I had to leave now!

I wrote a little note for Andrew. I'd ask Miss Parizzi to give it to him. I didn't tell him the real reason for my sudden departure. He wouldn't understand. I just gave him my number. Maybe we could see each other again.

I'M CAFFEINE POSITIVE

I had no time to lose, I had to see Kate. I grabbed my morning coffee to go — thankful Alex wasn't working — and practically ran to Kate's office where Irene was sitting in her usual spot.

"Hi, Sophie," she said. "How was Italy? I heard you took a few extra days in Capri. Good for you."

"Well, they signed, and Capri was a welcome distraction." I managed a smile. "Is Kate in?" I was in a rush, and I didn't want to waste time chit chatting with Irene. Not today.

"Uh yes, she's in," Irene said, a little miffed at my shortness. "Just a minute. I'll let her know you're here."

A few moments later, Kate opened her office door and welcomed me in enthusiastically. "Sophie! You're back. Come on in, please." She ushered me in, telling Irene to call upstairs.

It was the first time in my entire career I'd seen Kate look so happy. She'd opened the door for me! Normally I had to search for her.

She shook my hand. "Well, congratulations. You nailed it. Good work, Sophie."

"Thank you, Kate," I said, while thinking, *Come on, Sophie. She's in a good mood. Go for it. What do you have to lose?* I took a deep breath. "Kate, I want to discuss my future with the firm. I just brought in a huge account, and I want to know what Leaf can do for me."

She nodded. "Okay. You've got a point. Go on."

I sat down in one of the Chesterfields facing her desk. "I've brought in a lot of new business in the last few years —

especially this huge deal. I've always put the company first. I'm not afraid to work long hours. I'm an asset to the company."

"It's true, you're one of our best lawyers," she agreed.

"I want a position in higher management, I want to move forward," I said quickly. "I deserve it."

"You've grown a lot, Sophie. Your approach is bold and straightforward. I love those qualities in my staff. When you called to tell me Copco had signed, I knew I'd chosen the right person for the job. You're a superb lawyer and I'd hate to lose you to another firm. But I'm also aware — if I don't invest in your future — you'll leave. And I don't want to take that risk," she said.

I smiled and started to say thank you, but then she continued.

"When Copco asked for you, I hesitated. Brian was already on it. But I heard he was blowing it, and we couldn't afford to lose this account. So I did what they asked and put you in the lead. Best decision I ever made," she said. "So you're right on time." She glanced at her watch. "They're waiting for us upstairs."

I shifted in my chair and swallowed hard. Copco chose me to close this deal? Fuck. I pushed myself out of the Chesterfield and followed Kate to the elevator.

"You'll enjoy this, Sophie," she promised.

I was baffled. Why were we headed to the top floor? Why was my demand being granted so fast? Why was she willing to go the extra mile to keep me? I'd dreamed about an opportunity like this. And this deal had made the difference. I just hoped my relationship with Patrick wouldn't affect my future at the company. *Enough sidetracking, Sophie,* I admonished myself.

The elevator came to a halt, and I followed Kate into Mr. Baker's office determinedly.

"Ah, there she is." Mr. Baker, Leaf's most senior partner, rounded his desk and shook my hand firmly.

Mr. Derringer, another partner, lagged behind but quickly followed Mr. Baker in greeting us. He handed me and Kate flutes of champagne. "I guess a glass of champagne is in order. Please have a seat," he said, gesturing toward the office's lounge area.

Mr. Baker said, "Sophie, you did a terrific job in Italy. We've followed you and your work since you were an intern. And it's always been outstanding. You've built up an expertise and greatly contribute to the firm." He looked me squarely in the eyes. "Look, I'll cut to the case. Our division in Vancouver lost its partner to another firm, and they're looking for someone who can take control, someone trustworthy, someone who can give it a push. They need a new, fresh perspective, and we're confident — with your expertise and skills — you're the right person for this role."

"We want you to take the lead in Vancouver and lead us into the future," Mr. Derringer added. "Kate will give you all the paperwork later today. And we want a decision before the end of the week."

Wow, they were handing me a partnership. That was fantastic news! I tried to stay calm.

"Thank you for considering me," I said. "This means a lot. I'll let you know my decision by the end of the week."

We clinked glasses. I was euphoric. This was everything I'd ever wanted, everything I'd worked for.

As the elevator doors closed, Kate whirled around. "I'm cheering for you, Sophie, but it's up to you now. I know it's Canada. But I know you. You're not afraid of a challenge. So?" She looked at me expectantly.

"Kate, thank you for your faith in me. I really have to think this through. It's a big change," I said.

"I understand. But you should know the board is considering a few other people."

"Then I have no time to lose."

I followed her to her office in a daze. She handed me a file containing all the information I'd need to make a decision: a list of the lawyers in the Vancouver office, their numbers, their cases, and of course the contract outlining my new salary and bonuses as a partner.

"Keep me informed, okay?" Kate said. "Let me know if you have any questions."

I could only nod and hug the file to my chest. "Thank you, Kate," I said as I left her office and closed the door behind me. I nodded at Irene and walked as composed as possible down the hallway. As soon as I turned the corner and knew no one could see me, I beamed. I couldn't believe it. They'd offered me partner. Wow. Was this it? I'd worked so hard for it, I certainly deserved it.

Calm down, Sophie, I told myself. *Don't go rushing your decision.* Canada? Why not? I'd never stayed in one place long. And Canada was familiar to me. It was a bit far from New York, from my friends, from Carol... There was a lot to think about, that I knew. But sometimes you have to take a leap of faith.

TOO HOT TO HANDLE

"Good morning. Thank you for calling Leaf. This is Cynthia speaking. How can I help you?"

"Good morning, Cynthia. This is Mr. Knowles. Could I speak to Miss Smith, Sophie Smith, please."

"I'm sorry, sir. Miss Smith isn't available at the moment. Can I take a message?"

"Yes, can she call me back? No, wait. I'll call her back later. Can you tell me when she'll be back in?" God. Why was I so flustered?

"Sorry, sir," she said, "I can't give you that information."

"It's fine. Thank you." I hung up, frustrated.

Sophie, come on, why aren't you calling me back? I've left a dozen messages. What went wrong in Capri?

It wasn't supposed to go like this. Dammit, I'd handled it the wrong way. Again.

Okay, Patrick, calm down, I thought. *She's probably busy. Or she never wants to hear from you again.*

I was hoping for option one. I sat back in my chair, trying to calm down, but it wasn't working.

For almost three weeks, I'd been trying to reach Sophie. But I couldn't. She was nowhere to be found. It seemed like she'd vanished from the planet. Again. That would be the second time. The first time she'd severed every connection, changed her number, moved to another country. It took me a long time to find her and now I'd lost her again, thanks to my poor judgment.

I owed her an explanation. The link between Leaf and Copco. I had to tell her, in person, that she's a great lawyer, she's got good judgment, she's an expert in her field. That's why I wanted her on the deal and no one else. I had to reason with her, but it was extremely difficult if I couldn't find her.

I pushed a button on the intercom. "Miss Delaney?"

"Yes, sir?"

"Did you send those flowers to Miss Smith? With the card?"

"Yes, sir. I sent them last week, like you asked."

"Okay, thank you." I pushed away from my desk. *Sophie, where the hell did you disappear to?*

I pressed the intercom again.

"Yes, sir?"

"Can you look up an address for me?"

"Yes, sir. Which one?"

"Leaf's headquarters in New York. I think they moved recently," I said. "Oh, and let Carlo know I'll need him tomorrow at nine o'clock. Please give him the address." It's a pity Darren and his wife and kids moved to the country. If he was still my chauffeur, I'd strategize with him. Sadly, Carlo wasn't a big talker.

"Right away, sir. Anything else? Would you like me to make an appointment? Or confirm one?"

"No, that won't be necessary. That's all. Thank you."

Sophie, if I can't reach you by phone, I have no choice but to come to your office. I hope you'll forgive me.

In the meantime in Leaf's Vancouver's office...

Great, only a few more hours and I can start my weekend, I thought.

I was counting down the hours. I needed some me-time.

I'd finally gotten what I wanted. After all those years of hard work, I'd finally made it.

Everything had accelerated the moment I signed the contract making me partner. Only a few days after I got back from Capri, and after I filled out all the necessary paperwork, I moved to Canada. For good. I found a spacious apartment — big enough for a family of four — in the center of the city, only a few blocks from the office. It even had a rooftop terrace, partially overlooking the city, which was perfect for my new dog, Izzy.

I'd always wanted a dog to keep me company. When we were kids, Carol and I had a black lab named Satan. She was lazy and quite fat. Whenever we took her for a walk, she'd lumber along but always made sure we were following her. I'd dreamed of owning a dog again, but I'd never had the space until now.

As soon as I saw the terrace and confirmed the building allowed dogs, I didn't hesitate. I adopted a golden retriever with honey-blonde fur a week after moving to Vancouver. Izzy had been abandoned by her family, and I'd found her in a shelter. She was two years old and a real doll. She followed me everywhere. Slept at my feet, and when I worked from home, under my desk. I always took her for a stroll in the park after work. And I'd tried taking her along on a few jogs. It wasn't easy. I couldn't keep up with her.

I hired a dog walker to take her out during the day and to take her to the dog park. On the weekends, we'd been going away a lot.

This weekend I was taking Izzy to Tofino, to my holiday home, for a few days of rest and relaxation. It was actually our family's weekend house. When I was young, it had belonged to my parents. I'd spent endless summers playing with my sister on the beach, surfing, taking long walks. After my parents passed away, my sister inherited the house we grew up in, the one in Tillamook, and I got the house in Tofino. I hadn't been there much since I'd inherited it, but Tofino was only a few hours' drive from Vancouver. But now that my work hours had changed, I could get over there nearly every weekend. It was the only place in the whole world where I could be myself. And Izzy and I made it our home.

Izzy and I were planning to leave around noon, so we could be in Tofino around six — if traffic allowed.

Working in Vancouver was so different from New York. The atmosphere was more relaxed, the attorneys were great, and I was getting decent results. I liked my new job. Traveling wasn't part of the job anymore — except for the quarterly meetings in New York or Amsterdam. But those only lasted a day or two.

This weekend in Tofino would be a long and relaxing one. I'd planned to stay from Thursday until Tuesday. I had five days to relax and enjoy the beach. And Andrew would be joining me. So, I was really looking forward to it.

After I'd fled Capri, Andrew had called and asked me out. So we'd gone out a few times. When I moved to Canada, he hadn't made a big deal out of it. He was open to a long-distance relationship. And since his daughter only stayed with him every other week, he had plenty of time for me. Our relationship was too new, so I hadn't met her yet, but it wasn't an issue for me. Moving out of the States was complicated enough, so we were taking things slow.

On Friday morning, at seven o'clock right on the dot, I couldn't sleep anymore. Andrew was still sound asleep, exhausted from traveling. He had arrived at eleven o'clock last night and we'd gone right to bed after dinner.

I slipped into the bathroom and changed into my running gear: a pair of black nylon running shorts and a short-sleeved black cotton t-shirt. Izzy was already up and followed me through the terrace door onto the beach without hesitation.

It was a beautiful morning, and I knew the run would do me good. Izzy kept pace the entire time, and on our way back, we sat down in the sand to take a break and watch the sunrise. Izzy laid down at my feet, nuzzling my sneakers, while I enjoyed the fresh morning breeze, which was slowly being warmed by the first sunbeams peeping through the clouds. I sat there for half an hour, mindful, clearing my head. It was one of the moments I cherished the most, being one with nature. I could feel the wind whooshing through my hair, caressing me softly. I tasted the salt hanging in the cool morning air. I could hear nature coming alive, the roar of the surf, the birds flying by. It was sublime but also so contradictory to my busy life in the city. The beach gave me the energy boost I needed to handle whatever was next.

Meanwhile a few miles away...

I had to speak to Sophie. This time I would track her down, no matter what. I had hopped on the corporate jet and flown out of La Guardia Thursday morning, minutes after I'd called her office and discovered she no longer worked in New York. She was in Vancouver. I wasn't surprised. She had fled the country. Once again. And I was probably the reason for her decision. Once again.

On the flight, I'd called her office in Vancouver, hoping to pry some information out of them. Ten hours later, we landed in Tofino. A car was waiting for me at the airport, and I drove to a local B&B Miss Delaney had found for me. Luckily, they still had rooms; otherwise, I would have had to sleep in the car. After checking in, I went straight to bed. I wanted to see Sophie first thing in the morning.

"Okay, I'm on the right street. Now where is 1482?" I scanned the street with hawk eyes and decided to get out and ask for directions. I parked and noticed an old lady getting the mail out of her mailbox.

"Excuse me," I said, "I'm looking for the Smiths' house."

"Oh, it's that house right over there." She pointed toward a bright and cozy wooden paneled cabin down the street. It was surrounded by fir trees. There was an old surfboard with a colourful geometric pattern on the back standing on the back porch. "But," she continued, "it's only Miss Smith who lives there these days. Mr. and Mrs. Smith passed away a long time ago. Sad story. They were so kind."

I nodded. I knew the story.

"Well, if you're looking for Sophie, she'll probably be on the beach with Izzy. Take that passage over there, between the houses. It'll take you right to the beach."

It was up to me. Hopefully I'd find her quickly. I was impatient. We'd been apart for so long and seeing her in Capri had only made it harder. I knew we'd need to talk everything through eventually. Not chit-chat but a proper discussion about everything that had happened.

Izzy and I were heading back to the house when I saw Patrick coming down the small path linking the road and the beach. It was a path used mostly by surfers and seeing him there felt incongruent.

He noticed me, waved, and walked in my direction. Why was he here? I hadn't seen him since Capri, and our encounter hadn't exactly been pleasant. I'd wanted to call him. I'd picked up the phone so many times but put it back down quickly. I was secretly hoping he'd understand the whole story. That maybe I could explain everything to him one day.

I didn't have much time to think about why he was here because he was only a few steps away.

"Hi, Sophie." He spoke softly, smiling sincerely. And for a moment he looked like his old self. Composed, serene, at ease.

"Hello, Patrick."

He looked down at Izzy in surprise but bent down to scratch behind her ear. She laid down on her back instantly. *Traitor.*

He looked up. "You sure are hard to find," he said, straightening to his full height.

"Am I?" I didn't understand. He was looking for me?

"Well, I called a couple of times, but you never answered. I tried your office. But they told me you weren't in. So I went to your office and asked to speak to you in person. To my surprise, they told me you didn't work there anymore. I thought they'd fired you or you'd resigned. Nobody could tell me what had happened. Or," he said, "wanted to. But as I walked out, a woman came up to me. Irene. You know her?"

"Yes, I do." I nodded and laughed, remembering all the delightful moments Irene and I had shared.

"She told me you'd been promoted and that you moved to Vancouver." He smiled. "That's awesome, Sophie."

"Thanks, I guess." I was still trying to figure out why he was in Tofino. On the beach. At my house.

"No really. I mean it. So, what's the big promotion?" he asked.

"I made partner."

"Wow, that's huge, Soph!"

"Uh-huh." I shook my head. "Wait. How did you know I was here in Tofino? Only a few people know about my weekend house. Who told you?" I demanded.

"Irene gave me your secretary's number. I called her yesterday morning. She told me you weren't in till next Tuesday. So…" He glanced down at his feet. "I kind of lied to her. I wanted an excuse to talk to you."

"What?"

"Well, I told her I was a distant nephew and that I'd tried to call you about a death in the family, but I couldn't reach you. She was very understanding and gave me your address." He at least looked a little guilty. "I took a plane out of New York first thing. I'm staying at The Cove," he offered into the silence.

"I'll have to have a few words with her when I get back," I said and couldn't help but smile. "How did you know I was on the beach?"

"Simple." He grinned. "Your neighbor, a kind old lady, showed me which house was yours. But she said you'd probably be on the beach because it's a lovely morning. So I followed the path, and the rest is history."

I had some idea why he was here. I hoped I could talk things through, so he'd stay committed to the deal. But something told me there was more to this. He could have waited until I was in the office. Why all this effort? Why fly over?

"Patrick, I..." I paused, gathering my thoughts. "I don't understand why you're here. After what happened in Capri... I know we didn't leave things on good terms."

"I know. It wasn't fair of me."

"Not fair?" Oops. That came out a little harsher than I wanted. "Patrick, you bought a firm, garnered this huge reputation, got my colleague fired. So what? So you could get me on a deal? So my firm worked for yours? And all this time you didn't tell me it was you? You lied to me. You deceived me. So, really, why are you here? You signed a contract with Leaf."

"I know and I'm not backing out of the contract." He looked puzzled. "Why should I?"

I threw my hands up in exasperation. "Because you want revenge! Because I broke up with you without a reason!"

Patrick snorted. "Don't be silly, Sophie. I'd never do that. Yes, you broke my heart a few years ago when you disappeared without an explanation. But you still have a special place in my heart. That will never change. When I saw you in Capri, at the bar, it all came back to me. Even stronger."

My world turned upside down. I didn't know what to say. A small part of me still longed for him too. I ended our relationship because of Carol, not because I stopped loving him. But I couldn't tell him that. I was with Andrew.

"Sophie, I wanted to help you. You had so much potential. After we broke up, after you reappeared, I followed your work. And I don't know if you realize it, but you're a brilliant lawyer. I mean, you made partner! I could have used any other firm, but I wanted the best of the best and that meant you. I don't regret my decision. I'm happy about what our firms — what we've — achieved. If someone else took over the project, it wouldn't be the same. I wouldn't have signed the contract. I mean it."

"Thanks, Patrick, that means a lot to me," I said. "But you have to understand how betrayed I feel. You kept me in the dark!"

"Sophie, don't." He tried to take my hand in his, to comfort me, but I tore it from his grip. It felt awkward. Izzy growled, and Patrick took a step back.

"I didn't just come here to tell you how great your work is, that I'm sorry about how I handled everything. You already know that." Patrick looked straight into my eyes. "But I just need to know if you still feel the same way about me."

There it was. He'd put all his cards on the table. After everything, he still wanted to give us a chance. He wanted to know if I still loved him. He didn't want to talk about the deal. I had a lump in my throat the size of a baseball. He had to know. I had to tell him the whole story, the truth, and hope for a fresh start.

"Patrick, I've got to tell you something. But it's better if we go to the house. It's a bit further down the beach." I pointed and Izzy took off sprinting. We followed her in silence.

We were only a few steps from the house when Andrew appeared on the terrace wearing a dark-blue t-shirt and grey sweatpants, his hair still messy and a little bit wet from the shower. He looked surprised when he saw Patrick but then smiled brightly and greeted him, friendly, like they'd known each other for ages.

"Patrick, man, what a surprise."

Patrick looked at Andrew, confused, and then back to me. I looked at Andrew, confused too. I was surprised. They knew each other?

Andrew shook Patrick's hand, before grabbing me by the waist and kissing me on the lips. "Good morning. You were up early. You had a good run?"

I nodded, at a loss for words.

"What a woman. She goes out with Izzy and comes back with you. But not a problem. Come on, join us for breakfast." Andrew gestured for us to follow him inside.

Patrick didn't budge. "Oh no, it's okay. I don't want to interrupt. I probably should have called first."

"You aren't bothering us — right, honey?" Andrew insisted.

I hesitated. "Sure, stay." This was so awkward. Patrick and Andrew obviously knew each other well, like they were good friends. Why hadn't Patrick ever mentioned Andrew?

Patrick and Andrew sat down at the wooden table, chatting quietly. I went into the kitchen, happy to escape. I got out some glasses and a bottle of champagne Andrew had brought. I would've preferred something else, maybe some white wine, but this was the only bottle fresh enough to serve. I stacked a tray with plates, breakfast, champagne, and flutes and carried it outside, straight into an uncomfortable conversation.

"Andrew, I didn't know you and Sophie were dating," Patrick said.

"I told you. Don't you remember?"

"You told me you were dating a Sophie. But I didn't think it was this Sophie."

"Does it matter which Sophie it is?" Andrew asked. "I didn't know you two knew each other."

I placed the tray on the table and poured the champagne. Andrew and Patrick watched me with confused looks on their faces. I stared back at them. "What?"

No one said anything for what felt like an hour. Andrew broke the silence first. "Sophie and I met in Capri. We connected right away, and we've been dating since then. You met her there, right? Right, Sophie?"

I had to tell him. He had no idea. I cleared my throat. "Well, to be honest, Patrick and I have known each other for a long time. We dated a few years ago. But we broke up. Well, I ended the relationship..." Patrick nodded and told Andrew the rest of the story. "We saw each other in Capri for the first time in two years."

I saw the moment Andrew realized it. He grabbed the table, his knuckles turning white.

"So, Sophie is 'the' Sophie?"

"Yes, she is." Patrick's voice trembled. "Look, I should go. I shouldn't have come. I'm sorry I interrupted your weekend." He stood up.

Andrew looked at him in pity. "I didn't know, bro."

"Doesn't matter anymore, Andrew." He shook Andrew's hand. "Thanks for the drink." He didn't give me a kiss or shake my hand. He only looked at me, beaten, and walked back the way he had come, down the beach, toward his car.

Andrew didn't say anything. The silent treatment. He sat on the terrace, gazing at the horizon, lost in thoughts.

I didn't want to argue. The weather had changed — clouds were rolling in from the sea, turning the sky grey — so I carried everything back into the kitchen.

Andrew came inside but avoided eye contact. "Patrick told me a lot about you, Sophie. But I never knew he was talking about you." He took a swig from the champagne bottle. "Our friendship goes back a long way, you know."

"I can tell," I said quietly. "Andrew, there's nothing between me and Patrick. It's been more than two years since we split."

He nodded. "Still, it feels like I'm betraying him. Like I've taken you from him. Look, Sophie, I have to know." He finally looked at me, searching my eyes. "Do you still love him?"

Now I averted my eyes. "Andrew, don't ask me that. It's been years. And I'm with you now."

"You can tell me." He reached for my hand. "I can see you and Patrick have unfinished business. But I need to hear it from you."

I looked at our hands, intertwined. "Anything I felt for Patrick has faded, Andrew. Because I met you. I'm happy with you. Can't you see?"

"No, you aren't happy, Sophie. Don't fool yourself." He squeezed my hand. "Maybe it's better if we spend some time apart. I want to talk to Patrick. And I think you need to figure some things out."

"I don't have to figure anything out!" I screamed. Didn't he understand? I was with him, not Patrick.

He smiled sadly. "Yes, you do, Sophie. You're still in love with him." He shook his head and dropped my hand as I started to protest. "You don't have to admit it to me. But tell him. Admit it to yourself. Go after him. Tell him how you feel. You didn't see what I saw when you left. His world collapsed. You were his everything. And from what he's told me, you must have felt the same. He went out of his way to find you. But you vanished, and he never recovered."

"Andrew..." I pleaded. He was letting me go, and I didn't want that.

"I'll get over it. Just go. I'll be gone when you come back." He waved me off.

"But, Andrew," I said, reaching for him.

"Go now," he growled. Tears welled up in his eyes, his jaw clenched. He wasn't fine. But he turned his back to me and walked away.

I wanted to go after him, console him, talk this through... But I couldn't. He was right. A part of me still loved Patrick. I'd put my feelings aside for years, hid them well.

I walked onto the beach and started to run toward the port. Andrew had made his decision clear: He could never be with me knowing he'd betrayed his best friend. He was extremely loyal. Their friendship went way back, before we'd met, so I understood his feelings. I turned to look back at the house, hoping to catch one last glimpse of him. He was looking out the living room window. He gave a small nod, as if to say it was okay, and waved goodbye.

POUR OVER

It had started to rain. At first it was a light drizzle, but after a few minutes rain poured from the sky. Soaking wet, I arrived at the B&B where Patrick was staying. My t-shirt clung to my body. I had run the whole way and was gasping for air. I had to calm down. Hopefully he was still here. Or had he already checked out? How would he react? He didn't know I was dating Andrew and definitely looked surprised when he found out.

Damn, I messed up. I liked Andrew. He was charming, cuddly, and calm. There was just one minor detail. As the father of a four-year-old who was living in New York with her mother, he and I couldn't move forward. He couldn't move to Canada; his ex-wife would never approve. And I couldn't ask him to do that. He'd miss his daughter too much. So the only solution was to move back to New York. I'd have to ask for a transfer back to headquarters.

But that wasn't an option for me. I was finally in the position I wanted. A position I'd worked so hard for. The beach house in Tofino was my dream house. I loved being here, being near the beach, nature only a few steps away. And Izzy, my dearest Izzy. She had space here. In New York, she'd only have a few square feet. Maybe it was for the best. I hoped Andrew and I could be friends, but I knew I couldn't count on it. He and Patrick were too close.

I knocked on the B&B's front door, hoping Patrick was still there. After a few minutes, an elderly lady opened the door. I guessed she was the owner.

"Yes, dear, can I help you?" she asked with a smile.

"I hope so. I'm Sophie, and I'm looking for a guest. Mr. Knowles?"

"Sorry, there's no one staying here under that name." She started to close the door.

Stall her, Sophie! I held the door open with my hand. "He's a friend of mine. Patrick, Patrick Knowles. Tall man, curly blonde hair, blue eyes. He told me he was staying here."

"Oh, Patrick!" She opened the door wider. "You're looking for Patrick! He's registered under Downey. Sorry for the confusion, dear."

Go figure. He was using his father's name.

"He left ten minutes ago. To the beach," she said, pointing in the direction of the marina. She gave me directions before I could say a single word.

"Thank you so much!" I bounced off the step, my desperation replaced with happiness.

"Good luck," she shouted as I jogged away. "I wish you two all the best. Follow your heart!"

How did she know? I turned around, wanting to hug her, but I just yelled my thanks and sprinted toward the beach. A part of me was hoping everything would be okay. If Patrick saw me, I didn't think I'd need to say anything to make it right. But another part of me knew it wouldn't be that easy. He needed to hear me out.

The beach was deserted, so I headed toward the marina. It had started to rain again, and my hair was a wet mess atop my head. If I were Patrick, I would've taken shelter in a bar or a restaurant. But I couldn't check them all. That would take forever. By the time I reached the pier, I still hadn't seen him. That was it. I'd had a chance earlier and I'd blown it. I walked down the pier, soaking wet, and plopped on the last bench. What other options did I have? Was I supposed to stalk him?

I sat with my hands in my hair. It stopped raining. I looked around. Not everywhere. Only the bench where I was sitting. An umbrella hung over my head. I turned around to see who was holding it. To my surprise it was Patrick.

"Why aren't you with Andrew?" he demanded.

"Patrick, it's over." I stood up and walked around the bench, so I could stand next to him. What I had to say I wanted to say straight to his face. No more secrets, no more hiding, no more walking away.

He stood there, holding his umbrella without saying a word. He didn't smile, his face was expressionless. He just looked at me blankly with his big blue eyes, begging me not to hurt him anymore.

I tried to reach out, but he didn't move. I dropped my hand quickly. "Patrick, I'm so sorry. I didn't know you and Andrew went way back. He... He broke up with me."

"He didn't have to do that. We aren't dating anymore, remember? You reminded me of that this morning. Or am I wrong?" He was so cold, he spoke with such hate. It broke my heart. He had every reason. I hadn't been fair to him.

"Look, I never really got over you. Andrew could tell, that's why he ended things. And it's true. I admit it. I never stopped loving you." Tears formed in my eyes. Was I too late? Could I still win him over?

"Sophie, I don't understand." His gaze softened a little. "You ended our relationship and now you're sorry?"

"You have every right to doubt me. I still regret it. I didn't want it to end. I never wanted to break up with you."

"So why did you?"

"It's a long story... I had my reasons."

He stared at me, waiting for me to continue. "I have time and nowhere else to be. So speak up. I want to know. I want to finally put this behind me. Get some closure."

We sat down on the bench. Patrick held the umbrella over our heads as the rain faded into a light drizzle. I was drenched, my hands felt ice cold, every bit of clothing sticking to my body. I rubbed my hands together. I had to get through this.

Patrick motioned for me to continue.

"Do you remember how you always thought you knew me but couldn't pinpoint from where? You even mentioned it the first time we met after that latte incident. Remember?"

"Yes?" he said slowly, thinking back.

"Patrick, we went to the same school. We graduated the same year. You even dated my sister."

"Really? Who's your sister?" He looked surprised.

"Carol, Carol Smith."

"Hmm. I dated a lot of girls back then. Wasn't long, right?" he asked, searching for a memory of Carol.

"No, not exactly. Carol caught you making out with a cheer-leader. She made a scene. Does that ring a bell?"

"Damn, yeah. That girl was furious. She's your sister?" He was dumbfounded. "Wow, that's strange. It's been ages." He frowned and scratched his head.

"I know. Every girl wanted to date the captain of the football team. You were a real player," I said dryly.

"But, Sophie, why don't I remember you? Your face always seemed familiar... But we didn't meet or talk back then. Did we?"

"No, we didn't. Oh, well, it was a massive school, and I was kind of a nerd back then. Studied a lot... I didn't date in high school, wasn't popular," I said, like that explained everything.

"So what does that have to do with you breaking up with me?" He was confused, couldn't find the connection.

I told him the whole story. How Carol and I went for coffee at Starbucks and she had seen him. The coffee incident. How we started dating and how much fun we'd had together. I told him how Carol got sick and how I couldn't look my sister in the eye and tell her I was dating him. How she would've broken all contact between us if she found out I was dating Patrick, the reason for her weight issues during high school, the problems she had with men, her relapse. I told him how Carol was the only family I had left. I couldn't stay with him. I couldn't betray her.

I took a deep breath. "So now you know. That's the real reason I broke up with you, Patrick."

Patrick sat quietly next to me, staring expressionless. It had stopped raining and the sun was slowly creeping from behind the clouds. The water was crumbling upon the shore beneath us. Scraping the sand up the beach and back into the ocean. It was so quiet, too quiet for my taste. I wanted to say something, but then I heard him inhale deeply, turning to face me.

"It's gratifying to finally know, after all these years," he said. "Thank you for being so honest, Sophie."

I could only watch him and give him all the space he needed.

"It seems like I'm the cause of a lot of misery in your family. Your sister, you... And now this with Andrew..." He shook his head. "I don't know anymore."

"Patrick, I'm so sorry. I still love you, really I do."

"Sophie, Andrew is my best friend. I need to talk this through with him and put what you told me in perspective." He raked his hands through his hair, threw his head back, ran his hands down his face, and sighed loudly. "It's better if we don't see each other for a while. Or maybe never again. I don't know what to think right now. I need to take a break and think everything over."

And here I'd thought everything would be all right between us once I told him the whole story. Maybe he would fall back into my arms. But it didn't turn out that way. I was shocked.

Patrick stood up and walked away. No hug, no goodbye, no nothing. All I could do was watch him walk away, further and further, till he was completely out of sight.

I wanted to scream, scream loudly, "Don't go, please stay. We can fix this." But nothing came out. A lump, the size of an apple, filled my throat, smothering every word. I sat on the bench, wet and cold, unable to move, lonely and deeply heartbroken. It wouldn't make a difference if I ran after him. I'd already tried that when he left my house and look where I was now. I stood up, feeling ripped apart, and walked back to my place. It took me twenty minutes. Besides Izzy, I came home to an empty house. Andrew had taken his stuff and left, leaving a note on the kitchen counter.

Dear Sophie,
It's better this way. I wish you all the best.
Thanks for the great moments.
Love, Andrew

Bam — second hit. The guy who loved me couldn't or wouldn't be with me because of a friendship. Fair enough, but that still didn't help me much.

I peeled off my wet clothes, took a long hot shower, got into my pajamas, grabbed a box of tissues and a bucket of ice cream, and crawled into bed, miserable. Izzy curled up next to me. To top things off, it had started to storm. It reflected the way I felt. Tears streamed abundantly down my face. I had lost a lot today.

It was only Saturday and I had nowhere to go, nothing to do, so I stayed in my PJs and wallowed in my misery.

I had to do something. I wanted to hear a kind voice, to talk to someone about it. I called the one person who had always been there for me. The phone rang twice before he answered.

"Sophie?"

"Alex, I lost everything..." I started to sob uncontrollably.

"What happened?" he asked gently.

"Well... Patrick came, and he knows. Andrew, I didn't know... And now they're both gone..." I gasped out between sobs.

"What?" Alex couldn't follow my story. I was blubbering and being too cryptic. "I'm coming. I'll call you as soon as I land."

"Alex, don't. I'm fine. It's too far," I said, sniffling.

"You are not fine, okay? I'll be there soon." He hung up without another word.

He was crazy. Vancouver wasn't a quick flight away. He literally had to go from one coast to the other. And it wasn't like he had a private plane at his beck and call.

I rearranged myself under the duvet and started to think everything over. I didn't deserve Patrick's love. When we were together, I worked most of the time, even on the weekends. I jetted off to foreign countries that I never truly enjoyed because of work. Work, work, work — that was my schedule.

I'd succeeded in destroying my relationship with my sister. I'd barely seen her since I'd moved to Canada. But she was happy, fully in control of herself and in a stable relationship. And because I was so concerned with her health, I had put everything aside for her. I'd ended my relationship with Patrick, a man I adored and loved so deeply, for her. He was the only guy I'd ever truly loved. He was the only one who'd ever captured my heart. And now it was over.

I had to do something. I had to make a change or I'd end up an old spinster, like Alex always warned. I had to take control of my life. I had to get something out of it. Enjoy it.

What had I really achieved? I had a great job, but my life revolved around it. I'd been all over the world but hadn't exactly seen it. I knew hundreds of people but didn't have any groundbreaking relationships or friendships. Alex and Jane were my best friends, but we didn't see each other much now that I lived in Canada. What a pity.

Did my life have some purpose? Was I happy? Looking back, sure, I had some good memories, pleasant moments. But I'd never been in the moment. I was always thinking about my job, my next trip... I'd never taken the time to carve those moments into my soul.

That had to be my goal. I had to be in the moment, seize every day as if it were my last. I had to be happy again.

The doorbell woke me from a comatose sleep. I had fallen asleep, turning my thoughts inside out. I rolled sideways to peek at my watch on the nightstand. Seven thirty in the morning! What the hell? I was weary and my head ached badly. *Maybe if I crawl back under the sheets they'll go away,* I thought, pulling the duvet over my head.

The doorbell rang again.

Aaargh. Okay, out of bed, Sophie. They won't stop until you open that stupid door.

I crawled out of bed, knocking the ice cream tub I'd emptied last night onto the floor. I jumped when the spoon hit the floor. I just wanted to go back to bed.

The doorbell buzzed again, not helping with my headache. I partially stumbled into the hallway, not caring about my outfit or how I looked. I didn't have time to change. Besides, I'd stopped caring last night.

I was almost at the front door. The doorbell buzzed continuously. They started to bang on the door.

"I'm coming!" I yelled. I wasn't in the mood. I wrenched the door open, ready to scream at the person on the other side.

"Finally!" Alex threw his arms around my neck. He pulled away and surveyed the damage. "I've brought some reinforcement," he said, leaning to the side. Jane was standing behind him.

"Jane!" I shouted happily.

My best friends were here when I needed them the most. Alex had already let himself in, bottle of tequila in hand, and wandered into the kitchen in search of glasses. Izzy was jumping all over him, happy to have a new friend in the house.

"You are in desperate need of a drink, and so am I. I only slept a few hours on the flight. Where the hell are your shot glasses?" he called from the kitchen.

I heard cabinets banging open and closed. I hurried into the kitchen, amazed he'd kept his word and come to Tofino.

"How did you get here?" I asked, watching Izzy follow Alex, hoping for some food. She recognized the sound of the cabinets opening.

"By plane, silly."

"Yes, that I figured out. But so quickly?"

"He has a new friend. Oscar," Jane offered. "Quite loaded if you ask me. He has his own jet and is handsome as hell."

Andrew smirked. "Just the way I like my men: handsome and loaded." He laughed loudly. "Does that answer your question?"

"Yes," I said. It surely did.

"So, glasses, Miss Sophie?" he asked, tapping his fingers on the counter.

"Right here." I opened the cabinet next to the fridge to reveal the cocktail glasses and spirits. I grabbed three shot glasses and handed them to Alex. "Okay, I obviously missed a few chapters since I moved, but, guys, I'm so happy to see you. What about work?" I didn't want them to get in trouble because of me.

"Don't worry," Alex said. "Mark's in charge while I'm away."

"Jane?" I asked, turning toward her.

"I had some time left. But doesn't matter. We're here for you." She sat down and patted the chair next to her. "Come on, take a seat."

"You look awful, by the way," Alex said.

"Love you too, Alex."

He blew kisses at me. With a wide grin he poured the tequila.

I thought it was a bit too early for tequila and with my head-ache... *Oh what the hell, I'm already fucked anyway.*

I filled them in on everything, starting with unexpectedly meeting Patrick on the beach.

Alex kept pouring the tequila so I wouldn't stop talking. And with every glass, the emotions poured out. We talked and drank for hours, ordered pizzas, drank some more, and by two in the afternoon, the three of us were so drunk we fell asleep in the living room. Just like the old days.

They were my best friends, always ready to help out. And it did sort of help. When I woke up that evening, I wasn't thinking about Patrick or Andrew, just my terrible, throbbing headache. I looked around and saw the devastation: empty pizza boxes and bags of chips, hardly touched cookies, bottles of tequila, shot glasses, DVD boxes scattered everywhere.

Jane sat up and dropped her head into her hands, trying to rub the ache in her temples away. Alex was snoring loudly. He had drunk the most — or maybe we all did.

It was wonderful having them around, and I wanted to make the most of it. Maybe they could stay a few days. I wasn't ready to face a whole weekend alone, miserable, with a heartache the size of a basketball.

I went to the bathroom and swallowed two aspirin with a glass of tepid water. After splashing some cold water on my face, I took the aspirin, a bottle of water, and two glasses back to the living room. Alex and Jane could definitely use some.

I tidied up the room a bit and decided to prepare a light dinner — Caesar salad and for dessert some raspberries and strawberries with a scoop of vanilla ice cream and some lime zest. Easy and ready in a jiff.

They stayed till Tuesday. We philosophized about life and what I could do to change mine, what would make me happy — and not just in my relationships. I showed them around Tofino, we walked on the beach, we visited the Pacific Rim National Park, and we saw some black bears strolling along the shore looking for food.

Tuesday morning I drove them to the airport in Victoria where Oscar, Alex's new boyfriend, was waiting. I could tell he was fond of Alex and Alex liked him too. He had escorted Jane and Alex to Vancouver the instant Alex had called him. Seeing how he went out of his way to help Alex I understood their connection. He would do absolutely anything for Alex. So lovely. He invited me to join him, Alex, and Jane at his house in the Hamptons for the summer, a great foresight.

I hugged Alex and Jane tightly and said goodbye to Oscar. I wished them a safe flight back and watched as they boarded the jet. Standing on the tarmac, I waved as the jet taxied down the runway.

Two days later, I was back in the office. And I made a life-changing decision. Never mind where it would take me. I resigned my position as partner. Within a month, after the firm had replaced me and the new partner had settled in, Leaf let me go. I moved out of my apartment in Vancouver and into the beach house in Tofino — permanently.

A huge weight had fallen off my shoulders the day I'd resigned. I didn't have to think about facts and figures, law, or my next trip anymore. I only had to think about what mattered today and what I wanted, not what others thought was best for me.

After renovating the house, I took Carol for a spa treatment in the Tofino Harbour area, I visited Jane in New York, and had a long weekend with Alex and Oscar in the Hamptons. From there, I decided to search for a new job. Not as a lawyer. I'm not stupid, you know. That chapter was closed. But as a masseuse. I enjoyed a good massage, but I enjoyed giving them to others too. After splitting up with Patrick, I'd taken different day courses for fun, inspired by that class with Carol back in New York. It felt good, helping someone relax. I found a job in a spa in Tofino, the same spa I'd visited with Carol. I worked there four days a week. The other days I helped out in the Kwisitis Visitor Centre near Long Beach. I guided people on their walks, told them about all the different trips and activities they could do, and helped out in the gift shop. I found it fascinating and soothing. I enjoyed every minute of it.

I finally had everything under control. I wasn't making a lot of money, but that wasn't my goal. I was happy with what I had and with what I was doing. And that was the only detail that mattered.

WHERE HAVE YOU BEAN ALL MY LIFE?

On days when there were a lot of tourists, like Saturdays and during high season, I put in extra hours at the spa. Today was one of those days.

I didn't mind. The spa was gorgeous. It featured a Finnish sauna, a Turkish bath, two huge pools, both indoor and outdoor, a variety of whirlpools, and an outdoor relaxation room. The back of the spa offered guests a clear and stunning view of the beach.

My boss, Corinne, and her husband, Frank, had opened the spa 15 years ago. The building was only a few streets from the marina and my house, so I could easily cycle to my job, like I did today. I locked my bike up and looked at the wood and glass building, surrounded by the conifer forest. It just went up into nature.

Grabbing my backpack from the bike rack, I headed inside. Nodded at Lucy, our receptionist, who was sitting in the large oaken reception area, and went through the wooden panel behind the front desk that pivoted on itself. Passing the spacious, luxurious, and soothing changing rooms, I entered the staff quarters, where I changed into my white massage tunic.

I'd just finished a one-hour hot stone massage and was taking a tea break in the staff room, a cozy space where staff could relax, eat, or drink, wash up, and prepare for the next client.

My colleague, Ashley, was waiting for her next appointment, a couple who'd booked a duo massage. They were running late, so she'd prepped my next client.

"His name is Mr. Cobb," she said. "He's already on the table. Monica did the intake. He went hiking yesterday, so he has some pain in the rectus femoris and the medial and lateral head of the gastrocnemius. He asked for a full relaxation massage and a sport massage to treat his legs. He has no allergies, so you can use whatever oil you'd like."

I finished my green tea in one gulp. "I'll probably be finished in ninety minutes. I'll take a break and then help out with that couple's second treatment. Three o'clock for their next treatment?"

"Yep, suits me perfectly," Ashley said.

"Great."

I washed my hands with warm water and rubbed them against each other so they weren't cold. I knocked once before entering the treatment room.

Like Ashley said, Mr. Cobb was already lying face down on the table. Ashley had draped some warm towels on his back and legs so he wouldn't get cold. I gently placed my hand on his back, a sign that I was going to start the massage. "Hello, Mr. Cobb. I'm Sophie, and I'll be your masseuse today."

He mumbled something incomprehensible and that was it.

Okay, not a talker, I thought. That's how I like men. I mean, on my table, not in real life.

I folded the towel in two and adjusted it beneath his sacrum. He had a staggering body. Muscles and tanned arms. Not bad for a Saturday.

I started slowly, from his neck to his shoulders, from the back of his neck down to his sacrum near his spine and back up again, working in small circles. I could feel his muscles relax beneath my fingers. His breath started to slow down, so I knew I was applying the right amount of pressure.

I finished with his upper body, placed a warm towel over him, and started on his legs. I unfolded one side of the towel so his right leg remained under the warm towel while I massaged the left one. I did the same for his right leg and finished with a foot rub.

I stood next to him and placed a hand between his shoulders. Bending down, I whispered, "Sir, can you turn over so I can treat the front of your body? Thank you."

I held the towel up so he could turn onto his back and looked away. I replaced the towel and adjusted it below his abdomen so I could start with his shoulders and chest. His eyes were closed, a faint smile covering his mouth.

It was only then I noticed.

It was Patrick.

I didn't say a word. What were the odds, him being here and me treating him? I stayed professional and massaged his head, his shoulders, his arms, his chest, his legs, and ended with another foot rub. I placed a warm towel over his body and his eyes instantly popped open.

"Thanks, Sophie, that was awesome. So relaxing. They told me you were a natural."

He smiled at me with so much charisma I didn't know what to say. I could only blush.

"Thanks, Patrick. It's lovely to see you again," I said softly.

"You too," he said.

I composed myself quickly. "There are some towels on the table over there. Take your time. You can shower in here or in the locker rooms. Then, you're free to use the spa at your leisure. In the meantime, can I bring you some refreshments or a cup of tea?"

"Tea please." He sat up and propped himself up on his elbows.

I turned to leave — I wanted to leave — but I couldn't. Patrick was holding me by the wrist.

"Wait."

I was curious to hear what he had to say. Seriously, I hadn't seen him in months and now he was in Tofino, on my table. He was the one who'd vanished this time.

"Look, I came here for a reason," he admitted. "We both did stuff we're not proud of. Andrew and I are fine. We talked. I'm sorry for everything. I wasn't honest with you about Copco. But I hope we can leave the past in the past and focus on the future."

I nodded, still trying to find some words.

"Sophie, can we start over? Is that possible? Or did you close the door on me for good?"

"I left it partially open," I said.

Patrick took a deep breath. His cheeks were flushed. I'd never seen this side of him. "Hi, I'm Patrick Downey Knowles. Will you have a drink with me this evening?" he asked shyly, holding his hand out to shake mine.

I had to laugh. He was right. This was the best way to handle it. Start over, a fresh, clean slate. I shook his hand. "Sophie Smith," I said. "Delightful to meet you. What time would you like to meet?"

He smiled. "Well, I'm not from here. I'm on holiday and exploring the area. But they told me you gave guided tours. Maybe we could do a drink and a tour?"

"Okay. You're staying at...?"

"The Cove."

"Of course. The Cove. Good choice. I'll pick you up at the Pier House at six o'clock. That's a shop down the street from The Cove, right before you enter the marina. I'll show you around town and then we can go to a local bar for a drink. And we can catch the sunset. It's wonderful out there."

"Six it is." Patrick stood up, tightened the towel around his waist, and gave me a peck on the cheek.

I left the massage room, walking on roses. Was it this moment? Was it him? It was definitely the beginning of something new, and I was excited. I couldn't stop smiling. I peered out the staff room window, drinking in the sky cracking open after last night's storm. Stripes of blue sky were pushing through the clouds. I was behind the steering wheel of my life and was quite happy with the direction I was headed.

ACKNOWLEDGEMENTS

I would like to thank the women in my tribe who've gone on this journey with me — Virginie Cnudde, Mieke Demeyer, Claudia Nakayama, Sylvie Roets, Nele Van Hecke — and my parents. Your constant support, friendship, and love throughout the years, your belief in me and my story, gave me the courage to keep on going and putting myself and Sophie's story out into this world. I'm forever grateful.

Tracie Kendziora, my editor and GIPHY supporter. Thank you for your relentless motivation, sharp eye, and necessary dose of humor. It helped me push through and create a story I am proud of.

My sister Laurence Stevigny and good friend Sarah Braekevelt but also Stephanie Van den Bulcke, Filip Van Petegem, David Norton — thanks for pre-reading my manuscript and your suggestions. They helped in streamlining the story.

And, of course, my husband Thomas and my son Sebastien — you guys gave me the time and space to sit in solitude and write whenever I needed. You supported me by listening or brainstorming when I got stuck. I can't thank you enough.

ABOUT THE AUTHOR

JULIE STEVIGNY (1983) is an author and coach.

She helps women go from feeling "not good enough" and "overloaded" to confident and re-energized.

It's her mission to guide others on their path of becoming the best version of themselves, by helping them reconnect with their true selves while optimizing their health.

She does this by coaching in her private practice, blogging, connecting people, and chasing her own dreams — like writing this book.

She lives with her husband and son near Ghent.

Visit her website at www.happymindguide.be or follow or connect with her on Facebook or Instagram.

© Daphne Matthys

*Give yourself permission to be every bit of the woman
you are destined to be.*